THE
MURDER
GARDEN

BOOKS BY ALICE CASTLE

A BETH HALDANE MYSTERY

The Murder Mystery

The Murder Museum

The Murder Question

The Murder Plot

The Murder Walk

The Murder Club

The Murder Hour

THE MURDER GARDEN

ALICE CASTLE

bookouture

Published by Bookouture in 2022

An imprint of Storyfire Ltd.
Carmelite House
50 Victoria Embankment
London EC4Y 0DZ

www.bookouture.com

ISBN: 978-1-80314-498-6
eBook ISBN: 978-1-80314-497-9

To Ella and Connie, with love

ONE

It was a wet Monday in September, the sort of day when you wanted to hang onto a radiator for as long as possible before going outside. Beth Haldane was sitting in her kitchen, grabbing a quick cup of tea before getting off to work. Beth's son, Jake, now at the gangly cusp of twelve and thirteen, had already plodded to school, and her boyfriend, Metropolitan Police detective Harry York, had disappeared at an ungodly hour that morning to work on his latest tricky case. Beth knew she should be enjoying the moment; gazing out over her garden, watching the antics of her tatty black and white moggy, Magpie, and Colin the ancient Labrador. Normally they would be bickering gently against a backdrop of dead and dying shrubs. Colin would be attempting a bit of arthritic ragging, and Magpie would be ready with a raised paw in case he dared get too rambunctious. Today, however, both animals were looking on in deep umbrage, as a gang of workmen bustled about by Beth's back fence.

Beth sighed. To tell the truth, she shared her pets' misgivings. She knew at one level she was absolutely right to be joining the current Dulwich vogue and installing a 'shoffice', or

shed-cum-office, in her back garden. After all, they desperately
needed the space. Jake seemed to be growing several centimetres a night at the moment. While this was a relief for Beth, who
had often fretted she might have passed on her own stumpy
genes to her boy, it was a definite problem in her little Pickwick
Road house. The place was all angles. There wasn't really
enough room to swing Magpie, even if anyone had been brave
(or foolish) enough to try. The recent arrival of Harry, six foot
four in his socks and accompanied by an absurdly large number
of whodunits, had only served to compound the problem.

She knew the shoffice was the sensible solution. It would
easily house Harry's books, and she was secretly hoping it
would also house him quite a lot of the time. She had even
wondered, lately, whether perhaps he and Jake could develop
some nice hobby they could do in the shoffice? This would leave
Beth, Magpie and Colin to enjoy the peace and quiet of the
sitting room sofa.

But there really wasn't much peace to be had at the
moment. When the builders weren't clanging around with
metal poles, chunks of wood and sacks of concrete, they were
shouting to each other as though miles apart, instead of working
shoulder to shoulder in a miniscule suburban garden. Then
there were the uproarious laughs which broke out periodically,
and tended to die down the moment she stepped outside.

It must be about time for her to stick the kettle on again for
them. It was at least half an hour since their last infusion of very
strong tea. If her irrepressible friend Nina hadn't assured her
they were some of the finest builders to be had south of the
river, Beth would have been quite tempted to abandon the
whole scheme and go back to bursting quietly out of the seams
of the house.

But she was being silly, she told herself. What were a few
days of noise and upheaval, if it bought them the space to carry
on living in her beloved home? They certainly couldn't afford to

buy something bigger, with prices in Dulwich floating high above even the crazy London property bubble. They had briefly considered moving out of the area, but just looking for a new home had been a disaster. So they were staying, and it wasn't as if she had to do any of the work herself. She just had to watch it. Today was already day two. It surely wouldn't be much longer. Would it?

She was just wondering how best to phrase the question, 'When exactly are you going to be leaving?' when a massive yell rang out in the garden. Like a furry missile, Magpie immediately threw herself in through the catflap and raced up the stairs, getting as far away from the commotion as she could. Colin was made of sterner stuff, wagging his tail excitedly and adding a volley of ferocious barks to the chaos. He'd clearly decided the builders had seen sense at last and were ready to stop work and play like sensible chaps.

But Colin had got it wrong. That wasn't the sound of builders having fun. If Beth wasn't mistaken, there was alarm in those shouts. Fear, even. From grown men, it was chilling. She shot up from her seat and pressed her nose against the window. But she couldn't see a thing. The rear view of a row of hulking builders was completely blocking out whatever had just gone so badly wrong. As she watched, two of them hitched their trousers up, which she was grateful for. That still left a lot of overexposure, though. And it was getting closer – they all seemed to be backing towards her, away from the fence.

What the hell? Had they made some dreadful blunder? Poured the concrete in the wrong place, or something? Wrecked her shoffice before she'd even had time to install Harry? Damn, if they'd messed things up, this could take forever. She needed to get a proper look. She dumped her empty cup in the sink and dashed for the kitchen door, not even pausing to get her shoes from the hall.

Outside, she shivered on the tiny paved area, which was not

large enough to merit the name patio. It was already sporting a lush autumnal coat of algae. Once upon a time James, her late husband, had talked about getting a pressure washer and restoring the tiles to their former glory, but the grim reaper had put paid to that idea. Beth, being unsure the tiles had ever really boasted glory, even in their heyday, had not resurrected the plan. Now the damp slime was starting to seep through her socks.

'What's going on?' she shouted.

At her voice, the men turned round, standing in a ragged row like footballers waiting to fend off a crucial free kick. No one seemed to want to meet her eyes. And no one said a word.

'Sorry, what on earth is the problem?' said Beth, leaning this way and that to try and see behind their bulk.

'Um...' the foreman mumbled.

Beth tutted and strode out across the wet lawn, trying to ignore her increasingly soggy socks.

The men looked shiftily at each other. Then the foreman tried again. 'Um. Perhaps we should wait for your husband to get home?'

At that, Beth surged forward, head down, and the men reluctantly moved out of the way.

Once they had parted, like a scruffy, shuffling version of the Red Sea, Beth could see her back fence at last. And the usual fringe of miserable-looking bushes, some of which had been uprooted in readiness for the shoffice. And something in front of all that. Something sticking out of the deep, newly dug pit in the corner of the garden. Something long and whiteish, that was poking up into the wet September morning like a macabre flag-pole. Colin, by her side, whined with joy and she grabbed his collar before he shot forward. This was exactly what he had dreamt of bringing home from Dulwich Park for many a long year.

It was a long, thin bone. And it was unmistakably human.

TWO

Even as dawn broke the next morning, Beth couldn't quite believe the enormity of what had happened yesterday. It was only the sight of the abandoned pit at the end of her garden which told her it hadn't all been a horrible dream. She stood at the kitchen window, clutching her tea, and looking out in despair. It was the mirror image of yesterday – only everything was much, much worse. There was mess everywhere. Abandoned supplies, pallets of tiles, even a few tools which had been left out all night. The builders were long gone, of course. Only twenty-four hours earlier, that had been exactly what she'd been praying for. But now that there was an eerie silence in place of their cheery banter, she actually missed their crashes and bangs. That had been the sound of normal life.

Worst of all was the tarpaulin roughly spread over the hole, like a sticking plaster over a festering sore. A couple of police constables had finally dragged this into place yesterday, after Beth's panicked 999 call when Harry had been too tied up to get away. The tarpaulin had been their way of 'securing the scene', as they'd put it, as though the arm was going to somehow leg it. But then, to her frustration, they had got some sort of alert on their radios and bustled off. Apparently, live crime trumped dead bones. She didn't know exactly when they'd be back, but the sooner they declared the bone officially dead and gone and allowed her shoffice installation to continue, the better.

The tarpaulin billowed suddenly as a breeze caught it. The quiet undulation made her skin crawl. It was as though something inside was trying to get out. The whole thing poked upwards, like a finger pointing accusingly into the sky. Except, as she knew only too well, the fingers were missing. There was just a large arm bone sticking out of the ground. God, she wished she could get the image out of her head.

How terrible, that this grisly thing had been down there, in her back garden, where Jake had played his innocent games of football, and where her pets had enacted their endless war of attrition. It was the stuff of nightmares.

It had taken her so long to get to this point. She had been bodging repairs and dodging repainting ever since her husband James's sudden death when Jake had been tiny. Moving on from the colours they had chosen together as newlyweds seemed like a betrayal – albeit a small one compared with the recent installation of Harry in her bed. If she glossed over all those yellowing skirting boards, was she also painting out her happy years with poor James?

Even the very loud blue on the walls in Jake's room seemed like a link with James – he had insisted on it, to Beth's horror at the time. Over the years, she'd grown fond of the violent shade for that reason alone. But the other day, Jake had said to his mum that, if they were *really* going to redecorate, could he pick his own paint?

Jake's readiness to move on was a reminder that clinging to the past could be unhealthy. It had unlocked something in her. So, before she knew it, Beth and Harry had decided to jump on the Dulwich bandwagon and get a shoffice of their own.

And now look what had happened.

Beth shook her head. She didn't want to see this as a portent, an omen that leaving James behind was wrong. Surely no one would judge her so harshly. Except perhaps Beth herself.

By the time Harry came rushing downstairs to grab his stuff and go, Beth was still standing in front of the kitchen window, frowning heavily under her flop of fringe.

'Cheer up, might never happen – and don't say it already has,' he said, stepping across the tiny kitchen to give her a quick hug. 'You do realise that bone is probably fifty, a hundred years old? Maybe much more.'

Beth looked up at him. 'Do you really think so?'

'Bound to be,' Harry said. 'It's probably a stray from that old plague pit in the village. Nothing to worry about.' With that, he kissed the top of her head, snatched the least brown banana from the fruit bowl, and hefted on his navy blue peacoat.

'Um—' she started. But it was too late. The front door had slammed. He wouldn't be back for hours. The case he was on at the moment seemed labyrinthine in its complications and, as usual, he didn't want to tell her a word about it until it was over. Trouble was, once it was wrapped up, he'd be on to the next thing and have even less interest in discussing it.

Nothing to worry about, he'd said. But what if the bone really had come from the little burial ground in the village? It was strange enough having a graveyard in the middle of a bustling high street, but it was Grade Two listed and couldn't be moved, a throwback from the days when Sir Thomas Wyatt had strode up and down these parts in his unfeasibly large ruff in the 1600s. Having made his fortune in the slave trade, Sir Thomas had used his shamefully gotten proceeds to found Wyatt's School, which Jake attended and where Beth worked as head (and sole employee) of the Archive Institute.

Could it really be some sort of relic from the Great Plague of 1665, then? If so, might it still be infectious? She definitely needed to google the half-life of the Black Death. And there was something else; something she was desperately trying to shut her mind to. She had seen the top of that arm bone yesterday, and the big, bulbous joint had ended in what looked like two strange nodules. Even in less than ideal weather, and with horror and panic running through her veins, there had been enough morning light to see clearly. There was a network of marks across those nodules, as though something, or someone, had sawed away at them.

Would this have happened with a bubonic plague victim? It seemed very unlikely. As far as Beth could remember from her history degree, the disease-riddled bodies just got chucked into the nearest pit and covered up pronto with quick lime. No one would have wanted to get near enough to touch a bone, let alone spend ages hacking away at it. So Harry's best-case scenario – not without its massive downsides anyway – was at best highly unlikely. The poor old bone, thought Beth. She only hoped all that damage had happened after death.

Beth put her cup down in the sink with a snap. No good could come of all this introspection, she knew that of old. Tuesday wasn't normally one of her days at Wyatt's, but she hadn't been able to make it yesterday as she'd been expecting the police to turn up at any second. They now had her number, though, so they could call her when they deigned to come back. Popping into the office would take her mind off things... and there was also the chance that she'd be able to see Jake and check how he was getting on.

It wasn't easy for Jake, having a mum who worked at his school. She knew he was mortified when she waved in passing, and she often resolved to try and restrain herself. But it was so difficult. Even though he was now getting so big, he would always be her baby and the sight of him never failed to lift her heart. Her hand rose of its own accord, even while her brain was telling it not to. Being cool was so important at Jake's age and she knew she was wrecking it for him. Sometimes she felt like just sitting him down and telling him straight: the Haldanes were many things, but they had never been cool, and that's all there was to it. But she couldn't bear to crush his spirit. And it was lovely to get these little glimpses into his day, even if he winced every time.

She picked up her handbag, quickly checking her phone was inside. Yep, and there was even a message. *Class cancelled this morning. Fancy a coffee?* It was from Katie, Beth's dearest friend. Seeing her was the next best thing to seeing Jake, and if she didn't take too long over the coffee, then she could still swing by Wyatt's, she told herself, though she secretly knew the chances of getting any work done today had just been shot down in flames. Katie knew nothing about the bone; she needed to be filled in on all the details.

* * *

'God, I hope it's really, really old, don't you?' Katie shook her head over their second cappuccino. They had already got through a brace of brownies, which Katie had pointed out were strictly medicinal in the circumstances. 'It's very important to keep your blood sugar up when you've had a shock,' she told Beth firmly. For once, Beth didn't contradict the village's self-appointed wellness priestess, even if said shock had actually taken place yesterday.

Jane's Café was quite peaceful for once, as they had hit the mid-morning lull. Yummy mummies were perspiring on their Pelotons, au pairs were pushing dusters around flatscreen TVs while covertly catching up with *Bridgerton*, and babies were napping. The lunchtime rush would soon start, and then Beth and Katie wouldn't be able to get a word in edgeways over toddlers loudly comparing *Peppa Pig* impressions, while their mothers solemnly agreed that sticking a preschool tot in front of the box was a form of child abuse.

'Does it really make that much difference, if it's an old bone?' Beth wrinkled her nose. 'It's still part of some poor person, who used to be alive and well and had no business at all ending up in my garden.'

'I know what you mean, but if it's a hundred or, even better, a thousand years old, it *is* sort of less bad, isn't it? I mean, museums are full to the brim with old bones, and no one bothers about that.' Katie always looked on the bright side. 'They even had a skeleton in my biology lab when I was at school. We called him Sherlock. Geddit?'

'Sherlock *Bones*.' Beth groaned. 'Aren't those plastic, though? And anyway, I'd still think it was creepy, even if the bone was a million years old.'

'But if we all felt like that, we'd have to close things like, I don't know, the Horniman Museum down the road.'

Beth grimaced. She'd once loved the Horniman, especially the overstuffed walrus that had appeared on the brink of exploding when she'd been a small child, and looked exactly the same now. But she hadn't felt the same about the place since her late friend Jen's ill-starred second wedding there a few years ago. 'Maybe that wouldn't be such a bad thing,' she said gloomily.

'Oh, come on, Beth, we've learnt so much over the years from bones. Look at Darwin and stuff! He might not have been able to develop his theories without, I don't know, looking at real bodies or whatever. And what about Wyatt's Museum of Art? Those sarcophagi you're always on about?'

It was just about the worst thing Katie could have said. Immediately Beth was reminded of another horrible case. She suddenly wondered if she shouldn't just get going and put in a couple of hours' work at the school after all.

Katie looked at her friend's long face. 'Listen. How about a walk in Dulwich Park? That ought to blow these gloomy thoughts away. It'll be good to give Colin and Teddy a bit of an airing, too. You know you always feel better after. And we can have one of those great big sandwiches at the café, too.'

Yum, sandwiches, thought Beth. And Katie was right, a walk always did her good. She owed Colin a proper run-about, too. Yesterday there had been no time to do more than trot round the block with him, between the builders leaving in a hurry and the police turning up at their leisure. Even going round the park with Katie's Teddy, literally the worst-behaved dog in history, would stop her dwelling too much on things she couldn't fix.

'Let's do that,' she said with her first smile of the day.

* * *

They were on their second lap of Dulwich Park, and Katie was trying to extract Teddy from the nethers of an outraged Bichon Frise, when Beth got another text. It was the Kendalls, who lived at the other end of Pickwick Road, inviting Beth and Harry to supper the next evening.

She frowned. If anything, she owed the Kendalls supper. Beth and Harry had been over only a couple of months before, and had had a very jolly time. But as usual Beth had been procrastinating about arranging a return fixture – Harry was always working, Jake had so much homework. And, more importantly, Beth was the type of cook who could quite easily burn water. Lizzie, by contrast, was one of that dying breed of women, nudging her seventies now, who'd done a cordon bleu cookery course and had a black belt in flower arranging, all the better to snare an investment banker. Her husband George fitted the bill perfectly (and also paid every single one of them on the nail) and they had both been extremely happy with the set-up for fifty years.

Beth knew she was being churlish, but she immediately wondered whether news of the bone had already travelled the length of their street. If so, the Kendalls – and everyone else – would be agog to know more. But surely her grim secret couldn't be out already? The police had been as discreet as police ever could be, and they weren't a rare sight since Harry had moved in. And, while the builders had certainly been as loud about putting all their equipment back on the van as they had been getting it out in the first place, she still didn't think they would have wandered the length of Pickwick Road yelling about their discovery. They were too shocked for a start.

She was safe to say yes to the Kendalls, she decided, without risking a grilling about the bone. And that last mental image immediately made her glad the weather was so awful – they definitely wouldn't be having barbequed spare ribs. A barbie was not Lizzie's style anyway. She was more likely to produce a rack of lamb with those little paper chefs' hats daintily shrouding the top of each bone, which had been so big in the 1970s. Beth shut her eyes and resolutely turned her thoughts away from the menu. She'd have no appetite for her sandwich with Katie if she went on like this. She'd just tap out a quick yes, then see where Katie had got to. She needed to add a caveat about Harry, though. He was so busy on the current enquiry that it was a miracle if he got home while she was still awake, let alone in time for dinner. Having said that, he might make more of an effort if it wasn't her doing the cooking. Lizzie Kendall was a whiz in the kitchen and her husband, George, had the softly domed paunch to prove it.

An evening out would be a welcome distraction, and might be a bit more peaceful than this dog walk was turning out to be. Teddy, although no longer officially a puppy, was still as frisky as a whole fieldful of spring lambs. Katie, red in the face and keen to put some distance between her charge and his latest unwilling paramour, was already halfway to the café. Beth finished her text and galloped along with a stiff-legged Colin, trying to keep up.

By the time she got to the wooden tables outside – even in this weather, there was no way anyone wanted to risk taking Teddy into the café, with all those babies in highchairs waving eggy soldiers around – Katie had managed to tie the dog up to a seat and was inside, getting their order. Beth tried to give Teddy a stern talking-to, while Katie wasn't watching. Much as she loved her friend, she believed Katie had a fatal soft spot for Teddy which made her incapable of imposing the boundaries he sorely needed. But Teddy was much too busy bouncing up and down to pay any attention. Colin, who stayed very wisely just out of the reach of Teddy's lead, contented himself with unfurling his raspberry tongue and panting at his young side-kick, looking for all the world as though he was enjoying a good laugh at his expense.

Beth knew she was lucky. She'd adopted Colin when the Labrador was well past youthful frolics, and at the pipe-and-slippers stage of doggy life. But she was sure that, even as a pup, Colin had been a kind and thoughtful boy. He would never want to show Beth up, in the way that Teddy embarrassed poor Katie on a daily basis. Having a badly behaved child was one thing, but in Dulwich, you could blame it on the playgroup, the school, the tutors... A badly behaved dog, however, was a badge of shame, and one which had been kicked out of multiple obedience training sessions, as Teddy had, was almost beyond the pale.

Beth knew there were people who now avoided going to Katie's, for fear their handbags or boots – it was very much a shoes-off household thanks to Katie's pale blond wooden floors – would be trashed by Teddy while they were having a coffee. Even Charlie's friends had apparently started giving him a wide berth, apart from Jake. Teddy had a tendency to jump on them at the worst moment in any session of a game, and had even worked out how to open doors by repeatedly leaping up and knocking them with his paws, so nowhere in the house was safe.

Katie sat down with her loaded tray, her cheeks now almost back to their normal colour. 'Honestly, I don't know why people bring their dogs to the park when they're on heat, it's totally irresponsible,' she said, sliding a sandwich and a cappuccino towards Beth. Teddy immediately started sniffing around so Beth moved everything out of his reach.

'Oh, was that Bichon Frise a girl?' Beth wrinkled her forehead for a second. 'I'm pretty sure I saw...' but then she abandoned the struggle. There was little merit in pointing out the obvious evidence that the dog had been male, which had been clear enough while the poor creature tried to evade Teddy's overtures. But she'd never convince Katie, who'd developed the mindset that the whole world was unaccountably against her darling boy. She wasn't wrong – but there was good reason. Teddy was a total menace.

Beth started unwrapping a corner of the cellophane packaging on her egg and cress doorstep. Teddy began to whine under the table. The slats were wide enough for bits of sandwich to drop through, he told Beth loudly, if only she would only oblige... She promptly decided very definitely that not so much as a crumb was going to fall. But then Katie opened up her own pack and placed a piece of bright pink ham on the floor. Teddy was a blur of silky black curls – he was a beautiful dog, Beth had to give him that – and it was all gone. He looked up adoringly at Katie. Beth exchanged a glance with Colin, and the old boy all but shook his head at her. He then sighed and lay down, head on paws.

It was almost a relief when Katie turned to Beth and said, 'Now, I know you. You're very quiet. Not still worrying about this bone business?'

'Well, yes I am.' Beth munched carefully. 'I mean, it's absolutely horrific. To think it was down there all the time... all those years.'

'You'll just have to try and put it out of your head completely. Could be a good time to try some mindful breathing!' Katie never gave up hope that Beth might get the yoga bug. She suddenly had to practise what she preached, though, when Teddy started trying to insinuate his wriggly, muddy body onto the bench beside her, the better to hoover up more of her sandwich. And probably Beth's. Beth withdrew a little further. Katie tried zoning Teddy out, but just got a faceful of licks for her pains. Then she pushed at him ineffectually. Finally she gave up, simply raising her voice so she could be heard above his urgent pleas for more ham. 'I mean, nothing has changed, really, has it? You didn't know it was down there for all these years. Just wipe the slate.'

Beth munched on. Ignoring stuff was a lot easier said than done, as Katie was currently demonstrating. But she wasn't going to argue.

'Mind you, one thing does surprise me,' Katie mused, taking another bit of ham out of her sandwich and chucking it as far as she could from the bench, probably in the hope that Teddy would stop bugging her. Of course he immediately decided this was the greatest game ever, shooting over at warp speed to find the treat, gulping it down and coming back for more. 'I mean, why didn't Colin dig it up?' Katie asked.

Beth couldn't help thinking her tone was a little disapproving. And certainly, Teddy would probably have converted her garden into the Somme if he'd so much as sniffed an inkling of a bone down there.

'Maybe that's another reason to assume it's old... maybe it just didn't smell of anything any more,' Beth shrugged. She secretly suppressed the memory of those cuts at the end of the bone. They somehow suggested something more recent, something more violent, than the ancient death from natural causes she was hoping for.

But they were eating, after all. Or trying to, she thought, with a glance at the unrepentant Teddy. It really wasn't the time to dwell on the unhappy thought that someone seemed to have been dismembered in her back garden.

THREE

That Wednesday evening, Beth left Jake allegedly hard at his homework, or at least cloistered in his room for the evening, and nipped up the road to the Kendalls' house.

The door was thrown open by Adua, who 'did' for most of the residents of Pickwick Road. When she wasn't being employed to scrub floors or hoover, she was cat- or dog-sitting, plant-watering, taking in post or baffling burglars by turning lights on and off up and down the street. Lively and interfering, and now well into her fifties, Adua was defiantly raven-haired with dancing dark eyes and often sported a bright slash of scarlet lipstick. She took pride in knowing everything about everybody – but had never shared details about where she was from herself, expertly fending off polite enquiries. Beth knew she came from a village in an Eastern European country but, despite having taken careful note of the clues Adua had dropped over the years, she couldn't have pinned the exact spot down on a map if she'd tried.

Adua greeted Beth with a quick hug and ushered her in. 'You're late, darling. Come in, come in.'

Beth couldn't help goggling slightly at the pristine frilly

white pinny her friend was decked out in tonight, but she
hastily took her seat in the Kendalls' dining room and greeted
the tableful of friends and neighbours. Then it all started to
make sense, as Adua immediately started doing the rounds with
a huge platter of artfully arranged smoked salmon and horse-
radish cream on dinky bits of toast. She was basically doing a
tremendous impression of a parlourmaid – Lizzie Kendall must
have watched *Downton Abbey* one too many times. When she
got round to Beth, Adua almost did a curtsey with her tray, then
ruined the effect with a big mischievous smirk.

Pressganging Adua into service for the night suited Lizzie
Kendall's style down to the ground. The house, the largest on
Pickwick Road, was hung with complicated chintz curtains,
dotted about with cut-glass bowls of delicately scented pot
pourri, and all the furniture was antique and as well-uphol-
stered as George Kendall. The effect was grand but rather jolly,
like Lady Grantham after multiple sherries, and Beth loved it. It
also always made her wonder where her own mother had gone
astray. She had enjoyed a similar set-up with Beth's late
lamented father, yet somehow her house lacked the warmth that
Lizzie's had in such abundance.

Pondering this took Beth's mind off her rather unsatisfying
walk with Katie yesterday. After her initial interest, Katie
hadn't seemed keen to carry on debating Beth's bones. Teddy
simply couldn't sit still for any length of time, and Katie had
been anxious about that evening, when she was starting the
latest obedience class she had enrolled him in, all the way out in
Penge. They had by now either been banned from sessions
closer to home, or had completed the courses but failed to 'grad-
uate', as everything had gone into one of Teddy's beautiful silky
black ears, and straight out the other. Beth had been quite glad
to get away, once Teddy had ravaged the rest of his mistress's
sandwiches, and she suspected Colin had felt the same. She

made a mental note to check up on how the first lesson had gone.

Oh well, she was going to enjoy tonight's supper anyway – even though Harry, as predicted, had been unable to make it. Apparently his case had taken yet another turn for the worse.

'Wouldn't a night off be a good idea?' Beth had said, trying to cajole him into accepting. 'Refresh you? I know when I'm doing a difficult crossword, putting it down and walking away for a while sometimes really helps. When I pick it up again the answer just leaps out...'

Harry had pursed his lips, and she'd known then that he definitely wasn't going to make it. 'With respect, my job is not like doing crosswords. Detection is a painstaking matter, it's not startling leaps of intuition,' he'd said.

Beth had said no more, while knowing that all her own cases had involved eureka moments, when knotty problems had suddenly and obligingly unscrambled themselves to lay the solution before her.

Maybe she should pretend her successes were down to nothing but hard graft, if she ever wanted Harry to take what she did seriously, Beth thought now, scooping up some of the broccoli that Adua was proffering. A plumply buttered stalk fell and landed on the white starched tablecloth. Beth looked up guiltily but Adua gave her a broad wink, flicked the offending vegetable onto her plate, and moved seamlessly on.

Had anyone else noticed? On her right, George Kendall was nose to nose with Sally Bentinck, Beth's next-door neighbour. On her left, Howie and Doug Christie-Smith were discussing kitchen tiles with Lizzie. The Christie-Smiths had only recently moved in, and already their little house was one of the most elegant in the street, with perfectly trimmed bobbles of box atop their hedge, like baubles on a tiara. Beth hoped they didn't find her place too much of an eyesore. Its façade was now tired to the point of total exhaustion. At least it matched the interior perfectly. Doug turned to her.

'You're the owner of that gorgeous Lab, aren't you?'

'Colin? Yes, he's mine,' Beth said proudly, though she sometimes wondered exactly who owned whom. 'And you've got cats, I think?'

'Two Bengals. Have you seen them around?'

'You can't miss them, they're so beautiful,' said Beth. She'd been fascinated by the elegant creatures since they'd moved in. They loped around the fences and walls like fleeting, glamorous glimpses of a suburban tiger and leopard. And they could definitely give Magpie a run for her money in the haughtiness stakes. 'What are their names?'

'Ah, well. We made the mistake of asking our lovely little niece to name them,' said Doug with a rueful glance at Howie.

'She called them Silver and Gold. It was Olympic year,' Howie shrugged.

Beth laughed. 'Well, they're beautiful. I once knew a Persian who'd been named Barbie, by the family's toddler daughter. So perhaps they've had a lucky escape.'

They were still giggling when Sally Bentinck leant over. 'By the way, Beth, have you mentioned yet to Howie that Adua is a fantastic cat-sitter?'

'Oh yes! She's great if you're looking for someone.'

'Great! That's an understatement. Adua is simply *a-mazing* with my Reggie, and he's got quite the theatrical temperament,' said Sally Bentinck. Beth exchanged a tiny smile with Lizzie Kendall. Sally somehow never let anyone forget her West End background. She'd worked her way up from set design and stage management to become the acclaimed producer of many of London's top musicals, full of the kind of numbers Dulwich residents liked to belt out in the shower – however much they claimed they only listened to opera. If Sally's clanking bangles and bracelets didn't give the game away, her dramatic flowing garments and interesting use of eyeliner always screamed *Olivier Award Winning Impresario*, even when she was putting her bins out at 7 p.m. on a chilly Tuesday.

Sally was definitely right about her cat, Reggie, though. Maine Coons were usually friendly, docile creatures, but Reggie was as big a character as his mistress, and would sit on the gatepost of Sally's house, silently judging Colin, Beth and everyone else in the street. Beth knew he found her wanting, though he did treat Magpie with grudging respect. Adua, however, adored him, and in her arms the huge creature was reduced to a cuddly purring kitty-cat again.

'Ah, Reggie, he's *such* a lovely boy,' Adua said now, as she came and topped up their wine glasses.

'We'll definitely make a note of your cat-sitting services if that's OK, Adua,' said Howie, as she hovered with bottles of red and white.

'Of course, Mister Howie. I have seen your cats in your garden already, they're lovely too,' she said. 'I can see all the gardens when I am upstairs working,' she added, looking round the table before taking the empty bottles away. She closed the door behind her.

A silence fell. Beth sipped her wine, a vast improvement on the plonk she usually dragged home from the Tesco in Herne Hill. It was still a source of much sorrow in the village that Waitrose had yet to set up an encampment anywhere near SE21, but Beth was secretly grateful for the cheap booze deals elsewhere. Every little helped, indeed. She idly wondered how much Lizzie's wine had cost, but it was right out of her league – it had a cork, not a screw top. It was a such a shame Harry was missing this.

Strangely, the lull in conversation continued. Beth looked up and down the table. Her late granny would have said there was an angel passing, but the lull didn't feel exactly blessed... it was a tad uncomfortable. And unexpected, when there were such determined talkers gathered. Lizzie and Sally could both hold forth for Britain when they wanted to. Just as Beth was wondering if she'd missed something, Adua breezed back in with a dish of dauphinoise potatoes. God, that looked good.

Lizzie's cooking was old-school, to the point where Beth was actually surprised that she didn't still use one of those heated hostess trollies which had once been such a thing. Murmurs of appreciation finally segued into little bursts of chat, now that everyone's plates were fully loaded. Soon the table was as lively as ever, with Sally holding forth at one end with speculation about why a smash hit West End show was suddenly minus its leading lady. 'Drink, my dears, drink. She never stops,' she said, cheerfully blackening the reputation of a household name in a stage whisper that carried the full length of the room.

At the other end of the table, Lizzie's head just peeped out above the stunning flower arrangement of autumnal chrysanthemums. Not garage ones, perish the thought, but the extravagant curly type that appeared in Japanese woodcuts. Lizzie was on her favourite topic, the sheer wonderfulness of her grandchildren. Beth found this heart-warming. It made her hope her own granny had sung her praises like this, though she acknowledged it was unlikely. Her grandmother was as reticent as Beth. Perhaps her mother rhapsodised over Jake? But she dismissed the thought immediately. There was hardly time in Wendy's Bridge schedule to pause long enough to see her grandchild, let alone dote on him.

By the time Adua had cleared the plates and come round with an enormous trifle in a big crystal bowl, Beth felt as though she really wouldn't need to eat again for the rest of the week, let alone have a pudding. But she was completely unable to resist a large helping. The trifle was a masterpiece, its layers of yellow custard, red fruit and white cream as sharply delineated as the sky rocket ice lollies Jake still loved slurping on when no one important was looking. His mother didn't count, obviously.

The conversation now moved inexorably on to the current favourite Dulwich topic, shoffices. Beth had been dreading this. Shoffices were springing up left, right and centre in Dulwich and the phenomenon could hardly be ignored by the SE21 stalwarts round the table, but she was immediately on the defensive. She hoped her own abortive foray wouldn't be brought up, because as soon as it was, the reason the project had come to such a screeching halt was bound to be disinterred too. As inexorably as the bone itself had been. She'd been really enjoying an evening without having to think about that damn thing, poking up from the pit... almost as though it was waving at her...

Sally was now leading the pack on shoffices. She'd been an early adopter, having installed a souped-up shed-cum-studio about a decade before. But this had been lavishly revamped not so long ago, and she now considered herself the world authority on how to do it right.

Beth had even toddled round to Sally's for a drink, a few weeks back, to discuss her shoffice plans before taking the plunge. Sally had very kindly demonstrated the wonders of her revamp to her, with all the 'ta-dah' vibes of the big reveal on an interiors show. 'Isn't it mah-vellous?' Sally'd said, arms outstretched. Beth had nodded enthusiastically, realising too late that bobbing her head just didn't cut it with Sally. Her neighbour would always prefer the sort of foot-stamping standing ovation and ringing cries of 'Bravo' that her shows had regularly received.

Outside, Sally's shoffice looked quite normal, apart from an elaborate fretted woodwork trim and window shutters that gave it the air of a charming little Swiss chalet. Except that it was painted in the most startling colours on the Farrow & Ball chart, the ones no one else in SE21 had ever been brave enough to touch: Pelt (purple), Arsenic (vivid green) and Charlotte's Locks (orange). Inside, it was equally stunning. It was like Dr Who's Tardis – miles larger than anyone could reasonably have expected. The comparison ended there, though, as it was decked out like a nineteenth-century courtesan's boudoir, not an intergalactic spaceship. There was a chaise longue and a sofa, a desk and, behind an old-fashioned panelled screen, even a telly. Sally said the wi-fi reception was also great. She intended it to be a shoffice for all seasons, so she'd installed both a log-burning stove and a huge freezer for ice cream, both cunningly disguised behind lavish drapes, so the family could make the most of it come winter and summer.

'I don't want to have gone to all this trouble, only for the kids to turn round and say it's too hot or too cold, or whatever.'

'I know how you feel,' Beth had sympathised. 'That "whatever" is a killer. I finally got Jake a new backpack for the start of term as a surprise, only for him to tell me it was a naff brand and he's sticking with last year's. Apparently the whole "falling apart" look is really cool at the moment. But your kids are past that stage, aren't they, Sally?'

'Mine are in their twenties so yes, normally they'd be off, out, out into the world,' she had shrugged, arms flung wide again and bangles a-tinkling. 'And actually, the girls have got flats now. But the boys... the three of them have had problems. You know what things are like, no job security and they can't get on the property ladder... And they're all creatives. Where do they get it from?' Sally had laughed uproariously and Beth had joined in. She wasn't sure she'd call working for a courier company creative, as Eddie, the youngest son, did – but maybe he was writing a screenplay on the side. With the Bentincks, anything was possible.

'They're all working from home a couple of days a week – different days of course – so there were either four of us round the kitchen table all trying to charge our phones at the same time, or there was no one. Crazy. And this place,' she said, waving at the shoffice interior, 'was *stuffed* with my ex-husband's rubbish. Such a pain.' Sally lowered her voice meaningfully. 'Between you and me, before the divorce last year I'd more or less stopped using the shoffice at all. Angus was in here the whole time, monopolising the place, doing God knows what with all his stupid collections. Philately and numismatics my *arse*. He was just a hoarder,' she hissed, making it sound like 'serial killer'. 'I was happy he wasn't in the house! But now it's brilliant. It's either me out here, getting a bit of peace and quiet, or the boys hunkering down, getting away from all the chaos,' she added, back to top volume again.

Beth had smiled dutifully, though the house wasn't really chaotic at all. It was just full of big, exuberant, brightly coloured objects that were as large as Sally's personality – the kitchen alone boasted light-up panels saying 'On air' and 'Applause' and a massive old bus sign for Dulwich Village, as well as a grand piano and lots of antlers that Beth privately wasn't too sure about at all. There was a lifesize cutout of Magritte's man in a bowler hat in the hall, doing service as a coatstand, and everywhere there were great piles of velvet cushions and throws, in peacock, burgundy and screaming pink, which reminded her irresistibly of wonderfully swishy theatre curtains. Beth did wonder how anyone could possibly concentrate in this sort of environment. But then, after spending several years not repainting her hall beige, she knew she was hardly clued up on interiors.

'Oh, and if you're looking for a recommendation,' Sally had said, dropping a large hand onto Beth's shoulder. 'You really won't do better than Rutlands. They did all this for me and it really cost almost nothing. No more than forty or fifty grand.'

Beth had swallowed once or twice at that. Whatever her own budget was, it definitely involved far fewer noughts. And a much smaller figure at the beginning, too. Beth hoped a lot of

Sally's money had gone on extras like the curtains, rather than a roof, floor and walls.

'I don't like to blow my own trumpet...' Sally had started. Here Beth had silently bitten her lip – Sally most definitely had a grade eight in brass. 'But after my years in the theatre, I do know a thing or two about proper construction. And they really have done me proud. As you can see.'

This had been Beth's cue to rave about the wonderfulness of the shoffice again. She did her best, but Sally soon kindly took over the burden and it wasn't really all that long before she was happy with the amount of praise she'd heaped on her own accomplishments.

Beth smiled at the memory, but then looked up to find everyone staring across the table expectantly at her. She tried not to start back in alarm – this sort of sea of faces appeared in her worst anxiety dreams – but she needn't have worried. Sally stepped in.

'Guys, guys, I really don't think we should all cross-question poor Beth about that old bone business. It was probably something her dog dragged back from the park, wasn't it, Beth?'

Beth was about to demur – it would have been a red letter day for Colin if he'd got his paws (and teeth, she thought, remembering those awful marks) on something like that. Then she realised she'd be rejecting Sally's conversational lifebelt if she did.

'Um, who knows?' she mumbled, looking down at her bowl of trifle, which somehow had been completely scraped clean while she had been mulling.

'Exactly,' said Sally. 'Fuss about nothing, while still no one's taking action about that dreadful Low Traffic Neighbourhood monstrosity in the village.'

It was as though Sally had lobbed a Molotov cocktail into the centre of Lizzie's beautifully appointed table. Thank goodness, the LTNs were much more of a bone of contention than an actual bone. Everyone had a view on them. It was rumoured the council had already made over £3 million in fines, all of which seemed have emanated from the other residents of Pickwick Road by the sound of things.

Having stage-managed this uproar, Sally now took it upon herself to calm things down, by throwing the Sinclairs' fish into the mix. 'Anyone fancy taking over from me on feeding Simon and Trudy's carp?' she asked, as George Kendall came to the end of his tirade about the LTNs, the new expanded Ultra Low Emission Zone or ULEZ and, of course, PCNs, or parking tickets. It was a good job London traffic wars involved so many acronyms, at least it made the rants a bit shorter.

Simon and Trudy Sinclair were a very well-liked Pickwick Road couple, in their eighties. They were missing tonight's dinner as they had more or less adopted a life on the ocean wave, spending months drifting round the Caribbean or the Greek islands on cruises, docking briefly in Dulwich, only to disappear off again. They lived on the other side of Beth's house, and she was very fond of them. A couple of years before getting the cruise bug, they had bought some koi carp. The Sinclairs never seemed to do things by halves; no sooner had the first few arrived than their back garden was taken over by two huge pools, and a shed – not nearly as glamorous as Sally's shoffice – which housed all the fishes' paraphernalia.

There was a silence. No one seemed keen to help out. Beth looked around with interest. Beth's mother, Wendy, had a neighbour who kept koi carp and Wendy loathed the things, saying they 'gave her the willies'. As usual, Beth didn't agree with her mother. She thought they looked rather dashing when she gazed out of her bedroom window down into the Sinclairs' garden, as the carp flitted and turned, their orange and silver scales catching the light. But then she'd always liked fish. There was a tropical tank in the dentist she dragged Jake to once every six months, and it took their minds off fillings very effectively.

And of course she was one of local fish and chip emporium Olley's very best customers. Though, she supposed, that wasn't quite the same thing.

Beth always hated those loaded silences when someone asked for volunteers and no one put a hand up. She knew, as the pause stretched like the elastic on one of her elderly ponytail scrunchies, she would eventually feel compelled to put herself forward, though she had enough trouble feeding Jake half the time, let alone her own pets. Thank goodness, Sally broke the impasse herself.

'Oh well then, I'll just carry on. It's not really any trouble. Once a day seems to see them right,' Sally said.

'You could ask Adua,' Beth suggested. 'She wouldn't mind, I'm sure.'

'Oh, Adua's got so much on her plate already,' Sally waved the idea away. From the muffled sounds along the corridor, it did indeed seem as though Adua had her hands full, loading the dishwasher and whisking round the kitchen to return it to Lizzie's preferred state of perfection. 'Anyway, she's already turned it down,' said Sally. 'What about you, Nigel? Fish fan, are you?'

Once upon a time Beth would have suspected that Nigel Wallace had been invited expressly for her. He was the only unmarried man at the table and, though he was sixty if he was a day, she was certain that wouldn't have prevented Lizzie Kendall from thinking he was an eminently suitable match for her. He was a single man in possession of a London house and a good steady job – she had a feeling he was a chartered accountant, and he looked like the type to tell anyone who asked. Many would consider Beth should be grateful to have him as a dinner party date, if nothing else. But, thank goodness, Harry's arrival in the street meant the stream of well-meaning attempts to pair her off had stopped. There were downsides – all the small glitches of Pickwick Road life, like stolen garden waste bags and broken street lights, were now diligently relayed to Beth, so she could pass them on to the top brass of the Met.

Nigel looked up from his bowl, which was scoured as clean as Beth's own had been. They were definitely compatible as far as pudding was concerned, anyway. 'Well, er...' he said, sliding his smeary glasses further up his nose. 'That is to say—'

But Sally didn't wait to hear his excuses. With a merry jangle of her bracelets, she was off. 'Oh, not to worry, muggins here will just carry on as usual! It gets me out of the house every day anyway, and I swear those fish even know the sound of my voice, now. When I get near the tank, they come rushing over to say hello.'

'Greedy blighters,' said George Kendall. 'Any more of that pud, Lizzie love?'

'Well, just a *trifle* for you,' Lizzie simpered like a teenager. 'You know what the doctor said about your cholesterol. Anyone else?'

Beth heroically refused, then had to watch everyone else digging in and really wished she'd said yes. 'My mother's neighbour has carp. Is it true they grow to fit the tank they're in, so if you get a super-size one, you'll get huge fish?'

Sally shrugged. 'I guess we're going to find out. Not that the Sinclairs could really get tanks any bigger, bless them. They do love those fish. They even send them postcards while they're away.'

Everyone shook their heads at this, conveniently forgetting they all asked Adua to give their pets special treats while they were on holiday themselves, to cheer the animals up in their absence. Beth realised she was even sillier – she hardly ever went away, as she didn't want to upset Magpie. The cat often shredded curtains in revenge if Beth was out too long, or went on the cat equivalent of a 'dirty protest' in return for any perceived neglect.

'I must say, I am not a pet fan,' said Nigel, then sat back in relief at finally getting his views out.

Sally laughed uproariously. 'My Angus wasn't keen either. But that's one of the many advantages of divorce! I *adore* those fish. By the way, have you heard that the Elwoods have split up too?'

This was news to most of the table, and the conversation turned to the number of other marriages which had gone down in flames recently. As everyone drank the decaffeinated coffee or mint tea that Adua handed round, Beth detected a certain amount of unease amongst the couples at the table. There but for the grace of God... It was almost as though dissatisfaction was catching. Would Beth herself be sitting here, or at a table very like this, in twenty years' time, wondering where the magic had gone? No. She decided it was more than likely that she would be alone, just as she was now – but only because Harry had decided he was unable to get away from something much more important than their relationship...

There were some sombre expressions as everyone thanked their hosts, picked up their coats and wandered off up and down Pickwick Road. The Kendalls' smug smiles didn't budge, however. Beth wondered if they were really as happy as they seemed, or whether they just had very impressive game faces.

She had dodged a bullet this evening, though. Thanks to Sally's irrepressible desire for the limelight, her bone had not had much of a look in. Not for the first time, she felt a wave of pity for its one-time owner. She hoped there was a grave somewhere where the remainder of its bits were resting in peace. And she hoped that grave was very, very old.

But, now that she came to think about it, wasn't it a bit odd that people didn't want to find out more about this mystery in the heart of Pickwick Road? Perhaps she wasn't the only one in the street who wanted to bury the whole business six feet under. It was almost as if, she thought slowly, someone might have something to hide.

Beth swallowed. A very strange mystery had opened up, right on her back doorstep. And that was just much too close to home.

FOUR

Beth got very little sleep after the dinner party on Wednesday night, but any hope of a lie-in was wrecked when a full-blown SOCO team turned up at her door before dawn, and spent the rest of the morning dragging in the state-of-the-art equipment essential for any modern-day police investigation – a catering-sized box of PG Tips teabags and five packets of chocolate digestives. Plus a job lot of little blue plastic shoe cosies and an extremely dour Scottish forensic pathologist. She would prob-ably have faced a few more questions from the neighbours if that little lot had already been in situ.

She soon worked out that the tea and biscuits were vital to minimise the gloom of the pathologist, whose name was Chris Campbell. When he had a mug and a McVitie's in hand, he would occasionally permit himself a grim smile at the rest of the team bustling around. When he didn't, and had his nose to the earth of the far corner of Beth's garden, he looked as though he was in severe physical pain. In some ways she couldn't blame him. It was the sort of September weather when the rain fell in such a fine drizzle that you almost didn't notice it until you were lured outside without a coat. Then it was too late, and the cold wormed its way into your bones.

She couldn't help feeling sorry for them all, stuck out there, so she brewed up another round of weapons-grade tea and took it out into the garden, only to find everyone clustered around the hole. Standing at the back, shorter than every single one of the SOCOs and having to peep through where she could, reminded Beth strongly of the original dreadful discovery. Her heart started to beat faster. Surely there wouldn't be? There couldn't be?

But there was. It was another bone, found a metre away from where the first had been disinterred.

Beth stood in the drizzly garden, clutching her tea tray as though her life depended on it.

'Oh my God!' she wailed, the cups rattling like her chattering teeth. 'That can't be another, can it? Please tell me it's not real...'

Consternation, horror and disgust whirled through her mind. What the hell was happening in her scrubby, safe suburban garden? What was this going to do to poor Jake? How could she bring her son up in a place full of bits of dead people?

Chris Campbell stepped away from the dig and rescued the tray just before it slipped from Beth's grasp, a wintry smile appearing on his face, while the rest of the team stood and watched. 'We have found additional evidence of human remains, yes indeed. Would you happen to know anything about this?' he said, as a weak beam of sunlight broke through the fine droplets of rain and caressed his high cheekbones.

'What-what are you saying?' said Beth.

His blue eyes, the colour of glacier water, gleamed with something that could have been excitement, or even amusement. Beth realised he'd actually cheered up immensely. Did he think he'd already found the culprit? He couldn't possibly suspect her of having something to do with the bones, though.

Could he? But on the face of it, perhaps it was a fair assumption. After all, they had been found in her garden.

'Just wondering what you might know,' he said, in a faux-casual manner that, to Beth, seemed much more sinister than an outright accusation.

'What *I* might…? But you don't understand,' she said quickly, as the SOCOs, apparently completely unperturbed by the discovery or the way she was taking it, helped themselves to teas from the tray. 'The only thing I *do* know is…'

Campbell leant forward, fixing her again with that unwavering gaze.

'It wasn't me,' she blurted.

As soon as she'd said it, she realised how ridiculous she sounded. Just like Jake, that time he'd smushed PlayDoh into the sofa as a small boy. He'd blamed Magpie, who would certainly have been up for it if she hadn't been busy scoffing hideously expensive cat food. But Beth had absolutely no one to pin this on. Her denial was as weak as water. And made her seem all the guiltier.

Chris Campbell stared at her as though she was something very interesting in a Petri dish. 'Is that so?' he said slowly. Beth had a horrible feeling he'd either decided he'd unmasked the villain already – or he was laughing at her. She flushed a deep scarlet and stumbled into the house as quickly as she could.

Safely back in the kitchen, Beth leant against the sink and took a breath. No one could seriously think she'd bury bones in her own garden. Could they? She'd just been overwhelmed for a moment. She was a middle-class bleeding-heart liberal, guilt was priced in. But she lived with a policeman, for goodness' sake. How stupid would she be, to stash bones under her own shoffice? A little voice told her that serving Met officers had done far worse recently. But Harry wasn't like that. And even gloomy Chris Campbell couldn't possibly think either of them had this on their conscience.

Well, she was just going to have to get over her guilt reflex, Beth thought, banging a few dirty mugs around in the sink and beginning to feel better. Now rage started giving her cheeks a rosy flush, as she contemplated the ruination of her garden.

Granted, it had never been exactly a potential Royal Horticultural Society gold medal winner. But now the scrappy patch of turf was dominated by one of those weird SOCO tents, like a tiny wedding marquee but infinitely more sinister. As well as Chris Campbell, standing about with a clipboard, a brush and that strange expression, there were assorted underlings bustling this way and that. Just then, the doorbell rang and Beth had to let in another great influx of white-suited figures trooping through her house to join the throng.

Christ, how many people did it take to sort out two damned bones? This was beginning to seem like one of those lightbulb jokes Jake loved. And what was her poor boy making of all this anyway? Once upon a time, when he'd been very small, he would have found it all very exciting and would have yearned to be out there with his own little plastic trowel, joining in with the digging. He hadn't really said much about it over the last few days, but anything that caused talk at school and horrified gasps amongst the neighbours was bound to be a Bad Thing.

At first Beth assumed that the police were throwing these huge staffing levels at her fairly minor problem because of Harry. But, as the next day dawned and yet more SOCOs turned up, she realised it was infinitely worse than that. The police must be thinking that Beth's bones had not wandered in on their own. They had most likely brought another two hundred and four friends with them, comprising an entire human skeleton, which could be lurking anywhere in her garden.

So, far from getting the makeover Beth had dreamt of, her garden and, indeed, her entire house were filling up with police debris. Beth and half of Dulwich were addicted to Scandi noir boxsets, where attractive people in Icelandic jumpers popped on the very same SOCO plastic bootees for a second or two before making a massive breakthrough and driving off in vintage Volvos. Sadly, things weren't playing out like that in Pickwick Road. Apart from anything else, the uniforms worn by Chris Campbell's team seemed to attract mud, so Beth's front path, hall and kitchen were soon almost indistinguishable from the garden itself. That never happened in Scandiwegia, where interiors remained impossibly chic at all times.

If Harry was right about the bones being escapees from the burial site in the village, the mud itself might well be a serious problem. Beth's researches had confirmed that thirty-five plague victims had been interred there in unmarked graves, and as Google had had nothing reassuring to say on the half-life of infectious diseases, the soil being tracked through the house was potentially pestilential.

Magpie was treating this turn of events with all the disdain it deserved, but also enjoying getting in the odd swipe with her claws if any of the SOCOs tried any of that 'Hey, cute little kitty' nonsense and tried to stroke her. Colin, meanwhile, despite his age and normal imperturbability, was getting very overexcited. Being in such close proximity to a potential treasure trove of bones, let alone those already harvested, was too much for his equilibrium. He had taken to standing and barking by the kitchen door, pleading to be let out to frolic in the unsuspected charnel house that had been unearthed. Though he had not sniffed a thing before the SOCOs arrived, all the freshly dug earth was definitely now signalling to him that there was something a lot more exciting out there than the dry old Bonio biscuits Beth kept trying to palm him off with.

After a night of the old dog's bloodcurdling yowling, Beth decided she had to act. 'I'm going to ring Katie and ask her to take Colin for a couple of days,' she said to Jake over breakfast on Friday morning. She then had to repeat herself, as Jake had his earbuds in and hadn't heard a word. She really needed to ban them from the breakfast table, but the truth was she wasn't really a morning person either and quite liked a bit of silence over her toast.

To her surprise, Jake suddenly piped up. 'Do you think she'd take me as well?'

Beth almost dropped her cup. 'Really? Why do you want to go?'

'Duh, Mum, do you think it's easy for me to do my homework while there's, like, a hundred guys in the back garden chatting all afternoon, right into the evening, with searchlights and everything?'

Beth was about to remonstrate – there weren't *hundreds* of them, there were only maybe six or seven. OK, ten yesterday... but Jake hadn't finished.

'And Col is acting like he's in a remake of *The Hound of the Baskervilles*! He was barking for hours last night. And clawing the back door this morning when I got down. I mean, look at him now!'

Beth switched her gaze to the dog, who was sitting with his nose hard against the kitchen door, slavering at the scents wafting in on the morning breeze, his tail wagging hopefully from side to side. She was pretty sure he'd only stopped yapping because he'd lost his voice.

Sensing eyes upon him, Colin turned to look at Beth. It was a gaze full of love, gentle kindness – and a desperate desire to get out into the back garden and eat a bone. Why oh why wouldn't she do the decent thing and unlock the door? He turned back to his station, his mournful doggy sigh full of reproach.

'You might have a point, love,' Beth said sadly. 'OK, I'll ask Katie. I don't suppose it will do any harm for you both to go... You can keep an eye on Teddy, make sure he doesn't run Colin ragged. As long as you do your homework as soon as you get in,

just like you do here. Finish everything before you even think of
doing any gaming with Charlie.'

'Yeah, yeah, Mum,' said Jake, screwing his earbuds back in
and nodding his head in time to some ghostly beat. The conversation was over as far as he was concerned. He was smiling,
though, a sight which always gladdened Beth's heart.

She didn't have a chance to reopen the discussion anyway
as the bell immediately shrilled. The morning shift of investigators had arrived, all cheery smiles and massive boots, clad in the
blue shoe covers she was coming to hate so much.

After all her complaints to Harry last night about the
mud, she was initially pleased to see they had brought a whole
batch of plastic duckboards with them this time, which they
laid down carefully like big square white stepping stones, all
the way through her hall and kitchen and into the back
garden. Then they retraced their footsteps to the police van to
get more, with their bootees already trailing dirt everywhere.
In minutes, the boards would be as muddy as the garden
itself.

Harry was long gone, of course, having got up at some ludi-
crous hour to work on his intractable case. He was the only
person in the house who spoke fluent police, and had the rank
to ensure he was listened to. If she pointed out to the team the
utter futility of what they were doing, it would make her about
as popular as naughty Magpie now was. Beth decided she'd get
them where it hurt, by not offering any tea.

Jake sloped off to school without even saying goodbye,
which didn't improve her mood. Once he would have been
quite upset at the prospect of not seeing her for a couple of days.
Now he seemed decidedly cheery about the idea. It stung, and
added to her feeling of disgruntlement. She banged out of the
front door with a reluctant Colin in tow, but not before spotting
one of the SOCO team happily rustling about in his spacesuit
in her kitchen, putting on the kettle and sorting out some mugs

with an infuriating degree of familiarity. So much for teaching them a lesson.

It was just as well that Beth bumped into Katie before her blood pressure reached boiling point. Neither had time for the long coffee in Jane's that the situation really demanded, so Beth just let rip in the street, about the many infuriating consequences of the investigation. To her surprise, Katie wasn't all sympathy.

'I'd have thought you'd be enjoying this,' she said, adjusting her workout bag on her shoulder. She was on her way to teach her first yoga session of the day, offering a different kind of overstretch to the exhausted mummies of SE21. 'I mean, it's a new investigation, isn't it?'

'There's such a thing as being too close for comfort,' said Beth, feeling a little miffed. Yes, she enjoyed puzzles, there was no denying that. She'd even started to have a certain sort of notoriety in Dulwich as someone who solved crimes. But human remains in her own garden? It was a horrific intrusion into her world, and just when she had finally decided to get going on her home improvement programme. No point in moaning on at Katie, though. Her friend was now moving from foot to foot, her expensive trainers silent, but somehow screaming that she had urgent stuff to do elsewhere. 'Listen, Katie, I wondered if you could do me a huge favour?'

Was she imagining it, or did a shadow briefly cross Katie's sunny brow? But her friend said as obligingly as usual, 'Course, Beth. What is it?'

'Could you take Colin and Jake, just for a few days? Both of them are going spare, for different reasons.'

Katie looked down at Colin, who was taking advantage of the pause in his walk to have a quick and well-deserved nap. 'He looks pretty calm to me?'

'You should have heard him in the middle of the night. Honestly, it was earsplitting,' said Beth, eyes wide. 'He's desperate to get his chops round a bone, and he doesn't understand why I won't let him. And Jake says he can't do any homework with all the disruption.'

Katie caved in straight away. 'Poor old guy.' She bent fluidly to pat Colin's suede-soft head, making Beth realise yet again that she really ought to give yoga another try. Her own knees had started cracking like pistol shots when she picked up sticks in the park for Colin to fetch. 'And poor Jake too. Yeah, no problem. Happy to have them both. They can come from tonight, if you like. Bring Colin over later. I'll just expect Jake after school. Charlie's walking himself home so they can make their way together.'

'Are you sure, Katie? It won't disrupt your weekend?'

Katie waved the idea away and Beth smiled gratefully. 'I'll send Jake a text.' Using mobile phones in school was strictly forbidden, but the boys always managed to peep at them during breaks, to catch up on vital WhatsApps from kids they sat next to in lessons – and occasionally also pick up instructions from their mums. 'Thank you so much, Katie. I owe you.'

'I'll collect one of these days, don't you worry,' Katie said firmly. 'Got to run now.' With that, she was off, her vibrant Sweaty Betty-clad form ducking and diving through the crowds of mothers dropping off children at the Village Primary and the College School. Beth took the well-trodden path to Wyatt's, and her job as archivist. But, as she walked, she couldn't help wondering.

Was it her imagination, or on top of everything else... was something wrong with Katie?

FIVE

By the time she got to her office at Wyatt's, Beth had decided she was being paranoid. Katie had stuck by her through thick and thin, and had even ended up a lot more involved in some of her cases than she would have liked to be. Never once had she complained. She was a wonderful, kind person who'd always had her friend's back and Beth was simply imagining things. Probably due to lack of sleep, thanks to Colin's yowling.

Her desk was heaped with a distressing quantity of new post, as it always seemed to be these days. Her colleagues tended to dump stuff on her, with a blind optimism that she'd take it off their own massive to-do lists. She then had to weed it all out and hand the rejects back to their rightful owners. But it was also partly Beth's own fault. Try as she might since she had so fortuitously landed this job, she had never got into a proper routine. While the work had saved her and Jake from looming poverty, Beth still couldn't fight her tendency to relegate it to last place on her agenda.

Well, all that was going to change, she vowed. She was going to treat her job with the seriousness it deserved, and turn up for her allotted three days a week without fail. After all, she now had a massive incentive to, as her house and garden had been taken over by white-suited mess-makers.

One of her problems had been that Wyatt's, and its fine head, Dr Grover, had placed implicit trust in her. No one ever checked up to make sure she was beavering away. They just expected the occasional exhibition marrying up the past and present of the school, which she always delivered by the skin of her teeth. And of course there was the promise, now as often delayed as any government pledge to sort out the economy, that she would eventually finish her definitive biography of Sir Thomas Wyatt. Wyatt had long been lauded for his philanthropy. But it was Beth who had discovered that he owed his fortune to slavery. Her book was going to lay bare this heinous truth and reassess the legacy Wyatt had left the school – and the people of Dulwich.

After spending the next ten minutes staring into space, she realised it had happened yet again. Her mind had drifted back to the bones in her garden. Who on earth did they belong to? Even if they were as ancient as Sir Thomas Wyatt himself, they had once had an owner. Someone had waved that arm, to hail a friend, to say goodbye to a loved one. Perhaps they had used it to cradle a baby or build a home. She didn't know what the second bone was, and she deliberately hadn't asked. A toe, from a missing foot? Or worse, a finger, which had once beckoned from the arm? The thought was grotesque. And the much bigger question was, how had both bones come to lie, unmourned and without benefit of clergy, in Pickwick Road of all places? Katie was right, it was a mystery she ought to get her teeth into, if that wasn't too revolting an analogy. The trouble was that it horrified her too much.

She needed to see it more objectively, Beth told herself sternly. After all, as Katie had also pointed out, old bones were fine really. The Natural History Museum in South Kensington, one of Jake's favourite places in years gone by, was about ninety-nine per cent bone – although admittedly most of them belonged to dinosaurs.

She permitted herself a smile at that and it was enough to carry her through the next few bits of post, until she got to a photocopied page of upcoming rugby fixtures that made her sigh. Jake was already showing worrying signs of keenness on rugby, which probably meant Beth would have to get up early on Saturday mornings for the next five years and stand at the edge of various pitches round south London, going blue with cold, while her boy covered himself in mud.

The thought of mud then took her inexorably back to her garden. She really ought to speak to the builders, let them know there'd be a bit of a delay. She got out her phone and dialled. 'Oh hi, it's Beth Haldane from Pickwick Road here,' she started breezily.

'Oh! Oh... hang on a second,' said the receptionist. Was it Beth's imagination, or did she sound a bit shifty?

After a moment, a man came on. 'Mrs Haldane?'

'It's Ms,' said Beth.

'Oh? Well the thing is, er, Mzz Haldane, since you were having a spot of bother with the police and a body and all...'

'Not really a "spot of bother" exactly, and definitely not a *body*, just, ahem, a couple of bones, it's probably only a mix-up...' said Beth quickly, but it was no good. The man was still speaking.

'...So we had no choice really, we've got so much work, we had to move on. But we might be able to fit you in again when it's sorted out, say in the New Year? Or the spring would be better... All the best till then,' he said, and there was an unmistakable clunk as the phone cut off.

Beth was left staring at her mobile. Well, that was definitely someone else, like Chris Campbell, who thought she'd had a bit too much to do with these damned bones. What was she going to do now? She couldn't live with the garden in that state for a week longer, let alone several months.

Just then came the buzz of a text. It was Nina.

A fellow mum from Jake's pre-Wyatt's days at the lovely little Village Primary, Nina had become one of Beth's best friends after they had solved a mystery together down in Herne Hill. They had since cracked a case in Sydenham, too. Admittedly, Nina's major contribution had been to bring the snacks, but that wasn't something Beth was ever going to sniff at. An army marches on its stomach, and private investigators in Dulwich, it turned out, subsisted largely on Wotsits and Lucozade. These were both substances that Beth had no hesitation in banning her son from touching, while surreptitiously very much enjoying on reconnaissance missions with Nina.

One of the best things about Nina was that she lived a distinctly colourful life, the antithesis of Beth's rather sheltered existence. She was a speed-reader of airport blockbusters, a temp who sorted out ailing companies with one hand tied behind her back and, most usefully at the moment, she seemed to have an encyclopaedic knowledge of south London builders. It was time to put her friend's mental database to the test.

Beth quickly checked the time on her phone. It was reasonably close to pick-up. Beth could try to persuade Nina to leave work early for a quick coffee en route to fetching her boy Wilf from the Village Primary. Luckily, it was never difficult to get Nina to do a bit of slacking. Within seconds, Nina had pinged back a message agreeing to meet at Jane's. Beth was soon trotting out of Wyatt's and into the deliciously coffee-scented fug of the café. She'd just got in the cappuccinos when Nina appeared.

Nina was a bundle of energy, wrapped in a white puffa jacket. Her wild curls, dimples and guileless smile made her a dead ringer for one of Raphael's little cherubs, and were a cunning disguise for lashings of native wit. However much time Nina spent away from her current temp job, she'd still slice through the workload in seconds flat when she decided to show up. Any employer worth their salt realised this about Nina pretty quickly. Her temp agency now sent her out as a sort of one-woman wrecking ball to cut through south-east London's worst paperwork foul-ups. Nina was also impervious to the usual Dulwich double-kiss greeting.

'Awright?' she said, as Beth pushed her cappuccino over to her in lieu of the ritual. 'Wossup then, babe?'

Beth sighed gustily. 'Well, it's this awful bones business. I've no idea how long it's going to take to sort it. And now my builders have taken another job, they've really left me in the lurch. So I don't know how I'm going to get the shoffice finished.'

'No worries, mate. Plenty more where that lot came from,' said Nina airily, now speaking with a lavish foam moustache.

Beth gestured vaguely to her own upper lip, hoping Nina would get the hint. Nina just took another sip and acquired more facial adornments. Beth gave up. 'How come you know so much about builders, Nina?'

'Through my cousin, Katrina, innit,' Nina said. 'She's the one, really, she knows chapter and worse. Worked in builders' merchants and that. No reason why you should, though. You've never needed nuffin doing till now.'

Beth knew this wasn't true; her house was falling apart. As she and Harry had been tussling over moving almost since the day they'd met, it had seemed pointless to spend good money fixing the dodgy extractor fan in the bathroom, or replacing the cracked tiles in the kitchen. But now they were staying, she was keen to work through her extensive to-do list. To say nothing of filling in the massive crater in the back garden that, at present, was the only thing she had to show for her grand expansion plans.

'So, of all the builders you know, who is the best, would you say? Given that I don't have much money,' Beth added quickly.

Nina gave Beth a look over the rim of her sugary coffee. 'You don't want to skimp on this, hon. Do it once, do it right, my old dad used to say. Mind you, turns out he was a repeat offender,' she added darkly.

Beth looked inquiringly at her friend, but Nina waved her interest away, and inadvertently removed her 'tache at the same time. 'Let's not go there, hon.'

'Oh... OK. So, who would you say is definitely the best firm of builders you know?'

'Oh, the ones you've got, girl, no doubt,' Nina said, back to her usual bouncy self. 'You got the number from me, dincha?'

'But they've just dumped me,' Beth wailed.

'Oops, yeah. But don't fret, hon. Tell you what, let me give Katrina a bell later. See what she says. She'll know another firm that'll be even better.' The words sounded comforting, but Beth knew when Nina was prevaricating, as she'd virtually invented the sport herself. Or she would have done, if she hadn't tarried that bit too long.

'You really think she'll know someone who can help?' Beth felt sceptical.

'Yeah, course. Don't even worry about it, babe.' With that, Nina finished up her cappuccino and dashed off. 'Got to go, don't want to be late for Wilf.'

As Jake was going back to Katie's, Beth had absolutely no need to rush for once. That ought to have been cause for celebration, but it was hard to feel jubilant all on her own. She certainly didn't want to be sitting in the café in lonely splendour when the usual droves of mothers arrived with their freshly collected offspring in tow, for an afterschool hot chocolate treat. She'd really feel out of kilter with the rest of the world then.

When Jake had been tiny, a few hours alone had been all she craved. And even now, if Harry had been around for a romantic evening, she would have been rather thrilled at having her son off her hands for a bit. But poor Harry was so tied up at the moment. She'd probably just be getting quality time with Magpie, and, if she knew her cat, she'd have plenty to say about the SOCO team. She collected her things and trailed back to Pickwick Road, deep in thought. If even Nina was a bit stumped about which builders to call next, Beth's garden might not get sorted for ages. And that was something else she was definitely not happy with.

It took her back to all the chat about shoffices at the Kendalls' dinner party the other night, and the time when Sally Bentinck had given her the tour of her own amazing new studio. She'd been so fulsome about her firm of builders. Rutlish or something, wasn't it? Sally had even taken a sneaky peek at proceedings in Beth's back garden from the vantage point of her own shoffice. But that was natural. Beth loved all her neighbours but sometimes it was like living in a colony of meerkats, there always seemed to be someone keeping a beady eye on everything you did. Not necessarily in a critical way – it had been a great comfort in the dark days following James's sudden death to find a casserole on her doorstep or a message on her phone, after she'd had what she'd thought was a private weep in her own garden – but sometimes she wished people were busier with their own lives.

It was inevitable, with such thoughts in her head, that she'd bump into a neighbour on the way home. Luckily it was lovely Zoe Bentinck, Sally's second daughter, who was one of Beth's favourite people. Zoe had a willowy beauty Beth couldn't help envying. She used to babysit for Jake (who now considered himself far too grown-up for such things), and had been endlessly kind and patient with him, building Death Stars out of Lego for hours on end and reading him *Thomas the Tank Engine* books without a murmur. Having three little brothers of her own had made her a natural.

Tonight, she was wrestling with the family wheelie bin. These, like supermarket trolleys, seemed pre-programmed to ignore whoever was pushing them, particularly anyone who happened to be under six feet tall and weighing less than fifteen stone. Beth always tried to cede this part of the Pickwick Road routine to Harry, but he seemed to think it was an annual event, not a weekly chore. Zoe greeted Beth with a slightly exasperated grin, as the bin veered off towards the kerb. Beth gave the thing a hearty shove from her side, and between them they nudged it into position. She made a mental note not to forget her own. Harry would be back too late and off too early to do theirs tonight, she was willing to bet. She said as much to Zoe, who chimed in.

'Oh, Mum always forgets too, that's why I'm doing it. She says it's her artistic temperament which puts her above such mundane concerns,' Zoe said with a sideways smile. 'Mind you, I think it's a bit like selective deafness. She never misses doing the jobs she enjoys. Like feeding those fish on the other side of you.'

'Oh yes, the carp! Your mum's such a fan, isn't she?'

Zoe laughed. 'That's putting it mildly. She's obsessed.'

'The Sinclairs are lucky she's so taken with them. Have you heard from them recently?'

'Not a thing,' said Zoe. 'They just trust Mum to get on with it,' she added, wiping her hands on the seat of her jeans and preparing to go back inside.

Beth hesitated, but she decided to risk a question that had been on her mind since the dinner party. 'Do you know if your mum was actually a bit miffed with me? Because I didn't choose the builders she recommended for my shoffice?'

Zoe thought for a second. 'I doubt it. I don't think she'd care. I mean, she does love our builders, always gets them to do her DIY, but it's not like she gets a commission or anything,' she joked. 'Anyway, she's in too much of a fury at the moment to worry about all that. Have you heard?'

Beth hadn't, and did her best not to look too avid for gossip.

Zoe lowered her voice and leant in, though there was no one else in the street. 'She's up in arms about Dad. He's just called her saying he's got a new girlfriend. Guess how old?'

Beth stared at Zoe. From the expression on the girl's face, it was clear she was either very young or very old. She decided it was more tactful to veer upwards, rather than suggest Zoe's dad was acting out a well-worn cliché. 'Sixty-four?' she ventured.

'I wish. Take forty years off that.'

'But that's...'

'Yep. Same age as Magenta.' Zoe's big sister was now a trainee lawyer, and so busy she was seldom seen in Pickwick Road. 'Gross or what?'

Beth heartily agreed with her, but didn't like to say so. This was still Zoe's father. She made a face which she hoped said it all.

'And he's staying in the States. Says he's never coming back. It's like he doesn't want to see any of us again. Not that we want to see him, if he's going to do that to Mum.' Zoe blinked rapidly. The tears she wouldn't let herself shed made her eyes almost iridescent. Beth prayed the girl wouldn't break down. Luckily, Zoe just sniffed prettily once and changed the subject.

'So, what about all your bones? Creepy, no?'

'Creepy, yes,' said Beth. 'Although there are only two of them. Harry says they're really old, nothing to worry about. But it's still awful, actually. I'm hoping they'll just take them away quickly and we can get back to normal,' she added with a shiver.

'Yes of course, so horrid for you,' said Zoe kindly.

All the Bentincks were so lovely, Beth reflected. Except, it seemed, for Angus, Sally's husband. Beth had always quite liked him, but it just showed how wrong you could be. He was as big a character as his wife, a bit like Brian Blessed. Zoe was Beth's favourite, though. Beth had seen the heart-shaped look in Jake's eyes when Zoe wafted past the sitting room window. She'd just finished uni, had landed her first job in marketing and was living in a flat-share in Clapham, but still found the time to pop home, checking in on her mum much more frequently since her dad's defection. What a devoted daughter. In fact, all the Bentinck kids had been brilliant. Beth just hoped Jake would rise to the occasion, if anything similar happened to her. She wasn't expecting Harry to run off with a woman half his age... yet stranger things had happened in Dulwich.

SIX

Beth let herself into the house, the conversation about mothers and daughters reminding her she hadn't spoken to her own mum, Wendy, for days. She was brought up short by a heap of forensic suits and more of those dratted booties, discarded by the stairs. Was she supposed to wash them? She poked a suit with her toe. It was made of a weird papery substance that she was happy to conclude would disintegrate in the machine. She heaped up an armful and went back out to the front garden to dump them in the bin. What a terrible waste of resources. All this, for two bones. She'd had to wait long enough for anyone to come round at the start, but that must have been before they'd realised she lived with Harry. Now things had gone the other way. Her garden was mud as far as the eye could see, and her house was rapidly filling up too, while the line of filthy duck-boards trailed between the two, like the yellow brick road but most decidedly the wrong colour.

Beth stomped back to the kitchen, sighed and flicked on the kettle. The house didn't feel right, and it wasn't just the mess. She missed Colin's comforting presence, his huge ear-to-ear

Labrador grin welcoming her home, his stumpy tail wagging so hard that it almost threatened to raise his hefty rump off the ground. She even missed his woofly sighs at her failure to provide him with constant walks.

And Jake! She missed Jake too, of course, she reminded herself with a parent's automatic twinge of guilt. How awful that she'd thought of the dog before her child. But Colin expected so little from her, apart from a pat, a kind word and, if he was spectacularly lucky, a dog treat that would bring him a piercing, if fleeting, joy. Jake, dote on him though she did, always brought a raft of problems with him. Sometimes it was the old familiar sorrow that he would never experience a proper, deep father–child bond, like Beth's with her own dad. He was now long gone, having expired after one too many of Wendy's treacle puddings, but at least Beth had known his unconditional love and support. Then there was the strain of being all things to Jake, in the absence of James. This was some-what mitigated now that Harry was on the scene, though Beth still felt she had to be super-careful not to imply, for a single second, that Harry was a replacement for James.

Perhaps it was the gloomy view out of the kitchen window giving rise to these bleak thoughts. The stupid SOCO tent was shivering slightly in the cold wind, the lawn obliterated by muddy footprints and strange boxes of equipment dumped here and there waiting to be pressed into use again. Beth hoped none of it would get nicked – though it would be a cheeky burglar indeed who'd steal equipment from a police investigation.

She turned her back on it all, blew on her tea a couple of times, and sat herself down. Before she rang her mother, she quickly checked the time – she was in luck, if she could call it that. If she rang right this moment she would catch Wendy between Bridge games. She tried to channel Zoe Bentinck's unswerving loyalty as she dialled the number and stretched a smile across her face.

'Hi, Mum!'

'Beth, darling. I was worried you might have fallen down one of those sinkholes!'

For a moment, Beth's mind went blank. *Sinkholes? What sinkholes?* Had she been so wrapped up in her own concerns that she had missed an enormous fissure opening up in the village? But then she realised it was just her mother's way of ticking her off for not having called for a while. Wendy was getting her 'news' via YouTube these days, so normal UK headlines were now jumbled up with major disasters all round the world. Beth dimly remembered a car had disappeared into a crater in Australia or New Zealand or somewhere, that must be what Wendy was on about.

'We've had a bit of a hoo-ha with the shed, Mum. It's been quite, er, time-consuming.'

'I don't know what you expect, if you must employ cowboys,' said Wendy. 'I gave you the name of a perfectly good firm, they did a great job on my fence.'

Beth hadn't liked to point out that her mother's builders had gone out of business fully twenty years ago. Knowing Wendy, they'd probably stopped trading the day after finishing her job, having been harried to within an inch of their lives by her extremely effective passive-aggressive style. It was like being browbeaten by a delicate Dresden shepherdess. She paused for a second. 'Anyway. You'll never guess what's happened.'

As was so often the case, Beth found herself telling her mother all about something she'd sworn to keep from her, just because it might distract her from something else. Predictably, Wendy was up in arms about the bones.

'I always told you not to buy that awful house,' Wendy said with a sniff.

This wasn't true at all. Beth remembered her mother informing her in no uncertain terms that the Pickwick Road house was the best chance she'd ever have of getting a foothold

in Dulwich, 'even if it is a tumbledown wreck that needs bull-
dozing', as she'd put it.

'I knew there was something awful lurking somewhere in
that place,' Wendy went on now. 'After all, why did James die
like that? I've always sensed an *atmosphere*,' she said, dramati-
cally enough to give Sally Bentinck a run for her money.

Beth took a sharp breath and began counting, but Wendy
seemed to realise she'd perhaps gone a tiny step too far.

'Anyway, dear, enough of all that. How is my wonderful
grandson?'

Beth suppressed the thought that her mother would have a
better idea how Jake was if she ever took it upon herself to see
him. She remembered Lizzie Kendall and her breathless
enthusiasm for children who were obviously not a patch on
Jake, in Beth's totally unbiased opinion. Even though their two
houses were walking distance apart, Wendy always acted as
though Beth had whisked Jake off to the other side of the
world, perhaps even to the spot where this blessed sinkhole
was. Still, it was just as well she was highly unlikely to pop
round, as Jake wasn't even there at the moment. Wendy was
absolutely sure to take a dim view of Beth farming him out to
Katie.

Beth was beginning to wonder why on earth she'd thought
this call would be a good idea. Was there anything she could
talk to her mother about, that wouldn't result in one of those
jellyfish stings of disapproval she so dreaded? Then she remembered the Sinclairs' carp. At last, a safe subject for Wendy to
sound off about.

'You remember I told you the Sinclairs had got fish?'

'Oh yes? I really don't think I recall them... you know at my
age it's so difficult to keep track...' said Wendy, retreating into
the trademark vagueness that led many to assume she was a
sweet and gentle elderly lady.

'You do know them, they play Bridge sometimes at your

club and you always say she's rubbish at bidding,' said Beth. 'Anyway, they've got carp – just like your neighbour Mrs Hill.'

Wendy was back to acerbity in a flash. 'Not those monstrous things! Ugh, they give me the heebie-jeebies, writhing round all day. And when they eat, their mouths are huge. Talk about sinkholes!' Beth could feel her shudder down the phone.

'I suppose you don't have to peer over the fence at them?' Beth couldn't help saying.

'I *don't*, the very thought! It's just that if I'm changing the spare room bed, I can hardly miss them, thrashing in that tank,' Wendy said with dignity.

Beth smiled to herself. Wendy hadn't had a guest staying since about 1998. But she was off again.

'You know, I can't understand it. People make such a big deal these days of being vegan and not eating even a little slice of roast chicken, and then they get fish like that.'

'What have the fish got to do with being vegan? Except vegans can't eat them, I suppose.' Beth was baffled.

'They're carnivores, Beth. Don't you know the first thing about carp?'

'Well, probably not,' she conceded. Then she said her farewells, without taking too many more direct hits. Her conscience was now clear. She'd done her duty. And she knew that, despite all Wendy's barbs, her mother liked to keep in touch really. It had to be on her own terms, though. It was a shame Wendy couldn't just ring her when she wanted to talk. But that was much too easy. No, Beth would always have to guess when Wendy was in need of contact, and would also have to put up with Wendy's habitual conversational jousting. Underneath it all, there was love. Though sometimes it felt like she needed a SOCO team of her own to find it. For the umpteenth time, Beth resolved to be better at all this when Jake was grown-up and the one ringing her.

She decided she'd just check with Katie that he'd got to her place safely. But, to her surprise, her friend picked up but then just whispered urgently down the phone at her, 'Can't talk now. Ring you back in a bit.'

What on earth could Katie be up to? Had Beth been right, was there something off with her after all? Usually, at this time in the evening, Katie would be looming over Charlie's homework, testing him rigorously on the long lists of Latin vocab that Wyatt's had started throwing at the boys. She might even be trying to 'help' him with one of his projects, though it wasn't like the Village Primary any more. In those days, parents had got away with sending in creations that were quite obviously their own work and had nothing whatsoever to do with their darling offspring. Wyatt's teachers were a little more clued up, however. Beth's nemesis, Belinda McKenzie, had recently come a cropper, having forced her new French au pair, Chloe, to write an essay for her son Billy. Unfortunately, Belinda hadn't bothered to proofread it, so the 'What I did in the summer holidays' composition included a lot of interesting details about the twenty-two-year-old girl's fling with her previous employer's husband. When cross-questioned about it, Billy had fallen well short of the high levels of Gallic insouciance necessary to pass the essay off as all his own work.

Beth immediately dialled Jake instead, but wasn't at all surprised not to get an answer. She sometimes wondered if he even realised his phone was a phone, as he used it to do everything but talk on. Boys of his age weren't great conversationalists at the best of times, but she had even caught him making an appointment to talk to Charlie once or twice. Apparently, ringing up out of the blue was now really bad form. She could see he was active on WhatsApp, so she sent him a quick message, then watched as 'Typing' appeared, then disappeared, then appeared again. Finally, his words materialised. Or rather, word. Beth tutted. It had taken him that long just to write *Sup*. Without even a question mark. She wasn't going to pretend to know what the trendy response was. She just launched into a paragraph hoping he'd had a good day, enjoyed a nice supper, was having a good time with Charlie and had, as promised, finished his homework before doing anything else. For her pains, she got a *Yup*. She had a final try, asking how Colin was getting on. A large yellow thumbs-up eventually appeared and she sighed and switched her phone off. That was clearly her lot for the night.

The house was so quiet without Jake and Colin. Jake made plenty of noise simply moving from one room to the next. And Colin always made his presence felt with a lot of panting, scratching and the occasional friendly bark. Harry was still toiling away, and she knew better than to try and extract an ETA from him. She briefly considered ringing his right-hand woman, DC Narinda Khan, and trying to get a ballpark time from her, but she decided against. Although Narinda was always extremely polite, Beth had a funny feeling the girl wasn't too keen on her. She didn't want to test their fragile relationship too far, unless and until it was completely necessary. Just as she was beginning to feel a little bit at a loose end, Magpie came shooting in through the catflap and rubbed herself against Beth's legs.

'Ah, Magpie, it's just the two of us tonight.' She leant down to stroke the cat in the velvety spot behind her ear. Magpie looked up at her, her green eyes seeming to say, 'Thank God for that.' Soon she was chomping away at the strange dry chicken pellets she ate day in, day out, yet still contrived to get excited about. Beth, meanwhile, was nuking one of her dwindling supply of ready meals in the microwave. When everyone was in, she did her best to make something a bit more nutritious, but on the nights when she was alone, it was rather a nice indulgence to hear that ping that meant job done, a single fork to wash up, and a night of crime ahead, via a juicy series on the telly.

She hardly gave the bones a thought all evening, thanks to a killer on the loose in an obscure corner of Finland, so when morning came and the first thing that happened was a prolonged ring on the doorbell, she just thought Harry must have forgotten his keys. Then she looked to her side, and saw he was miraculously still in bed, and sleeping like a log.

Beth grumbled her way into her dressing gown, calling out for Jake on the way downstairs before remembering he was at Katie's. She tied the old fleecy robe more tightly and opened up. Chris Campbell was on the doorstep, the weak September sun glancing off his chiselled cheekbones. Beth was beginning to wonder if he had some sort of deal with the Almighty to keep his best features illuminated at all times. She was suddenly conscious that her hair was a wreck, her face was blotched with sleep and her gown had seen better decades. Thank heavens he couldn't see the even rattier old T-shirt beneath it. Campbell passed her without a word and made for the kitchen.

'Um, it *is* Saturday today,' she said, trotting along in his wake. 'But do come in,' she added with what she hoped was unmissable irony. By the time she'd made it to the kitchen, Campbell had made himself comfortable in her favourite chair.

'Um, am I allowed to ask what this is about? It's not even seven o'clock yet. On a Saturday morning, as I mentioned.'

Even as she said it, Beth groaned to herself at the injustice of it all. One of the advantages of Jake being at Katie's should have been that his mother would be able to luxuriate in a well-deserved, and very rare, lie-in. And her boyfriend, for once, was on the premises. That lie-in might well have morphed into a lie-on... As she felt as though she hadn't clapped eyes on Harry for weeks, thanks to his deadly secret uber-important investigation, a little bit of alone time together would have been rather nice. Instead she was in her kitchen at a ridiculous hour with a man who seemed perpetually sunk in gloom, unless he was finding bones on her premises or ordering his poor underlings around. As she watched him, he fixed her with those icy blue eyes. He seemed to be weighing something up. Was it her? She knew she wasn't looking her best, but... She drew the dressing gown around her even more tightly and fussed with the belt.

'Got any biscuits?' he asked tersely.

'No!' Beth shot back.

'Oh. Well, anyway... I thought you'd like to know. Sooner rather than later.'

There was a pause. Campbell looked at her, his face showing as many fierce angles and planes as her long-ago trigonometry homework. And seeming every bit as baffling. Eventually, she shrugged her shoulders.

'Know what?'

'About the bones.'

Instantly, Beth's stomach lurched, the way it had in class when some fiendish teacher announced an impromptu test. Why did this guy remind her of the worst bits of her school career? She told herself sternly she was being silly. He couldn't really have anything to say that would affect her. He was going to chunter on about the investigation, that was all. Hopefully, he was going to tell her they'd be out of her hair really soon. Maybe Monday morning even... She straightened up, and looked hopeful. But Campbell's next words dashed all that.

'There was talk of the bones being archeological artefacts... three hundred years old or more.'

Beth nodded, and swallowed. He was about to say they showed signs of the plague, she was sure of it. But even if they did, it didn't necessarily mean the disease was still active... There was no need to panic. Yet.

'The thing is, they're a lot more modern than that.'

'Wait, what?' Beth, who had been silently congratulating herself on getting Jake away from potential infection, did a rapid mental recalculation. 'They're not old after all? You mean... they're from a *recent* dead body?'

SEVEN

For a second, the kitchen swam crazily around Beth as she tried to get to grips with Chris Campbell's bombshell. She sat down abruptly. Modern bones in her garden... they had to be from a murder victim, didn't they? At least, that was the only assumption she could make. Because why else would anyone have buried them out there?

She felt sick. So nauseous, in fact, that it took her a while to realise he'd merrily carried on talking. She swallowed convulsively and tried to concentrate.

'So, the fact that we've unearthed this fifty-pence piece near the few shreds of clothing remaining is highly significant...' he tailed off as he finally noticed her pallor. 'Here, are you OK?'

At this, she looked at him in astonishment. Of course she wasn't OK. Why would she be, after the news she'd just had?

'Um. Never mind me. What's so important about this coin?' she asked muzzily.

Campbell more or less rubbed his hands together with glee, like a contestant on a quiz show getting a really easy question. 'It's a specific fifty pence, brought out by the Royal Mint in the millennium year, to celebrate one hundred and fifty years of public libraries,' he said, looking quite chirpy for once.

Beth blinked. The millennium, and the glorification of the concept of free access to books for all, seemed a long time ago – but not nearly long enough. Suddenly she couldn't do this on her own any more. 'Look, Harry is upstairs… do you mind if I get him? I think he'd like to listen to all this.'

Campbell's smile suddenly withered and died. 'Of course,' he said, with a strange half-bow.

Five minutes later, Beth had mustered a sleepy Harry. He'd thrown on his clothes without even showering, but contrived to look a lot more presentable than she did in her dressing gown. It was either the commanding height, the broad shoulders, the blue, blue eyes, the carelessly rumpled blond hair, or the effortless air of being in control, she decided. Though Campbell wasn't much shorter, he suddenly looked colourless and weedy by comparison.

Harry, Beth and Campbell were now all nursing cups of tea. Poor Harry, thought Beth, glancing at him. This case he was on was eating up so much of his time and energy. He'd got in really late last night and his eyelids looked suspiciously heavy.

Just as she started to worry he might fall asleep again at the table, Campbell cleared his throat importantly, then went through his spiel about fabrics, coins, libraries and bones for the second time.

There was a pause, then Harry put a heavy arm around Beth's shoulders. 'So, to sum up, you mean these bones are looking like they're twenty-odd years old at least?'

'Yes, at present we're making that assump—'

'There you are then, Beth,' Harry turned to her with a broad smile. 'What did I tell you? Ancient history.' Just then his phone buzzed. 'Ah, it's Khan,' he said. He leapt up and, with a spring in his step, dumped his mug in the sink and pressed a quick kiss into her rumpled hair as he passed.

'Harry? Where are you off to?' Beth asked, as Campbell looked on.

'Got to get to the office. Case might be about to crack!'

Beth and Campbell were left gazing after him. 'But it's a Saturday!' said Beth plaintively. Why did neither of these men seem to understand that? She sighed. She supposed criminals just didn't care about the working week.

Beth sat, clutching her cooling cup of tea, acutely aware of Campbell's moody gaze across the kitchen table. But if he was expecting chit-chat at this point, he was going to be sorely disappointed. Harry might suddenly be fine with everything, but she needed to think this through.

The only way she had been able to contain her horror at the bones before had been on the premise that they were ancient relics. Now, however, they had been pitchforked right into the recent past. Not so very long ago they had been part of a working body and, presumably, enjoying all the joys and sorrows associated with the human condition. They'd been a person. A person who had suddenly become dead and found themselves in, of all places, Beth's garden.

It really wasn't fair. Beth was almost beginning to feel she was being singled out by whatever gods might be swirling in the ether. Manifesting was a big thing at the moment, and to Beth's horror, even sensible Katie had started blathering on about it recently. It was supposed to be a way of making the riches of the universe appear, simply by thinking strongly enough of what one wanted. Had Beth managed to get the process spectacularly wrong? Was she accidentally now dragging dead bodies towards herself and her loved ones?

She had thought this once before, when she had stumbled upon something dreadful in Wyatt's Museum of Art, previously one of her favourite places in the world. To this day, she had to edge past the spot in question, so traumatic had her discovery been. She couldn't avoid her own back garden, though. All right, admittedly she didn't exactly spend a lot of time tending it currently. Maybe it wouldn't be such a terrible loss. Jake could still play football there – she might even be able to shield him from this latest bit of news, as he hadn't been around to hear it. Magpie wouldn't be bothered. There could be bones waist-high all around her, and as long as she had a patch of unkempt grass to scratch at she'd be happy. And Colin? He would be about as excited as an ancient and dignified Labrador could get.

And, if the bones were a couple of decades old, at least they predated Beth's arrival in Pickwick Road. Otherwise, she would have been in the frame herself. She'd had previous experience of that, too. It was the finger of suspicion hovering over her which had got her involved in solving mysteries in the first place – and had led to her romance with Harry. Perhaps murder wasn't always *all* bad, she reflected. But she preferred it when it was a lot further away from home.

But there was much worse to come. Campbell, who'd been biding his time quietly, started stirring his tea with a rhythmic motion that Beth found peculiarly annoying. Now he gave a little cough. 'I should probably say, at this point, that we've found some more.'

'More?' Beth shrieked, rather like the master of the orphanage when Oliver Twist asked for seconds of gruel. 'More... *bones*?'

'Yes, yes,' Campbell confirmed. 'Are you OK, Beth? Do you want me to explain exactly what we've found? It's just that it's...'

'It's what?' said Beth wildly, a parade of grisly potential finds dancing through her imagination.

'Well, like you pointed out, it *is* a Saturday. I popped by to give you a quick update but I really do need to be...'

'Oh yes, of course,' said Beth, embarrassed. No doubt he had other places to drink tea and eat biscuits at the weekend – a home, even, though that was hard to imagine. But then why had he come over at such an ungodly hour? Chris Campbell's ways really were impossible to understand. 'I suppose... I suppose it'll keep till Monday, then?' she said.

'Till Monday. Bright and early,' he said, his usually sombre features alight at the prospect.

* * *

Honestly, thought Beth, during the rest of her quiet weekend. She knew forensic archaeology was very important, and goodness knew how many years you had to train to qualify. But what kind of person wanted to dig up bones for a living? And why hadn't she just asked if there was a full body's worth of bones down there? That was what she now needed to know.

The thing was, she just hadn't been prepared for the information on Saturday morning. Now she was ready to hear the worst – but Campbell was long gone. She could have found out for herself, she supposed, simply by popping down to the hole and having a good look. But she couldn't bear the idea – and it probably would have interfered with the investigation somehow anyway. So Beth spent Sunday with her back firmly to the garden, in a pointless quest to scrub the mud off the hall and kitchen. She knew it was all going to be filthy again, as soon as Monday dawned and the SOCOs reappeared. But it took her mind off her woes – and kept her busy while Jake and Colin were doubtless having oodles of fun at Katie's, and Harry was spending even this day of rest, when they could have done something nice as a couple, at his desk in Camberwell Police Station. With DC Narinda Khan. She was sorry he was having to work so hard. The case had obviously not cracked, as he'd hoped yesterday. But he hadn't bothered to discuss this little detail with her. At this thought, Beth redoubled her scrubbing, and by the time she finally went to bed, the little house was gleaming – particularly the yards and yards of skirting boards.

As Beth had suspected, Chris Campbell and his SOCO minions all seemed thrilled that her garden was officially riddled with bones. As soon as the doorbell rang on Monday morning, the team was galumphing muddy booties happily up and down Beth's briefly pristine hall, daubing her surgically swabbed surfaces generously with nameless filth. Magpie, perching on the sitting room windowsill at the front of the house, as far as she could get from the back garden, directed a particularly malevolent glare at Beth. *It was all so nice and quiet before you had this mad shoffice notion. Why did you have to go and do that?*

'Look, it's not my fault,' Beth told Magpie plaintively. 'I hate it too. In fact, I loathe it so much that I'm planning to put in a full day's work at the archives office for a change,' she said. The cat turned away from her so only her large fluffy bottom was visible, deeply unimpressed. And out in the hall, she heard Chris Campbell clear his throat in that distinctive way. Damn, he must have arrived just in time to overhear her losing an argument with her cat.

Beth was about to go upstairs and seek the comfort of Harry's arms for a sorely needed hug, since by some miracle he hadn't actually left yet, when to her disappointment he came thundering down the stairs at a hundred miles an hour. As she watched, he shoved on his shoes, kissed her in the vague vicinity of her fringe, and whisked out of the front door. 'Oh... hang on,' she said. But she was speaking to empty air.

There was nothing for it, Beth decided. It was up to her to find out, once and for all, what was down there in the vast pit in the garden. And if she had to do it alone, so be it.

She marched out into the back garden, where Campbell was busily directing his muddy minions to grub up the few surviving bits of her lawn. 'Chris? Chris!' she said. 'Have you got time for a word?'

Campbell turned. For a second his face showed the sort of

incredulous delight Colin displayed when Wendy sneaked him a morsel of meat, against Beth's express instructions. Then it disappeared and his normal, mournful expression snapped back. He climbed out of the hole, brushed himself ineffectually, and followed Beth to the kitchen. Then he waltzed around flipping on the kettle, getting out her favourite mug and searching the cupboards for more biscuits, before handing her a steaming cup of tea.

Beth sat looking at the mug, then came out with it. 'Can you just confirm... how many bones exactly are down there?'

She braced herself for the worst. But Campbell seemed impervious to her distress.

'Of course, Beth. I'm glad you asked. Well, the simple answer is, we've found about seventy,' he said, with an unmistakable grin.

EIGHT

Beth, who'd taken a sip of tea, now sprayed it out all over the kitchen. It dribbled down the walls to meet the muddy boot-prints, and created a particularly horrible morass of stains.

'Oh, God,' she said, almost hyperventilating. She fought for a few moments to get her breathing under control, while Campbell rustled the biscuit packet uselessly. Then she raised her head again and asked bravely, 'Seventy?'

'So far.' Campbell sounded almost perky again. 'And there are some very interesting specimens amongst the bones we do have,' he said, going on to treat her to a long lecture on post-mortem striations, colour variations, climactic conditions and microscopic flora and fauna. Beth did her best to concentrate, but it was hard going. She found the whole thing so disturbing. But, if she was going to get to grips with this business, the faster she wrapped her head around the details, the quicker she could solve it and get her life back.

As Campbell moved on to mansplain the process of putre-faction to her in loving detail, she decided her favourite piece of evidence so far was that millennium fifty-pence piece. But although that meant she was definitely in the clear, as it predated her arrival in Pickwick Road, the same didn't hold true for a lot of the street's other residents. Loads of her friends and neighbours had lived here for decade after decade, arriving as newlyweds, bringing their babies home from nearby King's College Hospital, educating them at the Dulwich schools, then sending them out into the world, all the while enjoying what she'd assumed were blameless working lives, followed by trouble-free retirements.

But now it was beginning to seem as though someone, in the street she loved so well, might have known these seventy bones twenty years ago when they had constituted a person. That could mean they also knew what had happened to them. And, worse still, one of them might well be responsible for converting them to their present sorry state.

Sensing he had somehow lost his audience, Chris Campbell stalked back out to the garden and got busy with his tiny brush, trowel and extensive SOCO team. Beth was left in the kitchen, in a daze. It was truly awful to think that someone in Pickwick Road might have put the bones into her garden. But she had frequently discovered, in the course of her recent adventures, that her beloved Dulwich was a pretty place where ugly deeds could, and did, get acted out. She'd always thought her own home was exempt from that stain of evil. Now, it seemed, she'd been wrong. Very wrong indeed.

Perhaps it wasn't as much of a surprise as it should have been. The bones were concrete evidence that something was amiss in Pickwick Road. But there had been inklings that something was awry for a while. It had been such a happy place, when she'd first arrived with James a lifetime ago. Everything seemed different now. She had always blithely assumed that most people felt the same way about major issues as she did. But the recent years of political turmoil had shown plainly that there were wide differences of opinion up and down the road. There had been times when heated debates had even raged over

the garden walls of Pickwick Road. The Bentincks had been
famous for disagreeing loudly over Brexit before they had split
up, and even the Kendalls, such a devoted couple, had differing
views about whether the milk in a cup of tea went in first or
second. Beth found it all quite unsettling.

Take the Kendalls' recent dinner. While outwardly
everyone had got on as well as they ever did, there had been
undercurrents. That peculiar lull halfway through the evening,
for example. Try as she might, Beth couldn't quite understand
what had caused it. She was definitely missing something. But
what?

These thoughts preoccupied Beth as she zipped up her
pixie boots, picked up her bag and trudged through the village,
right up to the gates of Wyatt's. She managed a wave to old
George in his porter's lodge, and then cantered quickly past the
head's window, facing onto the perfect half-moon of lawn that
always looked more like velvet than grass. Today wasn't the day
to get buttonholed by Dr Grover on why her forthcoming epic
biography on Sir Thomas Wyatt was still, um, forthcoming.

Beth managed almost half an hour of concentrated work
before there was a knock at her door. She was about to burst out
with, 'You'll have the first draft after Christmas, I promise' - a
pledge born of blind panic rather than any sort of realism –
when she saw with huge relief that it was Janice Grover, not her
husband, who had popped her head round the door.

The relief didn't last long, though. Janice, today dressed in a
floaty buttercup yellow floral number, made her way quietly
towards Beth's desk, and then drew out a chair and sat down.
She had been the school secretary when Beth had started at
Wyatt's. She was now Dr Grover's much-treasured second wife
and mother of Beth's darling godchild, currently nicknamed
Libby-Lou (Beth had high hopes this would be replaced by
something less icky by the time the girl was school age). Janice
had a huge wardrobe of adorable cashmere cardigans, some of

them now daubed with chewed-up rice cake and pureed carrot, and was almost as kind and smiley as Katie. But today she had an extremely serious, not to say anguished, look on her face.

Beth grew cold. She recognised that look and almost couldn't bear to hear what might come next. It reminded her of James's consultant at King's College Hospital, a kind woman whose grim pronouncements Beth had done her best to block out, until it was too late. What on earth was Janice going to tell her, warranting that awful expression?

'Say it quickly,' Beth said breathlessly. Under her desk, her nails dug into the soft underside of her thighs and her whole body tensed up.

'It's... something bad,' said Janice gently. 'I've just heard from Harry...'

'Harry? Harry rang you?' Instantly, Beth felt the injustice of this. When had he last rung Beth? Not for days, he'd said he was so busy on his highly confidential project. What on earth was going on?

'Look, he's only just had this bit of news. He thought you'd probably be coming into work today, because of the, erm, situation at home. And he, well, he thought you might need a bit of support. Since, um, things have got a bit stirred up.'

'Well, that's literally true. You should see my back garden, it's like a bomb site,' Beth broke in with a nervous laugh.

'I know. It must be awful. And the, erm, discoveries.'

Bless Janice, thought Beth. That delicately inserted word, so much less triggering than 'bones' or, God forbid, 'body', showed the sort of tact that had made her friend such a natural at Wyatt's, doing a job that required a constant tightrope-walk between parents, teachers, children and the head that would have most trained acrobats complaining of vertigo and having a quick lie-down. But that didn't stop Beth's heart from leaping into her mouth. What could possibly be so awful that Harry thought Janice should break it to her?

'Is it Jake?' Beth's hands flew to her cheeks.

'No. It's not Jake. No, no, nothing like that,' said Janice. Beth knew Janice, as a mother herself, would realise that allaying that fear was crucial. Beth could pretty much survive anything, if it didn't involve her son.

'So what on earth can it be? Is it Magpie? Colin? Has the house fallen into the hole in the garden? Oh my God, this is painful. Just tell me.' Beth grasped the armrests of her chair, now, instead of her own flesh.

'It's Adua Wozinsky.'

Beth nearly said, 'Who?' The surname was completely unfamiliar. But after a second, her mind cleared. There was only one Adua – the cleaner who ensured virtually the whole of Pickwick Road was sparkling. The Kendalls' pinafore-touting maid. Her own wonderful Colin-sitter. And her slightly less successful Magpie-sitter. A good friend, for many years, with her dancing eyes and irrepressible attitude.

'Wozinsky? You know, I don't think I've ever heard her last name before. She's just Adua. A bit like Madonna, you know?'

Beth knew she was going off at a tangent. Janice would hardly have sat herself down like this to reveal the truth about Adua's surname, would she? But Beth couldn't help herself, her mouth was like a runaway train.

'I mean, it sounds Polish, doesn't it? But she's never really let on where she came from. I know the Sinclairs always say she's Lithuanian...'

'Yes, her surname was Wozinsky,' Janice said gently.

The use of the past tense suddenly lay between them, as awkwardly as a corpse in the room.

Beth stared at Janice. Then stared some more. 'You can't mean...'

Janice nodded sadly, her little pearl earrings bobbing. 'I'm so sorry, Beth. She's dead.' Today's cardigan was just the softest butter yellow ever. She looked a picture, but all Beth could now

see was Adua's face. Clever, mobile and knowing, Adua was –
had been – a trusted part of the family. One of the few people
she would happily leave Jake with in a crisis. Colin adored her,
and Colin was an excellent judge of character. And, although
Magpie had loathed her as an unauthorised intruder in her
domain, she had never once clawed her. That really said
something.

'What happened?' Beth asked, blinking furiously now.
Adua had been such a fixture in Pickwick Road. She couldn't
have died, could she? Beth was struggling to believe she'd gone,
on top of everything else that was happening. 'She's not old,
maybe in her fifties. What... Was it a heart attack? I always
thought she worked too hard.'

Of course, that had not stopped Beth hiring Adua to look
after her pets on the few occasions she and Harry had managed
to sneak a day or two away, or taken Jake on a break. It didn't
happen often, as the Metropolitan Police sometimes seemed
hell-bent on wrecking Harry's sex life and Beth's holiday plans.
But when they had, wonderful Adua had been there to make
sure Beth's habitual anxiety about Magpie and Colin was kept
to manageable proportions. What on earth were they all going
to do without her? She covered her mouth with her hand, trying
to stifle the horrible selfish thought. How could she think of
such a thing, at a time like this? But Janice was speaking again.

'It wasn't a heart attack. I'm afraid it was worse than that.'

'Worse?' Beth stared at her friend.

'From what I've heard... well, there's no easy way to say this.
But it's looking like it was... murder,' Janice said.

NINE

'Oh my God,' said Beth very quietly.

Janice had got all her information from Harry, Beth remembered. So it was true. Adua had been murdered.

Already, the wheels were turning. Who could have done this? Who could possibly want Adua out of the way?

It just didn't make any sense. She was one of the most popular people in Pickwick Road. She was the one everyone turned to, in all their domestic crises. Adua always had a way with a cracked heirloom vase, or a stubborn stain on a precious sofa – usually involving vinegar, superglue, bicarbonate of soda and, her secret weapon, good old-fashioned spit. And she still had time to do a stellar job as a cleaner for half the street.

'Was it some kind of random attack? A mugging that went wrong? Motivated by prejudice, even?'

But no sooner had the last thought occurred to Beth than she realised that was unlikely to be the case. You'd have to have a pretty broad spectrum of race hatred to encompass Poland, Lithuania, Estonia, Latvia, Ukraine, Romania and Bulgaria – all suggestions as to Adua's home country over the years. Of course, someone could have ended all the speculation easily enough, by simply pinning Adua down on her origins, but it was clear she'd enjoyed being a woman with a secret, so the neighbours all stuck with their own pet theories.

'Harry hasn't told me much apart from the bare facts. I expect he'll be able to give you more details,' Janice said, patting Beth's hand where it lay, limp, on the desk.

Beth did manage a wry smile at that. Harry would rather give her his last chip from Olley's than pass on a single iota of information from a live investigation.

She had run out of words, now. She just sat there, staring mutely at Janice, until her friend got up and put one soft yellow arm around her. They stayed for ages like that, with Beth feeling like a chick being clasped to the bosom of a particularly fluffy mother hen. It was very comforting. But she could still see Adua's mischievous face, as she had flitted round the table at the Kendalls' the other night. And the way Adua had winked at Beth when no one else was looking.

But had it been Beth Adua had been winking at? Or could it have been someone else all along?

* * *

By the time Beth trailed home that afternoon, she'd heard more about Adua's death. The place where the murder had happened ensured absolutely everyone knew about it by school-run time, if not way before.

Poor Adua had had her throat slit right by the controversial electrics recycling bank, in the centre of Dulwich Village, outside the burial ground containing, amongst others, the plague victims Beth had googled – the very bones Harry had hoped might have somehow sneaked their way into Beth's garden. The recycling bank was an ugly black box which squatted by the venerable railings. According to its many critics, it massively lowered the tone of the area. The graveyard, which

closed to new bodies in the nineteenth century, housed local
luminaries including John Willes – the corn merchant turned
bigwig who had built Belair House in the eighteenth century –
and possibly even Sir Thomas Wyatt himself, though luckily for
him his tomb had fallen into disrepair a century or so ago and
his last resting place was now unmarked. Nowadays, thanks to
Beth's spotlight on his appalling wrongdoing, Sir Thomas
would surely have been a prime target for tomb-toppling at the
least.

Adua had been found by a gaggle of teenagers; a couple of
lads from Wyatt's and a matching set of girls from the College
School. They had each told their parents they were off to hear
the Budapest Festival Orchestra performing Stravinsky's *Rite of
Spring* at the South Bank, which sounded just about highbrow
enough for their parents to waive the 'not on a Sunday night
before school on Monday' rule, and could even be used to flesh
out the 'loves classical music' sections of their eventual univer-
sity applications. Little did these parents know that there was a
newsagents on the South Bank notorious for allowing underage
kids to buy alcohol. The teenagers had had quite a different rite
of passage in mind for their evening. But such dreams of revelry
had been cut short when, waiting for the bus and joshing each
other in an important teenage mating ritual, one of the boys
made the horrific discovery that poor Adua was neatly sand-
wiched between the electrics bank and the wrought-iron railings, bleeding away into the night. A Global kitchen knife lay
right beside her, rusty with gore.

Beth couldn't argue with a slashed throat as unequivocal
evidence of murder. But she was still finding it very hard to
accept the idea of Adua as a victim. Everyone had loved Adua;
everyone appreciated her skills. Everyone *needed* Adua. Beth
knew for certain that she would not be the only person in Pickwick Road wondering what on earth she was going to do now.
There would be a lot of beds going unmade, plants dying of

neglect, and hungry bored pets, now Adua was not around to sort everything out. The last time Beth had come across a stabbing victim in Dulwich – quite literally, unfortunately – he had been someone who had been pretty universally loathed. And, even when his murderer had been brought to justice, there were many who felt their actions were perhaps justified. With Adua, this would absolutely never be the case. She had been a wonderful woman, Beth thought, as yet another tear escaped her reddened eyes.

But there was one unmistakable truth which she couldn't dodge, no matter how hard she tried. Everyone loved Adua – but someone had also hated her enough to kill her.

She didn't see how it could possibly be connected, but it seemed only reasonable to wonder whether there was a link between this awful killing, and the bones in her garden. Pickwick Road was the common factor. But that was ridiculous, surely? The bones were a couple of decades old... Beth was letting grief get the better of her.

Getting back home was no easy matter today. There were knots of people everywhere, strewn in her way. As if the chatter at the Wyatt's school gates wasn't enough, Beth had to dodge clutches of young mummies with children at the St Barnabas playgroup too. The parish hall, strangely shaped like three pieces of Toblerone jammed together, hosted one of the most exclusive babies-and-bumps sessions in the area. Everywhere there were mothers shivering in their Lycra exercise gear, or clutching their Missoma layering necklaces (the two sartorial options currently acceptable) at the very idea that their precious Jocasta or Louis's buggies might have been driven past *the exact spot* by their nannies, ignoring the fact that Adua's earthly remains had actually been carted off by the mortuary van at about 3 a.m. the night before.

The only sign left of the horrible deed was another of those white SOCO gazebo things that Beth stared at with a baleful eye. Even the sight of it was quite triggering. But she did suddenly wonder whether this atrocity would mean Campbell and his white-suited team would be rustling their way out of her garden and heading to the burial ground instead. It was surely more important to find the killer loose in the middle of Dulwich Village than it was to investigate Beth's dry bones. It would mean yet more delay before her shoffice got finished, but it would be worth it to avenge Adua.

Beth put her head down and trudged on. The crush was even worse outside the Village Primary. Beth had very fond memories of it, but she hadn't much liked its mum mafia even when Jake had been at the school and, judging from the crowd outside, nothing had changed on that front. Gossip was a currency, for women who'd probably had big jobs in the outside world once upon a time, and had now, for whatever reason, decided to pour all their energy into life with small kids. Gaggles of parents had collected everywhere. Beth did her best to skirt round them. Eventually, she was forced off the pavement into the road, though that was now much less perilous than it had once been, thanks to the controversial LTN road clearance scheme that had so incensed half of Pickwick Road at the Kendalls' dinner.

She was striding along as fast as she could when she was hailed by one of the mums. 'Beth!' She feigned deafness, until she recognised the raucous 'Oi!' that followed. It was Nina, in her trusty white puffa coat as usual. And, just as typically, she didn't waste any time at all with the niceties. 'Shocking about that char, innit?' she yelled over the school railings.

'Char?' For a second, Beth thought about fish. Were the Sinclairs branching out? But then she remembered Adua's profession. She hadn't really thought of her as just a cleaner. She was so much more than that. She had been one of the few who had known James. She had watched Jake grow from a tiny blob of a baby into the young man he was rapidly becoming.

Adua had also welcomed both Colin and Harry to Pickwick Road. She had even been known to tell Magpie that she was a 'lovely little catushka'. And then step hastily back out of range. 'Yes, it is shocking. Really shocking. Poor Adua.'

'Knew her, dincha?'

'Yes, yes I did. She was one of the first people I met in Pickwick Road.'

Adua had turned up on her doorstep shortly after the removals van had left. In her hands had been a box of teabags and a packet of biscuits. It wasn't until later that Beth found out the tea was filched from the Kendalls and the Sinclairs had inadvertently donated the biscuits – Adua had a habit of redistributing wealth. She had always been a law unto herself – but surely only in ways that benefitted other people.

'How did you know, though?' Beth asked.

'Stands to reason. Dead person in Dulwich. Don't take this the wrong way, hon. Got your name all over it.'

Beth wondered if there was a right way to take that. Perhaps, when this was all over, she ought to think about some sort of rehabilitation of her reputation. Solving mysteries was one thing, and as a long-time puzzle aficionado it was a hobby she definitely enjoyed. But becoming known as some kind of vulture, or coffin-chaser? That wasn't great. And more than anything, she would hate it if her desire to get to the bottom of things had any negative impact on Jake. Teasing was always rife in schools. She'd had enough of it herself, just for being short and somehow always terminally unhip. She didn't want any slights about her sleuthing being transferred to her poor boy.

No doubt a spin expert would tell her that her brand was becoming toxic. Or maybe that was just life in Dulwich? But there wasn't time for all that now.

For Beth had come to a conclusion, during the time that had passed between Janice breaking the news and running the gauntlet of gossips outside the schools. Once again, the place where she lived was under siege. There was something rotten in the state of Dulwich Village and, while Harry would no doubt do his excellent best to sort things out, no one knew better than she did how overstretched he was at the moment. Yes, he was worried about her, concerned enough to take Janice into his confidence and make sure Beth was comforted when she heard the horrible news about Adua, but it was still unlikely he was going to be home at a reasonable time tonight. She didn't even have the energy to badger him about it. He'd been working endlessly before Adua's death, when she'd just had the bones to cope with. Things weren't going to get any easier now. Beth took a breath and joined Nina on the other side of the railings.

'Right. What have you heard, exactly?' she asked her friend. If she wanted to get in on the ground floor of this investigation, now seemed like a very good place to start.

But Nina had no time to give Beth the full briefing on what everyone was saying about Adua's death. She had to get her son, Wilf, home as he had an unbreakable appointment for after-school gaming with his best friend. Besides which, Nina pronounced herself 'proper knackered'.

'Sorry, Beth. It's well sad if she was a mate. But I can't help tonight. This job is running me haggard, innit?' she explained to Beth. Nina always picked up the most complicated roles in double-quick time. But this week she had a boss who insisted on micro-managing her every move, and it meant she was getting behind on her reading.

'I haven't managed so much as a page today,' she complained. 'If it wasn't for the bus journey I'd have to be giving this back to the library late,' she brandished her current book around the playground, its garish colours attracting the odd raised eyebrow from other mothers. 'Can't wait for this post to be over.'

'God, poor you! Well, maybe the weekend, then?'

'Nah, you're all right. Let's try and meet tomorrow. Going

to tell the agency I can't hack another day. Or mangle a bit of time off somehow.'

'Great! Let's do that. After drop-off, then.' Although what she was going to hear would probably be very sad, Beth knew she needed every nuance of the current wave of rumours to start off her delving. The mummies of Dulwich could be relied upon to produce a very fair picture of events surrounding Adua's death, and Beth had to be on top of it.

'Lovely jubbly. See you then, hon.'

Back at home, Beth made some tea, then let it go cold while she fretted. What on earth was she going to do about Jake? Should she tell him about Adua straight away, while he was at Katie's? But if she did, she'd have to tell him over the phone. And that really didn't seem ideal. With WhatsApp as his preferred channel of communication, how could she say everything she needed to? Just send a skull and crossbones or a coffin emoji? God, how ghastly. It hadn't even sunk in properly for her, yet. She decided she needed to get a bit more distance before passing the awful tidings on.

She wasn't even really sure how upset Jake would be. He knew and liked Adua, of course, but at his age he no doubt felt invincible and Adua, who really wasn't old at all, would probably have seemed comparatively ancient. She'd been older than his mother, after all.

Would he tie her death in with the massive loss that was the death of his father? Though the awful thing was, Jake had been so young when James died that he scarcely remembered him. Beth had noticed most of his memories, cloudy at best, revolved around events in the photos of James that Beth kept in the sitting room, and had placed in Jake's own bedroom when he'd been small. Things like his first couple of birthday parties, a Christmas, a trip to the park when a kindly stranger had taken a picture of the three of them together. It wasn't much to show for all James's excitement at becoming a dad, and the joy she knew he had felt about his son's birth.

James hadn't had time to create one of those memory boxes people put together now. And, even if he had, would he have thought they were a bit mawkish? Beth was finding it increasingly hard to remember James's views on things, let alone predict how he might have felt on hypotheticals. It made her feel disloyal, though she knew that was illogical. If anyone had deserted the relationship, it was James himself, leaving her so abruptly and so permanently. His memory was bound to blur over the years. It was as inevitable as it was sad.

It wouldn't be long before Harry would have been *in loco parentis* longer than James had been an actual father. And now another connection between Jake and his dad, in the shape of Adua, had been severed. Thank heavens he was still at Katie's, away from the fray.

Just the idea of the conversation to come had Beth in tears again. She sat on the sofa, and thought about Adua. Eventually she decided to distract herself by thinking about the bones instead. Then that felt overwhelming, and she flipped back to Adua. And the hours ticked on. All the common sense things she had told herself about not expecting Harry that evening, and how busy he was doing important work, flew out of the window one by one.

She rang him, only for the phone to go immediately to voicemail. She rang the general station number instead, and asked to be put through to his office.

'DI York's phone,' purred a voice. Beth recognised the soft tones: it was Narinda Khan. Harry sometimes described her as his bag-carrier, which Beth had always automatically tutted at. It was so patronising, not to mention sexist. And surely Harry couldn't be blind to the gleam of ambition, at the very least, in DC Khan's lovely brown eyes?

'Hi Narinda,' Beth said, trying to sound like her usual self.

She knew she looked a wreck, having been sighing and crying all evening. Luckily the poised policewoman would be none the wiser, but Beth's throat also felt raw from all the emotion stirred up by Adua's horrible killing. 'Erm, is Harry still there?'

'I'll just have a look for you,' Narinda said. There was a brief pause, during which Beth hoped she was searching very hard. She really wanted to hear Harry's comfortingly deep voice, though she'd settle for the news that he was on his way home to her right now. But, after a series of clicks and thuds, and a moment when she was pretty sure she could hear Harry coughing somewhere in the distance, Narinda came on the line again.

'I'm so sorry, Beth, I can't find him anywhere. Shall I leave a message? That is Beth, isn't it?'

Yes, Narinda, of course it's me, and not one of his other legion of girlfriends, Beth thought a little crossly.

'Yep. Um, listen. Do you happen to know anything about the excavation, at my house? How long it's likely to go on for?' She hated having to ask – but she was desperate to know.

'Ooh, quite a while, I think. The SOCO leader needs to keep everything on site instead of bringing it back to base,' Narinda said. 'It could be ages. Anything else I can help you with, Beth?'

'Um, no. Could you just tell Harry I called?'

'Absolutely,' said Narinda, and put the phone down.

Beth closed her eyes. Damn. It looked like she was stuck with Chris Campbell and the team for the foreseeable future. And she was having to cope with it on her own. She felt for poor Harry, when he was working so hard. But a tiny voice also whispered, what use was a boyfriend, if he wasn't there in her hour of need?

* * *

Beth wasn't feeling a whole lot better about things in the morning. Harry, when he eventually turned up after midnight, had been much too tired for a discussion. He had been asleep as soon as his head hit the pillow.

She had tried shaking his shoulder mercilessly, whispering into his ear, 'Adua's dead!'

But he'd just mumbled, 'Yeah, yeah, I know. Got Janice to tell you.' Then he'd looped one long arm around her and snuggled her into his side.

'I know you got Janice to do your dirty work for you. But now I want to talk to you about it all!' Beth was furious, and about as far from sleep as a small enraged person could be.

'Look. Let's discuss it in the morning, I'll tell you everything I know. Promise,' he said softly, subsiding back into sleep.

Beth lay there, trying to breathe deeply, trying to get herself to relax like the now gently snoring Harry. But she was shot through with adrenaline. The annoyance of knowing he had so much more information than her on Adua, and was not sharing it, was too grating. If he had broken the news to her himself... True, he had got Janice to stand in for him. But what had previously appeared considerate, now seemed like passing the buck because he couldn't be bothered to deal with her emotions. And, no doubt, the plethora of questions she always flung at him at moments like this.

By the time she'd got to sleep, the birds had started tweeting in their raggedy south London chorus, interrupted every two minutes by planes edging into position to land at Heathrow and Gatwick. She'd snuggled against Harry's big broad back, thinking at least when she woke up she'd be able to get the full story out of him.

But, when she finally opened her bleary eyes, it was past eight o'clock and the other side of the bed was cold and empty. Harry was long gone.

TEN

Beth immediately jolted upright in bed, thinking of the school run. But Jake was still over at Katie's, no doubt ingesting a carefully curated breakfast filled with all the nutrients necessary to power a young boy through a packed day of learning. Poor thing, he'd be so missing the Coco Pops she always gave him at home. She tried to get him to eat his five a day, she really did. But he was too old to force-feed. Not that it had ever been easy. She had a whole album of pictures of Jake and his surroundings splattered with the many foodstuffs that didn't meet with his approval. Coco Pops meant he had something in his stomach, at least.

There was no chance of Beth drifting off to sleep again today. She was too sad about Adua, too alarmed at the idea of a killer still at large and too anxious about the bones in the garden. And, even if Harry was up and out, and Jake and Colin were off her hands too, that didn't mean she could laze in bed all day. She had to be dressed and ready to let in the blasted SOCO team.

Would they still turn up, though? If Harry had kept his promise to her, and filled her in on what was going on with the

investigation into Adua's death, she might have had a clearer
idea of whether or not the large looming figures in white suits
were on their way to her, or whether they'd be diverted to the
ghastly murder site in the village. As it was, she thought, taking
a hasty shower and flinging on her clothes, she literally didn't
have a clue.

It was just as well she was soon downstairs and fuming
over her own breakfast of rather burnt toast, because the
SOCOs did arrive bright and early, despite the rival claims of
the much fresher dead body round the corner. Chris Campbell
explained that 'he'd started so he'd finish,' with his usual
deadpan delivery. Beth didn't know whether to laugh or cry,
but she supposed it was a measure of Harry's influence that
her old bones were reckoned to be at least as important as poor
Adua. Another forensic team had been assigned to the burial
ground site, Campbell said, helping with the ongoing investigation.

'You can't seriously be expecting to find anything else here,
though?' she asked Campbell when she staggered outside with
the first loaded tea tray of the day. As everyone dived in to grab
their mugs – by now all the officers had their own favourites –
Campbell looked at her with those piercing eyes. When the tray
was empty, she turned away, realising she wasn't going to get
any sort of an answer.

Being out of the house was infinitely more appealing than
staying at home. She threw a few things into her bag ready for
the hours ahead, reflecting that if she started totting up days at
work like this, she might be in severe danger of actually accom-
plishing a completed draft of her biography. She didn't know
who was going to be more astonished, her mother (who had
laughed outright when Beth had told her of her plans long ago,
assuming it was a joke) or Dr Grover himself.

Beth kept her head down while she trailed through the
village, past the fateful site near the graveyard. But she had to

look up when a familiar voice pierced the morning air as she passed the florist's.

'Oi, Beth!'

It was Nina, fresh from dropping off Wilf. She was late as usual, but at the Village Primary the consequences were not severe. Jake now faced the threat of detention if he turned up a minute late at Wyatt's, but as he usually took himself to school these days, and was currently running on Katie's efficient timetable, he was in no danger.

'Ready for that coffee, then, babe?'

'Definitely!' Beth linked arms with her friend and they strolled along together.

Nina cocked her head in the vague direction of the forensics tent by the electrics recycling bank. 'Heard any more about all that?' she asked. There was now a uniformed policeman outside, with another toiling up the beautiful Georgian stairs of the Grade II listed mansion next door to the burial ground. A third on the other side of the road was talking to a couple of the shop owners. Beth assumed they were conducting a house-to-house – but it would have been nice to have known for sure.

'Not a thing,' said Beth, hoping there wasn't too much bitterness in her tone. 'How about you? Hope you're going to tell me everything you heard yesterday.'

'Do my best, mate. But you want to work on your official sources, innit?' she said with a nudge. 'And what about your bone, then?'

Beth grimaced. 'It's a lot more than one, now...'

'Getting on your bits, is it? One thing when it's a murder down the road in Herne Hill, innit? Right on your doorstep's not so much fun,' Nina said shrewdly. 'Don't worry. A coffee'll pep you up. I'm at the dentist's now, though, so I gotta keep an eye on the time.'

'Oh, but I don't want to keep you, not if you have an appointment?'

'Nah, babe, you're all right. Dental is what I told them at work,' Nina said, tapping the side of her nose. 'It's a bit of a white lion, know what I mean?' As usual with Nina, Beth wasn't quite sure she *did* know. But she was beginning to guess. 'Full time can get a bit intense. As you know. It was either get a break today, or dump the whole assignment.'

Beth ducked her head again. She was sometimes shocked at Nina's constant pushing of employers' boundaries. But she was just as bad herself. Look at her, scurrying off to Jane's coffee shop again. It wasn't Beth's favourite, because it was usually chock-a-block with Dulwich's finest and yummiest mummies. But things had shifted a little in the coffeeverse recently. A new place had opened up just down the road, replacing the luxury stationery shop which, appropriately enough, had folded. The café, called Meribel's, was rapidly poaching business from Jane's. Dulwich was all about novelty, and Meribel's not only had a fancier name but was also decked out in the very latest ethnic-cum-twee style, all unbleached calico, rattan and fairy lights.

Sure enough, Beth and Nina were able to secure quite good seats in Jane's for the first time in living memory – not too close to the front door and its draughts, yet far enough away from the queue for the loos, where impatient toddlers had been known to jump the gun. Beth did the honours at the counter, ordering coffees and brownies.

'So, what do you really make of this fing going on in your garden, then?' asked Nina, head on one side, curls bobbing as she sank her teeth into the squidgy cake.

'Well, it's awful, obviously. And now all this with Adua as well! I still can't believe it,' Beth said, swiping a napkin from the table and dabbing her eyes. 'I've been trying to get hold of Harry, see what he knows, but he's just so busy at the moment.'

'Hmm,' said Nina. 'I think I'd be busy too, if you were at home doing your nut the whole time.'

'Well, I'm not at home, am I?' said Beth a tad acerbically. She'd like to see how Nina would deal with bones in her garden and a dead friend in the village, too. Though it wasn't going to happen; Nina lived in a nice block of flats in Herne Hill. If any bones or bodies were ever found, they'd be a communal problem, and Nina would be surrounded by concerned friends and neighbours. Beth had great neighbours, too – as long as one of them wasn't somehow a killer, that was. But there was no doubt that everyone seemed to see the bones as exclusively Beth's problem. Unfortunately. And that seemed to include Harry.

Nina gave her friend a speaking look over the rim of her coffee cup. Beth didn't need telling that she wasn't taking this whole business well. Even before Adua had turned up dead. She tried to relax. She was having a lovely coffee with a friend. Everything was good. Everything was *fine*. Then Nina piped up again.

'Your bones... they were found by the fence, right?'

'I wish people wouldn't call them *my* bones,' Beth said, but a little less briskly than before. 'Right there, yes.'

'Dincha have a shed before?'

'We did, when we first moved in. Well, I say shed, but really it had pretty much fallen apart. The whole house needed work...' And it still did, thought Beth ruefully. 'One day James just gathered all the bits of wood up and took them off to the dump.' Beth remembered him doing it. It had been a day like today, cold but bright. Now James was dust and the bones in the garden had only just poked their way into the light. It seemed unfair that they were so present, while he was nothing now but absence.

'Got me finking. I wonder...'

Beth looked at Nina in surprise. Long periods of introspection were not really her speciality.

'What's up?'

'Oh... just. No, well, it couldn't be that.'

'What? Wouldn't be what?' Beth was leaning over her coffee now.

'Hold your Horlicks, mate. It's just that it sort of fits with the whole blood feud thing, you know?'

Beth certainly didn't know. And she made that abundantly clear. 'Blood feud? What are you talking about?'

'Well, it's an old story. I'm surprised you haven't heard it, you've been in these parts so long.'

'Maybe I'm not as up with the gossip as you are,' Beth said with a shrug.

'Maybe it's not the sort of thing you lot talk about,' Nina said, cocking her head again. Beth didn't rise to this, and merely sipped her coffee. Nina could never usually resist a chance to spread a good tale. And this time proved no exception.

'OK, all right. I'll spin the beans. Well, you see, it happened this...'

Just then, Beth's mobile shrilled. Normally she wouldn't have picked up the call, but the screen filled with a name she wasn't expecting... Jake's form teacher at Wyatt's. Why on earth would he be ringing?

'Sorry, Nina, do you mind? I'd better get this, it's the school,' she said.

'Course, hon. Might be important,' Nina mumbled, through a heroically large bite of brownie.

'Mrs Haldane? Can you come in straight away? We've got an emergency on our hands. It's Jake.'

ELEVEN

Beth galloped up the street, hair sticking to her hot face despite the autumnal chill. The world had stood still when Mr Waring had said those few dread words about her boy. She had thrown down some money on the table, grabbed her bag and run, mouthing 'Bye' to Nina over her shoulder. Whatever story she wanted to tell Beth about blood feuds – what on earth had she meant? – it would just have to wait.

By the time she'd puffed her way to Wyatt's and presented herself at the teacher's office, she was barely capable of speech. But that was all right, as Mr Waring had plenty to say.

'Are you aware, Mrs Haldane, that your son has a problem?' he said, as soon as Beth collapsed into the seat in front of him.

Beth shook her head as emphatically as she could.

'Well, he has. He has been falling asleep in class.'

Beth's first thought was relief. This wasn't nearly as bad as her fevered imaginings as she had pelted to the school. She'd thought he must have been terribly injured, broken a leg at least. Or been expelled. Though, as his worst crime ever was to shirk optional homework, that would have been quite a punishment. She couldn't help giving Mr Waring a shaky smile. But he just glared at her from the other side of the desk.

'This is a serious problem, Mrs Haldane.'

The trouble was that Beth had difficulty believing Peter Waring was a proper teacher at the best of times. He looked about fourteen. She didn't know him that well, as he was new (very, very new) to Wyatt's, but of course she'd taken much more of an interest since Jake had started in his class in September. He had a quiff of dark blond hair and was still painfully thin, in that way of an adolescent just past his first growth spurt. His trousers didn't quite flap around his ankles (as Jake's were doing at the moment) but none of his suits really fitted. He was no commanding figure, but today annoyance twisted his boyish features and lent him some gravitas.

'I don't have to tell you, surely, how important it is for our students to *remain conscious* in class, Mrs Haldane?' he said scathingly.

Beth adjusted her expression quickly. She also shrugged away her annoyance at being called 'Mrs'. She'd asked the school umpteen times to use Ms, but in some ways the place was still mired in the values of its seventeenth-century founder. Not all of them, thank goodness.

'I really don't understand. Falling asleep? Jake has never had a problem with drowsiness during the day. He gave up having naps when he was two. Are you sure about this?'

Mr Waring glanced down importantly at his notes. 'Well, yes, Mrs Haldane, I am absolutely sure. Jake had to be woken up by a classmate in Latin, yesterday, and today he apparently nodded off in Maths. So we have to look at this very seriously indeed,' he said, now staring at Beth as though he'd never seen a worse parent in his life.

Beth was stunned. Oh, Jake had refused to go to bed with the best of them, when he'd been small. There had been a terrible 'witching hour' when his attention span and behaviour had nightly gone downhill. But more recently there hadn't been a murmur from him at night. The Wyatt's daily routine was punishing, and the evening homework burden was heavy. Yes, he often had a short gaming session with Charlie or another friend in the evening, but the console was attached to the telly in the sitting room and he didn't want to play under the scrutiny of Beth and Harry after supper. His phone was an old model, with rubbish storage, and that meant he couldn't use it for much after he'd gone upstairs. Plus their wi-fi hardly reached his bedroom. So, one way and another (pretty much accidentally if Beth were honest) she'd avoided some of the pitfalls of houses where the tech was laid on more lavishly. There was no way he could be up half the night on his phone. And, as far as she knew, he never really stirred once his light went off every night.

'I just don't get it. This has never been an issue before,' Beth protested.

Mr Waring leant forwards across his desk, steepling his bony hands. 'Does Jake perhaps have something on his mind?'

Beth wondered. She hadn't spoken to him about Adua yet. But there was, of course, the uncomfortable fact that there were seventy-odd bones in the back garden. That was enough to give anyone sleepless nights. Beth remembered their conversation in the kitchen. She had initially just thought that Colin could do with a break from the chaos and temptation by staying with Katie. Then Jake had surprised her, and actually hurt her a little, when he'd asked to go as well.

'I mean... he's been at a friend's house for a couple of nights while we have some, er, work done.' Beth wasn't totally sure if a full forensic examination of the human remains in her garden constituted 'work'. Particularly in Dulwich, when it usually meant nothing more than light tinkering with the Osborne & Little curtain tiebacks. But Mr Waring didn't need to know all her business.

'Ah, I see. I wouldn't encourage sleepovers during the week, the boys tend to egg each other on, you know the kind of thing. Am I right in assuming the friend in question is young Charlie?'

Beth nodded. 'Is he having trouble staying awake too?'

'Let's just say, I think we've solved the mystery. Perhaps it's time for Jake to come home,' Mr Waring said, a deeply patronising smile on his youthful face.

'Er, perhaps,' said Beth. 'Well, thank you so much.'

She smiled and shook his long, fleshless, bony hand, which reminded her strongly of why Jake wasn't currently at home. She turned away quickly and left Mr Waring's office with a very grim look on her face.

What on earth had Jake and Charlie been up to? There was only one person who could help her find out – and Beth was going to ring them right now.

* * *

Beth got as far as the gates of Wyatt's before fishing out her phone. But, as soon as she started to dial, she was assailed by doubts. She couldn't just come out and say, 'What the hell has been happening?' Even Katie, her very best friend in the world, needed more careful handling than that.

It was a tricky situation. While Beth didn't want to apportion any sort of blame, she still urgently needed to get to the bottom of what had gone on with the boys. But Katie, like any mother, would be super-sensitive to the suggestion that she had been less than vigilant. And, as she was the most caring and dedicated mum Beth knew, any undue criticism was bound to be wide of the mark anyway.

She took a couple of breaths, thought for a second longer, then leant against the railings, and dialled. 'Katie? Beth here,' she said with a quaver in her voice. Her headlong canter to Wyatt's, the distressing interview with Mr Waring and her fear of striking the wrong note now meant she was a bag of nerves.

Luckily she didn't have to explain herself at all as Katie immediately wailed, 'Oh Beth, I'm so sorry about this. You can't imagine how awful I feel. Getting dragged into the school! You must have been beside yourself with worry. And then to find out that Jake's been nodding off... Listen, are you free for a quick coffee at Mariella's right now?'

Beth had never been readier for a steadying cappuccino.

After carefully rehearsing her lines all the way to the café, the better to avoid any suggestion that she was blaming Katie for Jake's predicament, Beth's script flew completely out of her head as soon as she slid into the booth opposite her friend. Never mind Jake having fallen asleep in class. Katie herself looked as though she hadn't had a wink for days.

'Is everything OK?' Beth asked, scrutinising Katie's hair. Usually bright as a sunbeam, today it was lank. Even her blue eyes, which normally twinkled more than all the fairy lights twining round their rattan-trimmed booth, were shadowed in violet and downcast.

Katie gave her a haunted look. 'I'm fine. Teddy's had to leave the classes in Penge, though. They just didn't understand his temperament. He's a very sensitive dog.'

Aha, thought Beth. So that was poor Kate's problem. Drat that mutt. To avoid having to share her views on Teddy's artistic soul, she studiously examined her coffee mug.

'But listen,' Katie went on. 'I just feel so bad about Jake. You can't imagine. I mean, he's only been with me for a couple of days. You must think I'm the most awful parent, custodian, whatever, ever.'

To Beth's horror, a perfect tear started to make its way down Katie's cheek. She put out a hand and patted Katie's arm clumsily. 'Katie, look, don't worry. I know you're a really... dedicated mother.'

That was an understatement. Katie was usually so much of a helicopter parent that you could hear the whirring of her rotor blades from the bottom of Red Post Hill. And a day ago, Beth would have said Katie knew exactly what her son was up to, at any given minute of any given hour. But that couldn't be true any more. Because if something was this badly awry with Jake, it made sense that Charlie was involved somehow. They would be in it together – whatever this was that was keeping them up at night. And Beth wanted to know. Right now. Sooner, if possible.

'I know you will have been nothing short of wonderful with Jake,' Beth said. 'I just don't get why he's suddenly so tired? Have they been up all night gaming, or something? Without you knowing, of course. That's all I can think of... Obviously, I'm going to have to come back with you and ask him the moment he gets out of school, but until then... do you have any idea what's caused this?'

Katie dashed the tear away and swallowed. 'I do. Well, it turns out it's all there, on Charlie's phone. That's the cause of this, really,' she said, with that look of despair common to all parents. Who didn't feel like a modern-day Canute, trying to stand against the tide of technology coming at their children, bringing with it, as well as the blessing of being in touch at all times, other much less savoury possibilities? Wall-to-wall porn, access to gambling, twenty-four-hour bullying... you name it, Beth had fretted about it late into the night.

'But what is it? What's on his phone?' Beth prompted. She swished her cappuccino about a bit but was much too keyed up now to drink even the tiniest sip. She felt as though she were holding her breath as Katie sat opposite her, weighing her words. Despite herself, Beth started tapping her foot with impatience. *For God's sake, spit it out.*

'It's... well, do you know that boy, Gregory King, in the year above?'

Beth blinked rapidly. She wasn't nearly as au fait with the class lists as Katie. When Jake had parties, they were small affairs, usually involving only Charlie and maybe a couple of others if Beth was feeling really expansive. Katie, however, had the deep pockets, the space and also the generosity of spirit to invite the entire class, and kids from other years as well.

'Nope,' Beth said. 'Who the hell is he?'

'I mean, he's a nice boy... Dad's a doctor, I think his mother may be a dentist, something white-coaty anyway...'

Beth didn't quite snort, but Katie's assessment of the boy's good heart seemed entirely based on what his parents did for a living. 'OK... all very Dulwich. I get the picture.'

'Well... he's been WhatsApping Charlie. A lot. I wasn't sure if it was great, I mean those boys in the year above, well, we're talking *teenagers* really.'

'I hate to break it to you, but Charlie's about two months away from being a teenager himself.'

'Well, yes,' said Katie, stirring her own cup meditatively. 'So I didn't immediately put a stop to it. I wish I had.'

'Wait a second, how did you even know all this was going on?' Beth was puzzled.

'I check his phone every night,' Katie shrugged. 'Don't tell me you don't check Jake's?'

Beth glossed over the question. 'How do you get access? Jake keeps his phone closer than his old teddy, or even Colin.'

'Simple. I've banned Charlie from having it in his room overnight. He leaves it to charge right outside his door... job done.'

For a moment, Katie let maternal smugness override her worries. But Beth suspected it was going to be the last time for a while that either of them was going to be able to outwit their boys so easily.

'Katie. What exactly did these WhatsApps say?' she asked, leaning forward again.

But the trouble was, though she'd been so cunning in securing access to Charlie's phone, it turned out something about Katie's demeanour two nights ago had raised her son's suspicions. She'd arrived back wrung out after Teddy's last obedience class in Penge and been less subtle than usual in accessing his phone. The next day, he'd deleted the entire WhatsApp thread with Gregory King. If Katie hadn't spotted his name previously, she wouldn't even have known anything was up. And she couldn't break guest etiquette to demand Jake hand his own phone over. He'd been acting shiftily, though, Katie did say.

What could be bothering the boys so much that Jake was losing sleep, and Charlie was suddenly up with John le Carré-level tradecraft? It was so frustrating. Beth would just have to hope that Jake didn't do his usual impression of a clam when she put these questions to him.

'I'm so sorry about all this, Beth. Especially when you must be so stressed already – the back garden and now Adua. You're going through so much.'

Beth bowed her head. 'I can't believe Adua's gone.'

'Harry must be so busy,' Katie said sympathetically.

'Well, he's certainly clocking up the overtime,' Beth agreed ruefully. 'Not sure where he's got to with the investigation into finding Adua's killer, but I have seen some officers making enquiries.'

'Yes, and there's another SOCO team at the um, site, today, did you see?'

'I think I was running so fast on the way to see Mr Waring, I must have missed that. But tell me, have you heard anything about it on the cleaners' grapevine? Via your Rosita?'

'Are you investigating this as well, Beth? Don't you think you've got enough on your plate, with Jake? Not to mention the, um, bones.'

'Well, I don't want to,' Beth shrugged. 'But at the same time, what can I do? I mean, these things do keep happening to me, don't they? The back garden... well, that's literally too close to home. Adua was a friend. I feel I owe it to her. And don't forget, whoever killed her is still out there somewhere. Out *here*. So, will you ask Rosita for me?'

At once, Katie started fidgeting, but to Beth's surprise it wasn't at the idea of a murderer walking their streets.

'Rosita and Adua never got on, don't you remember? Adua said they had a word for women like Rosita in her village.'

'Yikes, I forgot about that.'

'I hope that doesn't make Rosita a suspect,' Katie said a little sharply.

Beth tried to laugh it off. But inwardly, she was already beginning to wonder exactly where Rosita had been on the night Adua had gone to the recycling bin. Now didn't seem quite the moment to say that, though.

'Well, listen, let me take one thing off your shoulders at least. I'll organise a meeting with the Year 8 head tomorrow,' Katie said. 'And maybe we can get to the bottom of this snoozing thing.'

'Thanks, Katie,' said Beth. Now it was her turn to have moist eyes. Charlie hadn't been in trouble with the powers that be at Wyatt's yet. Katie could have left Beth to get on with things. But she was showing solidarity with her instead. 'I really appreciate it.'

'Right, well. It's about time we got back. The boys might beat us to it otherwise.'

Beth took a deep breath. Usually she loved going to Katie's sumptuous house. But today she felt nothing but awkwardness. She had two horrible conversations looming with Jake. One about his Rip Van Winkle impression, and the other about Adua.

She didn't know which one she was dreading most.

TWELVE

In the end, as was often the case with something she wasn't looking forward to at all, talking to Jake about Adua, and his behaviour in class, wasn't quite as awful as Beth had feared.

Jake was pretty surprised to see his mum at Katie's, though. Once he'd fought his way good-naturedly out of her mammoth hug, and endured her telling him how much she'd missed him, he smiled at her sheepishly – and then saw her expression. Immediately, he asked her suspiciously, 'Is something going on? Is Magpie all right?'

'Everything's fine at home,' said Beth quickly, mentally crossing her fingers and shutting out the vision of seventy bones in the garden. 'But, now that you mention it, there are a couple of things we do need to have a little chat about...'

'Shouldn't I be doing my homework before we have this "little chat"?' he said sassily. 'You're always telling me school-work comes first.'

Beth ignored that, and said quietly, 'Listen, we're just going to pop into the sitting room for a second. Then you can get right back to the homework.' She nodded at Katie, who smiled encouragingly.

Jake, probably sensing resistance was useless, followed her into the very grown-up room that he and Charlie rarely set foot inside. Beth perched gingerly on one of the gorgeous violet silk sofas and Jake sat opposite her, for once sitting up quite straight. 'Go on, then, Mum. Get it over with.'

'I was called into school today by Mr Waring. Can you guess what that was about?'

Immediately, Jake's head went down and he started a prolonged scrutiny of his shoes. As she studied his curly dark hair, and thought yet again she really must make a hair appointment for him, she could see the signs of a young boy wrestling with his conscience.

'What would you do,' he said eventually, 'if you could say something, but it would get someone else into trouble?'

'I'd think, if I'd already got into quite a pickle myself, that it was time to tell the truth, Jake. There is obviously something worrying you. Worrying you enough to stop you from sleeping. You know how important it is to concentrate in class—'

'If this is about the school fees, then I can go to a cheap school. I'm not bothered,' he broke in, looking up with a flushed face.

Immediately Beth was cut to the quick. She'd always fondly hoped she had concealed her money worries from her son.

'Is that what's keeping you awake? You're worried about money? Because you don't need to be. I'll sort it. It's not a problem,' she said, sounding a lot more confident than she felt. 'This is about you not being able to concentrate in class. I just need to know what's going on.'

'I'm fine, Mum. Don't stress. It was just a... misunderstanding. With one of the older boys. Yes, I kept thinking about it at night... I couldn't get to sleep... but I'm over it now. Really.'

Beth considered this. It sounded reasonably convincing. Could it be true? Could this have been some storm in a teacup that was now sorted? She wanted to believe it... but she wasn't sure if she should.

'A misunderstanding? But why would that be stopping you from sleeping? Can you tell me more about it?'

'I just... had a lot on my mind. I didn't realise how late I was up. It won't happen again. I can't tell you more. Not without breaking a promise. And you're always saying how important promises are.'

Damn it, thought Beth. Her own obsession with truth and justice was being used against her. Jake was getting so wily. She looked at him again and saw his face bore that familiar shuttered look it got when he decided that was it, no more cooperation. She sighed inwardly. Maybe she had to leave this. For now. Because, after all, she had another horrible subject to broach.

'I wanted to talk to you about something else as well. Adua.'

'If you mean, had I heard she's been killed, well, yes I have.'

'Oh Jake, no! I'm so sorry you heard it from someone else. I wanted to tell you myself. I know you loved her.'

'Yeah. You know what school is like, I probably heard it before you did. She was fab.' His head went down again, like a sunflower deprived of the light. Beth felt her eyes welling up. She went and sat next to him, and put her arm round him, and they stayed like that until Charlie knocked on the door.

'Hey. Wanna play?' he said. Jake looked up at Beth for confirmation – something he hadn't done for a while – and she nodded, giving him a last hug before letting him go. She heard them scampering up the stairs happily enough. She wandered back into the kitchen.

'Tea?' said Katie.

Beth shook her head. She'd realised, in the last half-hour or so, just how fast Jake was growing up. It was sobering.

'I'd better be going. I didn't get that much out of Jake, and he already knew about Adua. I was thinking he might want to come back with me, but judging by the way he zoomed off with

Charlie, I think this will take his mind off things better. And my house is still such a dump, too. Is it OK if he stays a bit longer?'

'Of course, Beth. And they will definitely do their home-work, don't worry about that. There's someone who wants to say hello before you go, though.' Katie gestured to the huge windows, where Colin was standing in the garden, tail wagging so fast it was a blur. Beth went out to give him some big strokes and told him he'd be home again very soon. She hoped it was true.

* * *

Katie was as good as her word, organising a meeting at the school the very next day to discuss the whole business.

But even this was not problem-free for Beth. She'd already arranged to meet Nina that afternoon, after their coffee yesterday morning had been cut short. She'd had high hopes of getting to the bottom of her friend's cryptic comments about a blood feud. But there was no contest. Jake had to trump Nina any day of the week. Even the possibility of getting further on with a whole bundle of intrigues, involving the bones and Adua, could not weigh in the balance against her own son. Jake had been coming first with her since his debut at King's College Hospital's maternity unit twelve years ago, and he always would until the day she died.

Jake, and the mystery of his sudden-onset narcolepsy, could clearly be traced to Charlie's involvement with this Gregory King boy. Beth wondered for the umpteenth time what this promise was, that her boy had made. Was it to this King boy? She suspected it must be. And she was also pretty sure that even if Gregory King's father was a brain surgeon and his mother the finest dentist in all Dulwich (neither impossible, given that every second parent at Wyatt's had a PhD or ran a global concern in their spare time) it wouldn't prove that King was really what Katie termed a 'nice boy'.

Beth grabbed her phone and texted Nina, apologising profusely for putting her off, explaining she was having a crisis (another one!) and asking her to reschedule as soon as possible. And then she braced herself for another less-than-fun meeting at Wyatt's.

As soon as Beth toddled into the school and checked who was chairing the meeting Katie had set up, she knew it was going to be super-serious. It was Mrs Montgomery, the gimlet-eyed Year 8 head. The woman was terrifying enough when Beth made fleeting eye contact in the corridors. She'd never yet endured a one-to-one session with her. True, this would be one-to-two, but still she felt she and Katie were going to be hopelessly outnumbered.

It was not for nothing that Mrs Montgomery had been made head of this specific year. Everyone knew that boys went feral at the age of thirteen. Some went before, one or two went afterwards, but the vast majority turned into silent, writhing hormonal messes at some point between a minute to midnight on their last day of being twelve, and one minute past the hour when they became teenagers. Mrs Montgomery could cope; she was every bit as tough as her haircut. This was an uncompromising helmet of grey, an apparently irony-free homage to the pudding-basin styles of yore. She teamed it with a uniform of boxy black jackets and slacks that had more than a whiff of a warder from *Prisoner: Cell Block H* about them. Beth, who found even genial Dr Grover a bit much sometimes, was pretty much shaking in her pixie boots by the time she met up with Katie outside Mrs Montgomery's door. The fact that she'd got nothing at all useful done in her office while waiting made it all the more frustrating.

Katie greeted her with such a beaming smile, however, that Beth's spirits rose a little. Then she realised Katie probably didn't yet know exactly how scary Mrs Montgomery was. Well, she was soon going to find out.

Beth knocked tentatively and, instead of a voice asking them to come in, the door was abruptly whisked inwards. Beth almost fell into Mrs Montgomery's arms, and only Katie's firm hand on her shoulder kept her upright. She was thoroughly flustered by the time Mrs Montgomery had gestured to both women to sit on the hard, upright chairs positioned with mathematical precision in front of her bare desk. Beth thought of the comfortable clutter of her own towering inbox, her picture of Jake, her dusty lamp and her selection of slightly chewed pens. How did this woman keep her surfaces so clear?

The answer soon became all too evident. She was ruthlessly efficient. Although Katie had called the meeting, it didn't take long before Mrs Montgomery had shown her mastery of the whole affair. Jake's unfortunate lapses into unconsciousness, and Charlie's inattentiveness in class, were soon laid bare. Katie turned to Beth and gave her a sympathetic look. Then Mrs Montgomery swivelled her basilisk stare to Katie and started on her instead.

'You'll be aware, I suppose, of your son's, ah, involvement with Gregory King in Year 9?'

Katie, already a little less sure of herself than she'd been a minute before, hesitated before nodding.

'He seems like a nice boy,' she ventured. That phrase again! Beth immediately looked down at her lap and tried to find the contemplation of her short, bare fingernails utterly fascinating.

Mrs Montgomery gave Katie a particularly baleful stare. 'Does he indeed?'

Then the woman turned to Beth, as though expecting her to either second her friend, or possibly leap in and blacken the boy's good name. But Beth didn't really have a clue about Gregory King. She'd already decided it was naïve of Katie to rely on his parents' professions as a sure-fire indicator of his pure heart. But she hadn't heard of him at all before this business with Charlie and his phone. He could be a saint or he could be the devil personified. Although she rather thought she might have spotted him stalking around Wyatt's, if he'd really had cloven hooves, horns and a tail.

'Do you mind my simply asking what this is about?' Beth asked. On the one hand, Mrs Montgomery was extremely intimidating. But on the other, the suspense was killing her. If her Jake was involved in some sort of terrible compact with Charlie and this King boy, she wanted to know as soon as possible. 'It's not like Jake to be falling asleep in class. Obviously. He's usually keen to get to school, he's enjoying Wyatt's. Or so I thought. Something's going on.'

'Yes. Yes, it is,' said Mrs Montgomery, tilting her head towards Beth. Her hair didn't move at all during this operation. Beth found herself wondering if setting spray was involved, or whether the whole thing lifted off in one piece, like the styles sported by the little Playmobil figures Jake had once adored, in what was beginning to seem like a blissfully easy phase of parenting.

'I don't know if you ladies know much about the Year 8 disco?'

Beth and Katie looked at each other, jaws dropping slightly. Of all the words Mrs Montgomery might have come out with, 'disco' had not been on Beth's list. 'Expulsion' had been top of her worries. But this? Her mind instantly flicked to John Travolta's white suit and iconic pose in *Saturday Night Fever*. What on earth was the woman on about? But it was clearly beginning to ring some sort of bell with Katie. She started nodding her head and even began to look slightly relieved.

'We had a mail from Mr Waring about the disco. It was a couple of weeks ago. Don't you remember, Beth?'

Beth shrugged a tiny bit. She was always forgetting to read the school's pronouncements. She had to go through reams of them for her job. The last thing she wanted to do in the evening was to wade through even more for Jake's class. They tended to bang on about endless sporting fixtures and expensive bits of kit that urgently had to be bought, and she always tried to ignore them for as long as humanly possible. Until Jake nagged her about them, anyway.

'That must have, erm, slipped past me somehow,' she said guiltily.

'They're having a joint disco with the Year 8 girls from the College School. It's quite a big deal,' said Katie, clearly surprised that Beth wasn't across this. But wait a minute, it was now beginning to ring a vague bell. Beth heard about it every year from Janice. But she'd somehow never thought Jake would be old enough to go. It only seemed a minute since he'd been doing the actions to *The Wheels on the Bus*, for heaven's sake.

'Charlie actually mentioned it to me, said he wanted some new jeans. I nearly fell off my chair,' Katie said with a laugh.

'And so it begins,' said Mrs Montgomery in leaden tones. 'Well, as you'll already have worked out, the Year 8s often do start to develop, shall we say, a certain interest in the opposite sex. That's why we have the disco. To allow them a little contact, in a controlled way. There are always teachers from the College School, as well as Wyatt's, present at the Year 8 disco to make sure the mingling goes to plan.'

Immediately, Beth decided this 'mingling' sounded like the most ghastly sort of social experiment, like breeding pedigree dogs. As if there wasn't enough trouble in Dulwich with labradoodles, schnoodles and one cavapoo in particular, she thought. Jake hadn't said a single word to her about this disco, either. But she suddenly wondered whether that was because he was a bit embarrassed. If Charlie was going, and even planning what to wear (wonders would never cease – both boys had worn identikit jeans and tops since they'd been old enough to walk and not once expressed even a passing interest in fashion), then odds on Jake would be keen to go too.

'I see... but I'm not sure why this is causing problems for our boys? I mean, why would Jake be losing sleep about this? And...' Beth looked at Katie. She didn't want to dump Charlie in it about the WhatsApp messages.

'Yes,' said Katie. 'I mean, what does this have to do with Gregory King? I don't know if you know, but he's been messaging Charlie...'

'And do you know what those messages have said?' Mrs Montgomery's eyebrows were virtually on the ceiling. Or so Beth had to assume. They had ascended inside her helmet of hair and were now nowhere to be seen.

'No. No, I don't,' Katie said in a quiet voice. 'He, um, well. They seem to have been... deleted.'

'I see,' said Mrs Montgomery. She used the sort of sepulchral tone that Beth imagined the old hanging judges had picked when they put on the black cap signalling the death penalty.

Beth and Katie looked at each other nervously.

Mrs Montgomery leant forward. 'It's like this, ladies,' she said. 'Gregory King is known to have a certain amount of influence on the younger boys. People in his own cohort tend to sideline him, for good reason. But the lower years aren't yet proof against the, erm, persuasive charms exerted by his type. Both Charlie and Jake are good sorts.' Here Beth and Katie exchanged a rather more cheerful look. 'But they need to learn when to say no.'

'Say no to what, exactly?' Katie broke in.

Beth was impressed that Katie was being so feisty. Normally she was too sunny to need to be confrontational – life inexorably went her way anyway. What did she ever have to get heated about, except perhaps the tardy arrival of a shipment of Le Creuset cookware to her Cornish holiday cottage? But with her son under some sort of attack, Katie was a different woman. She was sitting bolt upright, her core effortlessly engaged thanks to all her yoga, and no doubt firing on all chakras too. Beth, by contrast, knew her face was burning and her fringe was flying everywhere, as it did in moments of high tension.

Mrs Montgomery fixed them both with a steely eye. 'Well, they need to say no to Gregory King, for a start. Unfortunately, as it is, they have both agreed – to assault girls from the College School.'

THIRTEEN

Both Beth and Katie reacted in unison to Mrs Montgomery's bombshell.

'What? No way, there has to be some mistake!'

'You're kidding, they would never... not in a million years...'

The idea that either Jake or Charlie would ever try and assault a girl was sheer madness. And both mothers continued to give their views on this in no uncertain terms. Mrs Montgomery bowed her helmet under the onslaught, and eventually held up a palm for silence.

'If I could just give you some further details?'

Both women shuffled in their chairs and sat back reluctantly. Beth's mind was racing. It just couldn't be true. Jake would never try and attack a girl... why would he? He'd never been subjected to any kind of violence himself, never watched anything on TV that might have given him ideas. All the men in his life were kind and gentle. James had been wonderful with him. Harry was endlessly patient. Beth's brother Josh, when he was around, was great at all the football-playing stuff, but nothing rougher. His love 'em and leave 'em attitude to women was not great, but that surely had gone right over

Jake's head. Jake had never been violent with Beth, even though he was suddenly (and disconcertingly) almost her height. It was just crazy. And Beth didn't need to be a mind reader to know that Katie, right next to her, was scrolling through a similar checklist and coming to exactly the same conclusion.

'There must be some mistake,' Katie said, her mouth set in such a firm horizontal line that Beth almost didn't recognise her smiley friend.

'I assure you, there is not,' said Mrs Montgomery equally firmly.

Beth, worried now that they'd be in some sort of weird stand-off all day, tried to get things moving. 'Perhaps you could give us the details, as you said? Just tell us exactly what you say has happened?'

Mrs Montgomery angled her helmet towards Beth. 'It's hard to know exactly where to begin. But perhaps the character of Gregory King is key here. As I've said, he has a certain charisma. He's also very interested in gaming, and spends a lot of time helping the younger boys by explaining, er, levels and shortcuts and whatever.' They were clearly reaching the end of Mrs Montgomery's knowledge of the subject, and Beth and Katie's too for that matter. 'This gives him what we might call an "in". He then starts to exchange this information, considered valuable by boys who are sucked into the gaming world too...'

Here Beth and Katie shifted uncomfortably again. Had Jake and Charlie been 'sucked into the gaming world'? That sounded so terrible. But both boys did spend hours on their consoles. Beth couldn't pretend, hand on heart, that she knew what that really entailed, now they could link up with other players online. Was Jake always playing with Charlie? Or was he sometimes playing with this awful Gregory boy? She simply didn't know.

'Then King begins to ask them to do things in order to

earn his tips,' Mrs Montgomery continued. 'Small things at first... hand over the odd snack, maybe fork out a pound coin or two.'

Had Jake been forgoing his snacks? Again, Beth had no idea. He was always ravenous when he got home – but then he was growing. The new shoes she'd coughed up for at the start of term, such a short time ago, were already pinching, he'd told her the other day. As for money, his grandmother slipped him the occasional fiver (about the only input she had) so Beth wouldn't know if more than usual was gone from the shoebox he put his fortune in, since deciding that his old Buzz Lightyear moneybox was too babyish.

'You can see how things like this might escalate,' Mrs Montgomery continued. 'Gradually, the boys are asked to do more compromising things... and once they're involved, then they're all the more vulnerable to pressure to, ah, "up the ante" as I think one might say.'

'Hang on a minute,' said Beth, her mind whirring. 'If you know so much about this boy's modus operandi, then why on earth isn't the school doing anything to stop it? Taking people's snacks and money is bad enough, without anything else going on. And I'm still not convinced that Jake has been asked to do anything at all by this boy, by the way,' she added, folding her arms across her jumper.

'I take your point, Mrs Haldane...'

'*Ms*,' said Beth wearily.

'...But the real consideration here, surely, is where we are today? Yes, people have observed Gregory's tactics before. But it's hard to nip these things in the bud. He is, not to put too fine a point on it, pretty sneaky.'

'Why have you got someone like him at Wyatt's at all?' Katie sounded almost at the end of her tether now. 'He's clearly a repeat offender, though I agree with Beth that nothing, not one word you've said, suggests our boys are planning to attack girls at all. The idea is ridiculous. But if you just kick him out, surely that's the problem solved?'

'Excluding pupils is a very serious matter. It could have severe consequences for their academic future, going forward.'

'Are you telling me you're putting the future GCSEs of a, a, thug like Gregory King above my own boy's wellbeing?' Beth was now just as angry as Katie.

'Look, ladies,' Mrs Montgomery swivelled her helmet and tried an ingratiating smile. 'We need proof of what's been going on. At the moment, we just have anecdotal evidence of what Gregory's aim *may* be, which isn't enough to act on.'

'All right, then. Tell us exactly what this aim is. Because you seem to be accusing our sons of something, when it's another boy's fault. And you're not taking action against that boy, the perpetrator. But you've dragged us here. Where are Gregory King's parents?'

Mrs Montgomery sighed. 'I can see the situation seems confusing and even unfair. What we understand is that Gregory has put your two boys up to something concerning the Year 8 disco.'

'We know that much already! Where does the assault come in? *Alleged* assault, I should say,' said Beth crossly.

'The idea, apparently, is to accost as many of the College School girls as possible, to get a kiss. While the other boy documents the encounters on his phone. According to Gregory King, this will constitute "a laugh". And if they don't do it, he will shame them in front of their contemporaries. But the thing is – he has said your boys were more than willing to go along with the scheme.'

'He would say that, wouldn't he? It simply isn't true, it can't be. I'm sure they've denied it. You'll just have to stop this! Cancel the disco, if necessary. Just make sure this Gregory creature can't go ahead with his threats,' said Katie.

'I understand your view,' Mrs Montgomery told Katie, in

her maddeningly calm tones. 'But unfortunately, we are not able to call the disco off, of course.'

'Why on earth not?' Beth thundered.

'Well, for one thing, there are one hundred and seventy-eight other attendees to consider, all of whom are innocent of this, ah, scheme and very much looking forward to the occasion. No, it's simply a case of asking you to keep your boys at home, if possible. Or otherwise watching them both, very carefully indeed.'

Beth and Katie exchanged glances again. Beth felt every bit as furious as Katie looked. The whole thing was absurd. Gregory King should be suspended immediately, at least until the disco was over. And then, if Beth had her way, he would be thrown out of Wyatt's for good. Stopping poor Jake and Charlie from going to the disco, when they had been picked on and victimised like this, seemed incredibly unfair.

Besides, Janice's tales about previous Year 8 discos were flooding back to Beth now. She remembered that whole thing was as stringently policed as any all-women candlelit vigil. There would be teachers prowling the corridors all night, ready to root out pupils from either school who tried to secrete themselves in classrooms or misbehave in changing rooms. There would also be a parent lurking behind every pillar in the Great Hall. Some would ostensibly be doling out the (alcohol-free) punch, some would be in charge of the limp sandwiches and sausage rolls on the refreshment table, but all of them would in fact be subjecting their children's every move to anxious scrutiny. Were their babies too ill at ease with the opposite sex? Or too blasé?

Either way, she was pretty confident it would be impossible for the boys to carry out Gregory King's dastardly plan, even if they had desperately wanted to.

Beth had always managed to evade Janice's entreaties to help out at the Year 8 disco. But she had certainly not shied away from hearing her morning-after descriptions. So she knew all the boys would spend their evening on one side of the hall, while the girls would be on the other. There would be a certain amount of arms-out, legs-out gyrating to the music from the boys – embryonic dad dancing, really – as well as some much more graceful moves from the girls. There would be an awful lot of clumps of these girls giggling inanely. But there would be no real mixing at all, until about ten minutes before the end. Then, the very boldest of each sex would make a quick sortie into enemy territory, mostly just to be able to say that they had. But she was willing to bet that neither Jake nor Charlie would be in this vanguard, even with Gregory King's threats spurring them on.

Beth would have preferred to give Jake free rein to spend an evening hovering on the edges of the action, or throwing some ill-judged shapes, without any maternal scrutiny. But that was not, now, to be. She would have to be on red alert, redder even than Katie's red alert. What would that be, she wondered, some sort of hyper-scarlet alert? Well, so be it.

'We'll keep an eye on them,' Beth said grimly to Mrs Montgomery. 'There's no need for you to worry. They won't put a foot out of line, I can promise you that. And as for Gregory King...'

'Gregory will not, of course, be present at the disco himself, as he is in Year 9,' said Mrs Montgomery, fiddling with a stack of papers.

'I mean what, precisely, are you planning to do about him?'

'Yes, exactly,' said Katie earnestly. 'Our boys are the innocent parties in all this. It's not their fault they're being blackmailed.'

'Blackmail is an ugly word, as I'm sure you understand,' Mrs Montgomery said loftily.

'Well, what would you call it?' snapped Beth. She'd often been told not to use the word by Harry, but really, was there another description for what was going on? 'They're under pressure to do something they don't want to do, because this boy has a hold over them. It's awful. They deserve your support and understanding. Instead they're being treated like the bad guys.'

'It's not a question of "bad" and "good", is it, though, Ms Haldane? Things are never quite that black and white.'

Beth could agree with that. She had already seen red, and nothing Mrs Montgomery was saying was making her revert to monochrome. She bit her lip to stop herself from saying something she might regret. She wasn't just a parent here; this was her place of work, and if she obeyed her current impulse to reach across the desk and give Mrs Montgomery's coiffure a good sharp tug, she wouldn't be able to come back tomorrow. It was safe to say there were enough ruffled feathers in the room to fill a decent-sized duvet. Luckily, Katie stepped in, to smooth things over.

'You have our undertaking, Mrs Montgomery. And we'll leave it to you to sort out what's going to happen to Gregory King,' she added.

Beth opened her mouth to remonstrate, but Katie had already got to her feet and was putting out a hand to get Beth to do likewise. Slightly grumpily, she stood up and shrugged her handbag back onto her arm.

'Right. Well. We'll see.'

'Thank you both so much, ladies, for coming to see me this afternoon,' said Mrs Montgomery with a nod of her helmet. She then turned back to her papers and gave every appearance of having banished the two women, and their boys' troubles, from her mind.

Outside the door, Beth turned on Katie. 'What did you say that for? That Gregory King could get away scot-free?'

'Oh, for God's sake, I just said that to keep her sweet, Beth. Don't you worry. My Michael will be drafting a stiff letter to the school trustees the minute he gets home.'

'Let's go to my office, we can talk there without anyone overhearing,' Beth said, conscious that Mrs Montgomery might well be listening in on Katie's fighting talk. Her friend was so angry that she hadn't lowered her voice at all. They quickly walked the short distance to the archives office and Beth let them in. She took a cursory look around, hoping Katie wasn't going to be shocked by the massive pile of documents in her in-tray, or the slightly dusty air of the place. Though Beth did her best to keep on top of things – sort of – there had been a lot going on lately. Filing the latest batch of copies of the school magazine had not seemed the most pressing item on her agenda.

Beth shifted a pile of books from the chair in front of her desk so that Katie could sit. But her friend was still so incensed at what had just happened that they could have been on the dark side of the moon for all she cared.

'That bloody woman,' Katie fulminated. 'How dare she talk about our boys as though they are some kind of... sex pests. I bet they haven't had a single thought about girls yet, anyway, let alone wanted to *snog* any.'

Katie managed to make snogging sound as appealing as mainlining slugs. Beth couldn't help smiling just a tiny bit.

'You know, the time is coming when they will actually be interested,' she said. 'I know neither of us wants to think about it, but we do need to be sure they're on the right track with girls, it's so important.'

'Oh, I know,' Katie said, deflating like a balloon. 'Our lovely boys. Why do they have to grow up? Why can't they stay the way they were? Remember when they met?'

Beth nodded. How could she forget? Jake's little head had been bent over some of that big, chunky Lego for toddlers. He was trying to separate the blocks, and Beth was sitting on her hands, desperate to help but knowing he should learn to do it by himself. But then Charlie had bumbled over, all wispy blond hair and a grin as wide as a house, sorted Jake out, then trundled off again. Jake had leapt up and gone over to play next to Charlie and the rest had been history.

The little vignette encapsulated both their characters. Jake, intense, absorbed by problems, yet sometimes becoming a little bogged down in things. Very like his mother, Beth reflected. And, while things came easily to sunny and sweet Charlie, he was more than happy to pass on his luck to any friend who might need it. Just like Katie.

Beth wondered if this Gregory King situation was the reason Katie had been a bit stressed lately. She couldn't blame her if it was. The whole business was a sign their boys were really growing up. There would, from now on, be more and more pockets of their lives that were off-limits to their mothers. It was right, and natural. But it was also frustrating and, in this world they all found themselves in, it could most definitely be dangerous. Or so it seemed to Beth.

'Look, we've both got to step up, understand that changes are coming our way, however much we wish they were still in their little dungarees in the sand pit.'

Katie nodded sadly. 'So, what do you want to do about all this, then?'

'Shall we just take out a contract on Gregory-blimming-King?'

'God, I wish we could,' said Katie.

'I mean, Harry probably knows someone... I suppose that's out, though,' said Beth reluctantly. 'But maybe we should do the next best thing.'

'What's that?' Katie was agog.

'Maybe we should set Belinda McKenzie on him.'

FOURTEEN

Katie was much mollified by the idea of getting Belinda McKenzie involved in the Gregory King business. Belinda had skin in the game, in the shape of her son, who was in Year 8 too. She had a right to know that the King boy was trouble, Beth and Katie told themselves. And if anyone could knock the boy into shape – or possibly out of the school itself – it would be Belinda. She was a bit like a Chieftain tank. Most of the time, she was quite redundant. No one needs a tank in peacetime. But if there was a sniff of war, she could be very useful indeed. She was quite happy to roll over anyone in her way, and would get the big guns out any time she felt her brood was threatened.

Although Beth was somewhat relieved that they were outsourcing the worst aspects of the disco affair, she was still blaming herself terribly for what had happened. Though she wasn't nearly as assiduous as Katie in tracking her son's every mood, she was pretty sure that she should have noticed something was up with Jake. This thing with Gregory King had been going on for a while. And she now wondered whether he'd elected to go to Katie's just so Beth wouldn't spot how exhausted he was. He'd clearly been worrying himself sick, trying to think of ways to dodge the evil kid. Poor Jake.

In normal times, she could have grabbed Adua for a quick coffee as the cleaner did her rounds up and down the street. They would have discussed everything – Adua would have been gagging to know all about the bones, for example – and Beth would have felt soothed and supported. But lovely Adua was gone. Maybe this was why she was getting nowhere fast looking into her friend's death. It was one thing, dabbling in occasional problem-solving when strangers (or people she didn't like) got bumped off. But it was another thing entirely with Adua. Her death was not a game or a riddle. It was a tragedy, simple as that. Nevertheless, she did want to sort it all out. But making enquiries was going to be tricky. For instance, she had to follow up on where Katie's Rosita had been at the crucial moment – but that was a delicate matter. Katie had been prickly about the whole subject already.

Beth, in her kitchen again getting ready for the day, put down her cup and turned away from the dispiriting view of the garden. She knew she wasn't as alone as she'd begun to feel. Harry was on her side – well, mostly. He was just horribly busy. And Nina was already offering to help her.

Jake was coming home after school today, and Beth was heading off to pick Colin up shortly. With this business going on at school, it was important to get Jake back into his normal routine. She'd decided to welcome them both home properly, by making a cake. Well, not Colin. Although he'd undoubtedly eat it, given half a chance, so she planned to pop it into her sturdiest cake tin the moment it came out of the oven. Colin would have to make do with a Bonio. He'd be getting extra walks, though, as Beth could hardly let him out in the garden with that charnel house to play with.

But the thing really playing on her mind was the prospect of having to have a conversation with Jake about sex. Try as she might to be modern and open, Beth knew she was actually a product of her upbringing, and Wendy was about as relaxed about matters biological as a bad case of vaginismus. She had never even told Beth about periods, so she had thought she was bleeding to death when she got her first one. The only thing she had confided to her daughter about boys was that they were really best avoided. Beth had picked up what she knew – and that was still precious little, really – from the more knowledgeable girls in her class, from books read under the bedclothes at night, and from her own fumbling experience.

When Jake had been born, she'd been determined that every aspect of his upbringing would be very different. But the sense of embarrassment about her own body, which was by now inbuilt and still sent her scuttling for her biggest towel when Harry walked in on her in the shower, had stymied all her attempts to be breezy about sex education. She had tried being very technical when Jake was young, calling things by their proper names and making everything sound as mechanical as any Lego instruction leaflet. But when PSHE lessons had started at school, she had been glad to abandon ship on her attempts to enlighten him. Now she cursed herself. The result was that he apparently had no idea about the major issues of consent and coercion.

Perhaps she ought to be glad this had come to light now, while he was still so young and the problem could be addressed.

But there was no disguising the fact that she was absolutely dreading having the conversation with him – and she knew he'd find it toe-curling, too.

* * *

By the time Jake made it home from school that evening, after football practice, it was late and he was tired. Beth had picked up Colin earlier and taken him around Dulwich Park a couple of times so the bone scent wouldn't drive him too distracted. Normally, she would have asked Katie if she fancied joining her but today she didn't get the chance to linger long on her friend's imposing Court Lane doorstep, and nor did Katie ask her in for one of their customary 'quick coffees' that could last for hours. The reason was that Beth had finally got up the courage to ask about Rosita.

'Listen, Katie...' She'd shifted from foot to foot, then just came out with it. 'I don't quite know how to go about this but, erm...'

'What on earth is it, Beth?' Katie had asked. But her tone was already a little sharp. It had spooked Beth. Before she'd known what she was doing, she had just gone and blurted it out. Where exactly had Rosita been on the night of Adua's murder? Katie's face had been a picture. And not a very friendly one.

'Just to be absolutely clear, Beth. As you seem to think I'm employing a killer. Rosita was away when Adua was killed. She was at our house in Cornwall. Getting it ready for our next weekend.'

Instantly, Beth had felt awful. 'Look, Katie, I never meant to imply—'

'Well, I think you did. But Rosita has an alibi. You'll just have to look elsewhere for your murderer, Beth.'

With that, the door had been closed. Not exactly with a slam, and not precisely in Beth's face. But with a deliberation that seemed, somehow, very un-Katie-like.

God, that had not been fun, thought Beth sadly when Jake dumped his schoolbag and coat in the hall. But the situation with Katie would just have to form an orderly queue with the rest of the dreadful worries piling up. And surely Katie would realise, once she calmed down, that Beth had needed to ask the question. As a result of her abstraction, Beth weakly accepted Jake's excuse that he needed to go upstairs immediately to do his homework. She urgently needed to tackle the largest problem in the stack, the issue of what he did or didn't understand about girls – but she wasn't up to it tonight.

Beth sat in the kitchen, desultorily sorting through his schoolbag. Her aim had been to find any useful clues to the Gregory King issue, and even root out any washing that needed to be done – but Katie had done her proud on that front. All Jake's stuff was like new, freshly cleaned and beautifully folded. It was a shame, really. He was bound to ruin the effect in seconds by shoving it anyhow into his drawers. There was nothing else of interest.

Colin snuffled around her feet, then padded his way inexorably to the back door, and sat gazing at it, wagging his tail hopefully whenever she came anywhere near.

'Dream on, Col. You are not going into the garden, and that's that,' she said, reaching down to pat him consolingly. Just then, Magpie exploded through the catflap, and took her time sauntering past Colin with her nose and tail in the air, every inch of her saying, *Ner ner, I'm allowed out there and you're not.* Colin turned on Beth with beseeching eyes.

'I know, I know. Life's unfair. Tell me about it. If you think you've got it tough, I've got to explain the facts of life to Jake,' Beth said, opening the fridge and sticking her head inside, hoping some interesting dinner options would emerge if she looked hard enough. She'd already been stymied in her attempt to make a 'welcome home' cake by realising too late they had no eggs. When she swung the fridge door shut, there was Jake, looking pointedly at her.

'Got something to say, then, Mum?'

Beth cringed. He'd obviously overheard. A flush mounted to her cheeks, but then she decided that was ridiculous. This was a conversation she needed to have with Jake, and she shouldn't be embarrassed at, er, talking to her dog about it. And besides, now might be her only chance to get the thing over and done.

'Look, sit down, Jake. Heaven knows I haven't been looking

forward to having this chat. But you know Katie and I were hauled in to talk to Mrs Montgomery yesterday.'

Jake said something under his breath. Beth didn't quite catch it, but it sounded a lot like 'Bitch.'

Good grief, this was all much worse than she thought. Her boy had turned into some sort of secret misogynist. Maybe Wyatt's wasn't everything it was cracked up to be after all.

'I hope you didn't say what I think you just said, about one of your teachers, who you ought to show a bit of respect to,' Beth said.

'Well, she *is* a snitch. I don't know why she had to drag you into all this, Mum. It was bad enough before.'

Beth sat down, mightily relieved, and looked her son full in the face. Gone were the soft lines of childhood. His boyish curving cheeks were hollowing out, his nose was more pronounced these days and his eyes, currently avoiding hers, were much warier than ever before. He still had eyelashes to die for, though. And she'd always love him dearly.

'Look, I know you've got yourself in a mess, and I know it's embarrassing to talk to me about it. Believe me, I understand, I really do. But we do have to discuss this. It's a big thing. This boy, this Gregory King...'

'He's a right...'

This time Beth heard Jake's word perfectly clearly. And she didn't feel the least need to correct him. Gregory King was all that and more, and if Beth ever got her hands on him...

'I just wish you'd come to me, when all this started. If you'd told me he was putting pressure on you...'

There was a long pause. Then Jake finally spoke. 'He said parents never understand. He told us not to tell, that things would be worse for us if we did. And he said the girls wouldn't mind.'

Beth sighed. 'That's one of the many things he is so wrong about. The girls *would* mind. The girls would be terribly upset.

It would be horrible for them, and horrible for you. They're people, too – how would you like it if someone just grabbed you with no warning and tried to kiss you?'

Jake mimed being sick and Beth leapt upon it. 'Exactly! That's exactly what I mean. If you feel you don't understand girls, that they're from a different universe, just remember they are actually the same as you – with some obvious differences, admittedly. But if you think something would be weird and horrible if it was done to you, you can bet your life they would, too. The thing is, you're going to end up bigger and stronger than most girls. You could hurt them by accident or force them into something without realising it. You have to ask before you do anything. Don't grab. *Never* force. And if you don't want it done to you, then don't do it to them.'

Beth was a bit out of breath by the time she'd finished her little speech, and Jake was studiously looking out of the window rather than at her. But she'd got through what she needed to say, and she really thought he had been listening. There were none of the obvious signs that he'd mentally switched off, anyway, like leaving the room or starting to talk to Colin. And she'd managed not to mention genitalia once.

'Right, well, I think that's all I had to say. How do you feel about all that?' she asked him.

'Fine, Mum. But how do *you* feel?'

She gave him a quick look. But he had a straight face. 'Fine. OK then. To sum up – always ask. Now then, supper. How about a takeaway?'

There was absolutely no mistaking his consent then.

FIFTEEN

By the next morning, though, Beth's brief feeling of certainty and relief had disappeared and she was as jittery as ever. Her silly plan to create the shoffice had caused such havoc. It was grim to think that a pile of bones must have been under the little plastic turtle-shaped sandpit Jake had had as a toddler. How many pictures did she have of him grinning from ear to ear, waving his tiny spade around? Now she couldn't really see him there without imagining that disembodied arm bone waving too. And there were probably others lying beneath the football goal that had been rigged up much more recently. Was that the reason the posts listed more than the Leaning Tower of Pisa? Was the whole garden built upon human remains?

Jake finished breakfast and shot off to school in double-quick time – presumably to forestall any more pep talks about the birds and the bees. But Beth had something else to get on with. A lot of her brain was silted up with Jake's potential #MeToo scandal, but she was still eager to know what Nina had to say about blood feuds. Was it possible she might be able to shine a light on the bones, at least? Beth really hoped so. It hadn't escaped her that the remains had been found right by her fence – the site of her former shed. The fence had been constructed at some point before she had bought the house. And likewise the shed must have got there somehow. Granted, it had been matchwood by the time Beth became its proud owner, but at one point someone had got a builder to put it together, she had to assume. Could the bones, therefore, belong to that builder? Or had they been put there by a builder instead?

Perhaps all the myriad conservatories and shoffices of Dulwich were in fact standing on foundations made of bones. It was a startling thought. There were so many of them. Sally Bentinck seemed to think she had invented the concept of the shoffice, but even when Beth's father had been alive, people had been building fancy sheds and conservatories in their gardens. All right, perhaps there wasn't the whole working-from-home mania that was currently gripping the nation, but glass and wood structures had been rammed onto houses in the area for decades. Back in her dad's day, they had been decked out with rattan furniture and rubber plants, both now amazingly having another moment of red-hot modishness at Mariella's.

Beth's parents had dithered for quite a while about joining the conservatory trend, with Wendy's gentle inertia getting the better of their plans, and then Beth's father had died. Beth supposed it was a good thing; they had been spared the creeping green mould that affected many of these older structures, and Wendy certainly didn't have the constitution to withstand their bracing micro-climates, boiling in summer and freezing in winter. Now that Beth thought about it, many of the conservatories, in her parents' road and elsewhere, had developed serious structural flaws of one sort or another. Replacing conservatories was almost as big a thing as building them in the first place. A shifting foundation of skeletons was definitely an explanation...

Meanwhile, in a corner of her brain, she was also wondering if it was a coincidence that her bones from the turn of the millennium had just been disinterred, and Adua had promptly been killed. Could there be a connection? It was hard to imagine what could link the two awful crimes, apart from the fact that Adua worked in Pickwick Road and the bones had been found there. But it was worth thinking about…

Oh, but all this speculation was fruitless, Beth realised. She needed to get some information from the horse's mouth, though doubtless Nina wouldn't be impressed at being described in such terms. Sitting at the kitchen table in her now habitual position with her back to the sea of mud outside, Beth shoved her cup of tea out of the way and reached for her phone. It was after eight, but before nine; she might catch her friend on her commute if she was lucky. And it was probably Beth's only opportunity to call, before the SOCO team arrived and started demanding their first five hundred cups of tea.

Nina answered after a couple of rings. 'Wotcha!'

'So sorry about yesterday… I had to rush into the school.'

'No worries, babes. Everything rickety?'

Beth paused for a second. *Tickety boo.* 'Yes, yes, absolutely.' Not strictly true – but the fewer people who knew what Jake had agreed to do for that bully Gregory King the better. She took a sip of her tepid tea.

'I heard Gregory King might get suspended,' said Nina cheerfully.

Beth choked painfully as the tea went down the wrong way. Magpie, who'd been sauntering past, stared at Beth with outraged eyes before stalking, very much on her dignity, over to her catflap and exiting with a snap. Beth coughed a few more times and took a swig of water from the tap before she tried to speak.

'How on earth…? Oh, don't even tell me.' One of Beth's first feelings was tremendous relief, that Jake's persecutor was getting his comeuppance. Then came the even greater joy that she wouldn't somehow have to finesse Belinda McKenzie into winkling the boy out of Wyatt's. It seemed the school was going to do the decent thing without being forced. Not for the first time, she blessed wise Dr Grover – and detected the hand of his wonderful wife, Janice, in this outcome. Immediately, she thought of Katie, and how thrilled her friend was going to be. Then she remembered the terms they had parted on. But surely this would make up for that misunderstanding?

'Wait a second. Does this mean everyone knows what happened to Jake and Charlie?'

'Nah, babe. You're all right. Got my connections, innit? No one else knows.'

Beth scanned through a list of staff at the school, wondering who on earth had a hotline to Nina. She had worked there for a while, so it was pointless to speculate. Her source could be any one of the staff, including the groundsmen and the porter. Nina was just a force of nature and if there was anything in SE21 to know, she would find it out, without even having a child at the school.

'You know none of it was Jake's fault, don't you? Or Charlie's either.'

'Course, babe. That Gregory is a wrong'un, everyone knows that. His mum's a really mean dentist, too. All "you don't need an injection", just so you feel the agony.'

'Oh God, that sounds horrible. Do you go to her?'

'Nah, you got to be kidding. I go to the NHS one down in Herne Hill. Wilf gets stickers.'

Beth shook her head at the idea of a sadistic dentist. It was bad enough getting your teeth seen to, without someone deliberately making things worse. For the first time, she felt a pang for Gregory King, having a parent like that. But she soon suppressed it, when remembering that he'd targeted her beloved only son.

'Well, listen, I didn't even ring about that... I was just

wondering about what you were saying about local builders, really. But you're probably off to work, are you?'

'There already babe, got here nice and early today, didn't I?'

Beth hoped Nina's question was rhetorical, and that she wasn't holding forth about the King family in front of an office full of interested listeners. You just never knew with Nina. She was as generous with information as she was with her friend-ship, and sometimes that wasn't really the best idea in the world.

'Well, if I came over your way, maybe you could slip out and meet me somewhere for coffee? Just for a quick chat?'

'Yeah, lovely jubbly. Cappuccinos are on you, babe,' said Nina. 'Oops, bloody customer, innit. Gotta go.'

Nina was working just off the Camberwell New Road at the moment. It was going to take a chunk out of Beth's day, to get down there and back in time for Jake's return, but she'd just have to make sure she fitted everything in. As usual, the first thing to go from Beth's timetable was her job at Wyatt's. Well, she'd been in quite a bit recently, she reasoned. And everyone would die of shock if she started going too regularly. Wouldn't they?

Just then there was the usual peremptory ring at the door-bell that heralded the arrival of Chris Campbell and his cohorts. Magpie, who'd stuck her nose back through the catflap, thought better of it and headed for the Bentincks' fence, turning back long enough to give Beth an infuriated glance.

'Tell me about it, Magpie,' Beth said wearily as she trooped to the door and opened it to the familiar spacesuited gaggle of officers, headed by Campbell. His mouth was even droopier than usual and he stomped past Beth with a mumbled 'Good morning.'

'What's up with him?' Beth asked the others, but wasn't at all surprised when no one answered. They were like members of a cult, slavishly following their leader. One of the younger women did give her a quizzical glance, though. Beth pressed herself against the wall as they all surged past, rustling in their gear, apparently eager to start their daily task of rendering her garden more and more uninhabitable.

'Tea?' she asked, hoping this would go unheard too. But no such luck, the orders came at her thick and fast, with a 'Two sugars' here and a 'Black please' there. The easiest thing, she'd discovered, was to make a job lot of unadorned teas and put a bag of sugar and carton of milk on the tray, and then let everyone sort themselves out. Otherwise she spent most of her day acting as a glorified waitress. But they still seemed to feel they needed to put their full orders in, as though she was a branch of Starbucks. She was only surprised they didn't demand oat milk or shots of hazelnut syrup. Suddenly the trip to Camberwell was looking like a very tempting prospect indeed.

She was hefting her bag onto her shoulder and checking she had her keys when the female officer, Abi, came up to her.

'He's really perked up, you know. The boss,' she said, cocking her head towards Campbell, who was now striding about in Beth's tiny kitchen looking grim-faced.

'Has he?' Beth was astonished. What was he like when he was *really* miserable, then? 'Seems pretty down in the dumps to me.'

'Love does funny things to people,' said the woman with a smirk.

Love? What on earth was she talking about? Unless she meant Campbell's unreasoning love of bones. Anyway, Beth had quite enough to think about. She automatically started trotting towards the 42 bus stop in the village, then realised it was uncomfortably close to the very spot where Adua had met her doom. Walking past it was something she was inevitably going to have to get used to. But standing so near, for maybe twenty minutes or more, if the bus was up to its usual tricks? Could she do that without wondering what had been going through Adua's mind... no, no, no. There was simply nothing for it but to take her old car.

Beth had hardly driven since giving up her short-lived quest to find a new house in Sydenham. That whole project had come to a sticky end, in more ways than one. The little green Fiat still bore the scars of the experience. The passenger seat footwell was, she was embarrassed to find, still centimetres deep in empty Wotsits packets, while quite a few Lucozade bottles had been chucked into the back. Lord. Beth's cheeks burnt for a second at the thought that all her neighbours had been passing her ramshackle vehicle for weeks and no doubt remarking on her reprehensible snack choices. *It was Nina*, she wanted to shout. Nina had been her wingman – winglady? wingperson? – on that adventure, and the role came with a certain health tax. While Nina looked fit as a fiddle on all the E-numbers, and her son Wilf never took a day off school, Beth had felt quite bilious by the time the case was solved. That was one reason, she supposed, that she hadn't sorted the car out. Another reason was sheer laziness, she had to admit. Her car, like her hand-bag, was a rare OCD-free area in a rigorously scoured life.

She bundled a few of the shameful exhibits into an old plastic bag and brushed a generous scattering of orange crumbs off the driver's seat. The little car started first time, despite all her neglect, and Beth was soon chugging away down to Camberwell. The traffic wasn't too insane, at this time of day, though she always found the big junctions in Camberwell quite scary, largely because of the great shoals of buses that floated serenely up and down the roads, moving slowly, pushing every-thing out of their way, as they drifted in stately progression towards the centre of London.

There was another major problem with driving, and that was parking. As any London resident knew, finding somewhere safe and vaguely legal to leave your car was as hard a quest, these days, as paying your gas bill without having a panic attack. Beth started to look hopefully at side streets as soon as she passed King's College Hospital and edged into Camberwell proper. Eventually, past a NatWest bank on the corner opposite Camberwell Green, she saw a hopeful, stubby little road that didn't seem entirely plastered with double yellow lines. She eased the little Fiat into the one remaining space, checked the tiny writing on a sign high above her and locked the car with a happy sigh. She'd be fine for two hours. Her next job was to run Nina to earth.

Stepping out onto the main road again, an ambulance zoomed past and almost took her eyebrows off. She took a pace back, and nearly trod on a woman wheeling a shopper containing what looked like the entire contents of the local Lidl. Just then, she saw a very welcome sight – Nina, waving at her fit to burst, from the other side of the road.

As soon as there was a gap in the traffic, Beth nipped over and was soon enveloped in a lovely Nina hug, all snuggly thanks to her white puffa coat.

'So where are you actually working, then? And how come they've let you out?'

Nina waved a hand vaguely in the direction of the green. 'Oh, little place over there. Just doing the filing. It's not rocket salad.'

'Right,' said Beth. 'Shall we get that coffee, then?'

'Yeah, hon. There's a good place down here. Just a bit further,' Nina said, leading Beth past the noodle bar with the beautiful Chinese lanterns in the window, and almost as far as the gorgeous plant shop The Nunhead Gardener. Then she pushed at a door which opened with a merry jangle, and soon Beth found herself welcomed by her favourite aroma – a swirling blend of cappuccinos and pastries.

'Like one?' Beth asked, gesturing towards the cakes on the

counter. Nina didn't hesitate but grabbed a vast iced Danish creation and plonked it on a plate.

'Remind me to get four lattes when I go. I said I'd do the coffee run.'

'Oh, I'll make it quick, then,' Beth said, a little disappointed. She'd counted so much on getting every drop of information she could out of Nina. She was really her only lead on the builders who might have constructed the previous shed in Beth's garden. Plus she still needed to hear about this blood feud Nina had mentioned.

'Nah, you're all right. I'll just say the machine broke down, innit?'

Not for the first time, Beth marvelled at Nina's insouciant attitude to work. But then, she thought, she was little better herself. After all, she wasn't exactly putting in time at the archives office today, was she? But that was because she had so many other things going on at the moment, she tried to rationalise.

'So, you mentioned a blood feud?' Beth said once they had both slid into comfortable seats, overlooking the bustle of the street outside. It felt good being able to get this straightened out at last.

Nina looked at her for a second, head cocked on one side like a particularly intelligent sparrow. 'Yep. You heard about it?'

'No! Well, yes, but only from you. And I'm super keen to find out more. Where there's blood, there might be bones... and that would be really helpful right now.'

'Yeah, I see where you're coming from. Hope you won't be disappointed.'

It wasn't the introduction that Beth had been yearning for, but she knew Nina well enough by now to realise she some-times downplayed her stories. Hopefully this would be one of those occasions. Nina leant forward, until the dangling cords on her white coat skimmed the top of her cappuccino. She brushed

them out of the way impatiently, looked quickly to the right and
left to check no one was listening, and hissed to Beth:

'Have you heard about the Prices?'

Beth shook her head and moved closer in turn. There were
only a couple of other people in the café. And they both looked
pretty wrapped up in their phones or their food. But you never
knew. Beth had plenty of experience of eavesdropping; it didn't
take much to look busy, while your ears were wagging faster
than Dumbo's.

'No. Who or what are the Prices?'

'Well, they were the top cats round hereabouts, building-
wise,' said Nina, indicating pretty much the whole of south
London with one airy hand gesture. 'Until the Rutlands came
along, that is.' Then she tapped the side of her nose.

There was a pause. 'Um, is that it?' asked Beth, hoping she
didn't sound quite as disappointed as she felt.

'Nah, babe, nah. Just checking what kind of starting level
we're at with this info. Don't want to flood you too early with
detail if you don't know nuffink.'

'Oh, OK,' said Beth, reassured rather than affronted. 'Well,
let's assume I do know nuff... nothing. So, tell me more.'

'Well, it goes back a long way. How far do you want?'

'Um, the beginning?' Beth said it with a smile, but she was
conscious of time ticking by. Nina's excuse about the broken
coffee machine would surely soon be looking as flimsy as a wet
paper cup.

But Nina, once she'd properly got started, was nothing if
not concise. The Prices and the Rutlands, it turned out, had
both come to the area around the time of the expansion of
Crystal Palace, after the Great Exhibition of 1851. The two
families had spent the many subsequent decades tussling relent-
lessly for the business of the burghers of the area. Crystal
Palace, which had started off as majestic and very affluent, had
fallen on hard times but was now rising again. Dulwich had

remained solidly prosperous, Norwood had wavered on the fringes and Herne Hill was becoming increasingly well-heeled as time went by. But one thing remained the same throughout these ups and downs in the property market – the deadly enmity between the Price and the Rutland families.

'Do you know what started it?' Beth asked, by now agog at such a spectacularly long-running feud. It made her mother Wendy's decade-long on-off no-speakies with her carp-keeping neighbour, Mrs Hill, look like ridiculously small beer.

'That's lost in the moist of time,' said Nina. 'But all's I know is that it's still running to this day. It was really bad, I mean, *awful*, about twenty years ago, though. Oof,' she said, frowning at the memory.

'How was it so bad?' Beth asked. She then had to wait while Nina finished chewing and swallowing an impressive mouthful of Danish pastry.

'Yum. Well, ever heard of Fiona Price?'

'Doesn't ring a bell.'

'She was from round here. Just a young girl. Then she went missing.'

Beth stared at Nina in silence for a second. Nina looked back at her blankly.

'She went missing! Don't you see, Nina? This missing girl, Fiona Price – she could be my bones.'

Nina stared back, then dismissed the idea with a peal of laughter. 'Nah. It wasn't that sort of missing, babe. No. Nothing to see there. She just moved out of London. Fell out with her parents and off she went.'

'Oh.' Beth felt deflated by Nina's certainty. 'So how was that so terrible, then, with Fiona Price, if she left town in one piece?'

'Well, it's more the effect it had on the two families. Before Fiona, they didn't see eye to eye, sure, but it wasn't danglers drawn. But after Fiona, it was war. Chased out of her manor.

The Prices felt it wasn't right. See?' Nina said it as though it all made perfect sense.

'Hmm,' said Beth. She wasn't sure she really did see. But maybe a strong sense of family was super-important for the builders of south-east London. It definitely all added up to Nina.

But, despite Nina's certainty that Fiona Price had simply upped sticks and departed for pastures new, Beth wondered. It would be easy enough to say someone had moved out of London... and then put their bones in a back garden. Particularly if you spent your working week installing sheds all over the area. She was going to have to investigate this carefully.

The feud did sound vaguely familiar now, though. It would have been just about then that her late father had had huge trouble getting their garden fence repaired. It hadn't been a particularly big job, but her dad had approached it in his usual careful fashion, getting three written quotes from different firms. She remembered his consternation when two of the firms started undercutting each other. It was a bizarre reversal of the norm. The final price from both companies had been derisory but, rather than grabbing at this bargain, her father decided to go for the third, more expensive firm. Her mother, of course, had been against this but, in their very traditional marriage, the final say went to her father. Usually this was considerably modified by her mother's well-honed passive-aggressive tendencies. Wendy was an expert at stealthily chipping away at opposition until it was completely undermined. But not this time. Her father had been against any form of corruption or misbehaviour, and he had not liked the way the companies were undercutting each other. It had smacked of some kind of subterfuge to him and he would have no truck with it. Beth was now willing to bet the two firms had been the Rutlands and the Prices.

Wendy's back fence was still standing, a testament to Beth's father's instincts. The same could definitely not be said for a huge number of the construction projects in and around the Dulwich area, those from the same era and much later too. A lot of families would have found those low prices very hard to resist; the result seemed to be work which did not stand the test of time.

'Yeah, we've all seen 'em, innit? Rubbish old conservatories with the glass all mouldy, sheds falling over when you blow on them. And what about Belinda McKenzie's home office?' said Nina.

'What about it?' asked Beth, eyes wide. This structure, which she had glimpsed a few times from Katie's garden (the two were near neighbours in uber-posh Court Lane) was gigantic. It was like a wooden Hogwarts, complete with turrets and actual stained glass, all tastefully painted in a bold and moody mid-grey. The creation was so monstrously large it would have covered every inch of Beth's garden, not to mention the house and much of the pavement outside. Even in Belinda's enormous acreage, sweeping down to Dulwich Park, it still took up a fair slice.

'Falling down, innit?' Nina shrugged.

'No!' Beth felt an immediate jolt of glee. She tried her best to stamp it out. It really wasn't very nice to be so thrilled when something went wrong for someone else, she told herself firmly. Especially when she had actually considered roping Belinda in to get rid of Gregory King. Well, yes – but this was Belinda McKenzie. Belinda had been trying to make Beth feel small, even smaller than she actually was, since the day they'd first met. And she almost always succeeded. But according to Nina, Wyatt's was doing the decent thing with Gregory King, so Beth didn't need to be nice to her nemesis. She couldn't stop a grin peeping out and Nina gave her a wide answering smile.

'Well, that's made your day, mate!'

'I feel bad... but she has been pretty mean to me over the years,' Beth acknowledged. 'And it's not like she can't afford to get it fixed. But God, she must be beside herself. I dread to think how much that thing cost. It's absolutely huge. I bet you can see it from the moon.'

'I heard it wrecked the last attempt to dock the Space Station, the astronauts were so busy arguing about whether that dingy colour was a big mistake.'

This time Beth gave up the attempt to be a better person, and just laughed out loud. Once she'd got herself back under control, she couldn't help asking, 'Seriously, what's gone wrong with it? She must have spent a fortune on that thing.'

Nina shrugged. 'Electrics are buggered, whole roof leaks, and I think bits of one of the towers are falling off. Nearly killed one of their dogs, I heard.'

'Wow. That sounds quite comprehensive,' Beth said.

'Yep. That's the trouble when you get the Rutlands and the Prices involved. They'll do anything to beat each other to the job, then they're left without the money to do the thing properly. It's stupid. S'why I gave you that other firm's number, not theirs.'

It was certainly giving Beth a lot to think about. It perhaps explained the restless drive in Dulwich to keep on tinkering with outbuildings. Maybe it wasn't about change for the sake of it, or even endless bodies buried beneath foundations, but was rather a case of carrying out constant essential repairs to shore up shoddy building work. Much though the chat had cheered her up, it still wasn't quite what she'd thought it would be about, though.

'When you said "blood feud", I did think there might be actual, well, blood,' said Beth, over the rim of her coffee cup.

'Yeah, well, what can I say, babe? Watch this space. I got more to tell you... but that'll have to be enough for this time. Got to get my round in now and get back to the office.'

Beth gave Nina a big hug. 'I'm really grateful. Hope you won't get the sack for being out so long.'

'Nah, mate. They wouldn't dare! They needs me. At least until next week when the real girl comes back,' Nina said with a wink, as she prepared to head off with her little cardboard tray of offerings. Beth hoped she was right.

Nina had given Beth a lot of background on the building situation in Dulwich, and one of the names she'd mentioned was certainly jogging a memory, but there was only one topic she was desperate to find out more about. Fiona Price, the girl who had left town so abruptly years ago.

Nina didn't believe it was Fiona Price in Beth's garden. But that left Beth with just one question.

Who the hell *was* down there, then?

SIXTEEN

It wasn't until the middle of the night that Beth suddenly remembered where she'd heard one of those names before. It had been when Sally Bentinck had been banging on about her builders. Was it at the Kendalls' dinner party? Or even before... Beth was sure she'd used Rutlands.

Oh dear, she thought. She wondered if that would mean poor Sally's shoffice would soon be listing badly at one end, or leaking, or worse. It was all the woman needed, with her husband prancing around the States with his much younger paramour and her houseful of strapping grown-up boys. Not that kids coming back to roost was a bad thing. Beth certainly hoped Jake would stick around for a bit when he was finally an adult. But maybe not forever. She and Harry could probably use a bit of time to themselves. Though, at the moment, she hardly remembered what Harry looked like in daylight. As she rearranged her pillows in the dark, she flicked a look at the shape hunched in the bed next to her. She could just see Harry's coarse blond hair sticking up above the duvet, but he had his back firmly to her.

That's how it felt at the moment – as though he was shutting her out. She was probably overthinking things, and not being sympathetic enough about his extremely demanding job, but she couldn't help questioning whether he really had to be doing *this* much overtime. Not when she was facing trouble on so many fronts, and could do with him here. It would be easier for her to understand his absence if he'd just tell her what he was working on. If it was really as crucial as he seemed to think, she wouldn't feel nearly so resentful.

She took a chance, and said his name softly. Nothing. She turned up the volume a little. He still slumbered on. Abandoning subtlety, she shook his arm while saying, 'Harry!' into his ear.

'Blimey, love. What time do you call this?' he said, rubbing sleep out of his eyes.

'Time to catch up,' said Beth, trying to sound beguiling, but knowing she had a short window before he either went back to sleep again or, worse, got up and went to work. 'What's happening with Adua?'

Instantly he was contrite. 'I'm so sorry about that, Beth love. I wish I could have been there... got so much on,' he said, rumpling his hair.

'Yes, yes, but what's going on with the Adua investigation? Have you found anything out yet?'

Instantly he looked a lot less sympathetic. 'Look, you know I can't... Enquiries are ongoing, Beth.'

'Any witnesses?' There was a telling pause, which Beth jumped on. 'So someone saw something?'

Harry was silent for a moment, then he seemed to give in. 'Someone was seen running away. But who and where to, we don't know. We'll get there, though.'

Beth hugged the information to herself, like Magpie with a choice nugget of cat food. At least they were making some progress, however slow. She felt better for Adua. But the pace did suggest she should probably look into things herself, if she wanted to get things sorted out sooner rather than later.

'Right. Back to work,' Harry said, blowing her a kiss. Beth, who'd have preferred the real thing, pouted for a second. But then she rationalised. At least all the many extra hours of over-time he was racking up would be swelling the family coffers. They'd have the best constructed shoffice in Dulwich. Assuming she could get some builders sorted for when the bloody SOCO team had finally left the premises. She had a bad feeling those SOCOs were going to have as many comebacks as Elvis. She lay back down and dragged the duvet over her face.

* * *

Harry made his way downstairs as soon as he'd had a shower, noting the continuing chaos downstairs. He knew it must all be taking a heavy toll on the lady of the house. Colin wagged his tail frantically at Harry, signalling his availability for immediate walkies, but Harry just patted him and said, 'Soon, old boy, soon,' as he shut the front door behind him.

As he walked to his car, he kicked away the first few fallen leaves of the season. He'd take Beth out, once this awful case was over. Make it up to her.

He couldn't really blame her for trying her best to see where he was on the Adua investigation. Well, he could – but knowing Beth as he now did, he realised there was little point. That nose of hers might be cute as a button, but she spent a lot of time poking it into things that were really none of her business. It wasn't the moment to tell her that despite all the officers he'd put on the job, they'd turned up a big fat zilch so far, apart from their one witness. This was a vague old dear who'd come out without her bifocals, and couldn't be sure whether the figure she'd seen was a man, a woman or just a very large blurry mark on her glasses.

If Harry did let on, Beth'd feel honour bound to wade in herself, to avenge her friend or some such nonsense. No, it was vital that he gave her a wide berth for a bit, until he had some proper progress to report. And who knew when that would be? Khan had him working his socks off on his other big case, which was proving an absolute nightmare to break.

In fact, if it had been any of his other officers, he'd almost suspect Khan was deliberately making things difficult. He'd spent several days last week looking for some vital folders, which had finally turned up underneath her desk, of all places. But Khan was one of the hardest-working members of his team, always in before him in the mornings, waiting with a cheery smile on her face, and she only left when he did at night. No, if he had more like her around him, goodness only knew what he could do.

This mad workload was simply a blip, that was all. An unfortunate bit of timing. It would soon be over, and he'd be back on the sofa with Beth, where they both belonged. With that thought, he dismissed all at Pickwick Road from his mind, and focused instead on the massive workload waiting for him at the office.

* * *

When Beth finally woke again at 9.30, she stretched luxuriously for a moment, then reached for her phone. The accusing digits on the home screen danced before her eyes. Three-quarters of an hour after school had started! She jumped out of bed and raced along the corridor to make sure Jake was up. Thank goodness, his bed was empty and there was silence from downstairs, apart from the distinctive slap of the catflap as Magpie went about her complicated manoeuvres, moving in and out of the house in an obscure cat ballet. There was blessed peace for a moment.

Then the doorbell shrilled. From the upstairs landing, Beth could see shadows jostling outside the front door through the little round porthole of frosted glass. Damn it all, the SOCOs had arrived. They were actually late, for a change. But here she was, still in her dressing gown!

There was nothing to be done but to hurry down and swing the door open, then stand there as a parade of white-suited experts trailed past her, looking her up and down. She clutched the old fleecy thing tighter around her throat. She'd been meaning to upgrade it for years, but the moment had never quite come. When Campbell raked her with a particularly gloomy glance, she decided her first chore this morning would be to hit the online shops.

Honestly, just because they'd been up for hours and had commuted from all four corners of the capital to get to her house on time, there was no reason for them to be so sniffy, Beth thought, slopping hot water into myriad mugs of tea five minutes later. She stirred them briskly, then dashed back up to shower and get ready in record time. Her morning routine wasn't extensive at the best of times – it didn't take long to select one of her habitual jumpers from her wardrobe, or to shrug on her trusty jeans. Once she'd stuffed her feet into her pixie boots and slung on her handbag, she was good to go. But she'd forgotten something. There were two pairs of hopeful eyes gazing up at her by the door; Colin's liquid brown ones and Magpie's sharp triangular emeralds. Drat. She dumped her bag at the foot of the stairs, rushed to fill Magpie's bowl with her nuggets and got Colin's lead down. The old dog's tail was now wagging fiercely enough to propel him along the street, while he grinned his appreciation and inadvertently added a bit of drool to the muddy footprints all over the hall.

'Oh, Colin, what am I going to do with you?' It was clear the old boy wasn't going to be contented with a quick turn up and down Pickwick Road. Yet again, Beth felt a pang at Adua's passing. Beth had sometimes roped her in to give Colin a quick run to the park when she was too busy. It made her feel guilty, though there were plenty of dog owners in Dulwich who rarely even touched their pooches' leads. Belinda McKenzie was a case in point. She owned a whole pack of dogs, but delegated all their exercise to an exhausted dog-walker – despite living almost next door to Dulwich Park.

Beth thought for a second. Maybe this was a way to mend fences with Katie? She hadn't had time to ring her yesterday, with the glad tidings about Gregory King. But this was the perfect pretext. Teddy always needed a good long run around the park. And if Beth and Katie went together, they could have a proper chat and maybe put the events of the last few days behind them. Beth was well aware that their usually calm and trouble-free relationship had been rocked. It was her fault. She had been so upset about Jake. Perhaps Katie even thought that Beth blamed her, as it had happened during his stay at her house? But Katie's hands had been full, no doubt all too literally, with Teddy's obedience classes. It wouldn't have been surprising if she had taken her eye off the ball for once. Maybe that's why she had been so touchy with Beth, when she'd blundered in with her questions about Rosita. Beth really hadn't meant to be flinging accusations about... but it must have come across that way. If she and Katie got together, they could also discuss a strategy for the disco, think of ways to activate Belinda McKenzie just in case the school didn't do as Nina had said and oust Gregory King pronto, and walk their dogs at the same time. Four birds, one stone.

Beth stood in her little front garden and phoned her friend. One ring, two, then three... She was just about to give up hope and resign herself to a solo park mission, when Katie answered. But Katie sounded different – guarded, a bit hesitant even.

'Just wondered if you fancied a turn round the park with the dogs?' Beth said breezily.

There was silence for a beat.

'I'm so sorry, Beth. I can't. I've got a class starting in ten minutes.'

Now it was Beth's turn to think. She was pretty sure she knew Katie's yoga timetable off by heart, and most of her classes started at about twelve – the time when toddlers were down for their naps and au pairs could be left in charge, so the stressed mothers of Dulwich could achieve a serene mountain pose in peace for a while.

'OK,' she said quietly, and they said their goodbyes.

So that's how it was. She was hurt, she couldn't deny it. But she supposed it was just about possible that Katie had had to play switcheroo with a class at the last moment. Although she hadn't gone into any explanations, had she? She must still be furious about the Rosita thing.

She'd had so much to say, not least the great news about Gregory King's imminent suspension, which would surely cheer Katie up. But it would have to keep, Beth told herself. She gave poor old Colin the quickest possible run to Dulwich Park (noting that she did not spot Katie rushing off to teach her class at any point) and then returned him to the house. He didn't much like it but she shut him in the sitting room, as far as possible from the enticing scent of old bones.

It looked as if Chris Campbell was zooming up the garden path to give Beth an update, but for once she didn't feel inclined to listen. She grabbed an apple and was on her way again. She had another meet with Nina organised, thanks to a swift bit of texting in the park.

This time, Nina had consented to come into Dulwich proper. She'd been enticed by Beth's promise that they'd give posh new place Mariella's a go. Beth knew there were lots of things about Mariella's that would usually have her avoiding it like the plague – like the bang on trend décor, made all too literal after she'd got a thwack on the head when she'd visited with Katie. Who had known that being uber-trendy meant the risk of decapitation by macramé pot plant holder? But that apart, Beth did actually rather like the place. The seats were really comfy and none of the tables were wonky, both of which were big plus points. She was keen to see what Nina would make of it.

By the time Beth flung open the café door, Nina had already installed herself in one of the booths – and she had company. As promised, she'd brought her cousin Katrina along.

Beth slid into her seat, facing the two women. They were curiously alike, Katrina sharing Nina's bouncy curls and impish grin. But where Nina was petite, almost as short as Beth, Katrina looked as though someone had grabbed her at both ends and pulled, stretching familiar features over a larger surface area.

'Our Katrina, innit?' said Nina, tilting her head in her cousin's direction.

Beth smiled broadly. 'So lovely to meet you.'

'You too, babe! You're just like Nina told me,' Katrina said, looking at Beth assessingly. Beth suddenly didn't want to ask exactly what that meant.

'Um. Shall we order? It's nearly lunchtime... fancy a sandwich or something?'

Beth was amused to see Nina poring over the healthy but high-end list of possibilities. It wasn't exactly Wotsits and Lucozade. But, to her amazement, Nina chose one of the most nutritious options, the chickpea salad with quinoa, fresh spinach leaves and beetroot. If she actually ate it, it would be the largest quantity of vegetables Beth had ever seen her consume. With all the shocks she'd had recently, Beth decided to go for something more comforting. She picked the brunch, basically a full English breakfast – but the toast was hand-milled organic sourdough so that made it all pretty much health food. Katrina ordered the same.

While they were waiting, Beth decided to cut to the chase. 'Nina says you know everything there is to know about the building trade round here.'

Katrina laughed and gave her cousin a hearty shove, nearly forcing Nina off her side of the banquette. Nina pushed her back and for a second Beth worried both were going to end up on the floor.

'She'll say anything, this one,' said Katrina, when the jostling had calmed down. 'But yeah, as it happens she's not wrong. Went to work in the trade when I left school, didn't I? Still there now, as it turns out.'

'Katrina's the one with the steady job,' Nina winked at Beth. 'Safe as Hovis, it is.'

'*Houses*, Nina, houses. I'm amazed you can understand a word she says, Beth,' Katrina said. 'But yeah, I like to stay put and get on with things, not career around all over the place. Career, ha! You'll never have a career if you don't learn a bit of staying power, Neens.'

'Um, but on the building work stuff?' Beth broke in. She didn't want total warfare to break out between the women. She'd never get anywhere if they were distracted. 'The thing is, there's something really odd going on in my garden.'

Katrina looked sober all of a sudden. 'Yeah, Neens said. Dead body, innit?'

Beth swallowed and pushed her plate of sausages away. 'No, not exactly... just... an arm bone. And, um, a few others.'

'Yeah, but hon. I mean, who loses just an arm?' Katrina said, head on one side.

'Unless you're an ampersand or whatever,' Nina broke in cheerfully.

Beth and Katrina looked at her in surprise. Then Katrina's face cleared. '*Amputee*, you mean babes. Christ,' she said, shrugging at Beth.

'Well, anyway, it's just bones. No, erm, flesh,' Beth said,

eyeing the sausages again. 'So, Nina was saying you know all about builders in the area... mine have dumped me since the, erm, discovery. And the feud? I'm dying to hear about that.'

'Yeah, not sure anyone's going to touch your building work while you've got the police in there, love.' Beth slumped a little in her seat, but then brightened up as Katrina went on. 'But I can fill you in on the feud. How much do you know about the Rutlands and the Prices?' she said, a piece of sausage poised on her fork.

'Well, Nina's told me a lot... but I want to work out if there's a connection to my, er, garden.'

'Oh, OK babes. Simples, really. It's a bit like them brothers that fell out, what were their names?'

'Um, Cain and Abel?' ventured Beth.

'Nah, nah. Noel and Liam Gallagher, that's it,' said Katrina, sitting back as though everything was now clear.

'You mean they're related? And they argued?'

'Well, yeah. Cousins, not brothers though. Like me and Neens here.'

'But we'll never fall out, will we?' Nina broke in chirpily.

Katrina gave her a darkling look, and continued. 'Yeah, this was way, way back... before the Second World War, even. They got a contract to fix up the Crystal Palace. It was getting a bit ratty, not surprising as it was built yonks before. They were meant to fix a bit of broken glass here, sort out the frames, I don't know. Just bring it up to scratch. Pretty standard. But then it happened.'

'What happened?' said Nina indistinctly, through a mouthful of quinoa.

Beth swivelled from Nina to Katrina with a look of dawning comprehension on her face. 'This was in the 1930s, you mean? Wait, no, it can't be... can it? The fire?'

'Yep. Whole place burnt down. Winter of 1936, it was. They blamed it on faulty wiring and wooden floors, didn't they?

Easily done. Shoddy work, substandard switches... Four hundred firemen turned out to help. But they couldn't do a thing. Winds blew the fire from one end to the other. It only took a few hours to destroy the lot. People came from all over to watch the blaze, Churchill and all sorts.'

'Oh yeah, Cromwell. I knew that,' said Nina, digging in to her food again.

'But who was responsible?' Beth asked. 'The Prices... or the Rutlands?'

'That's the big question, innit, Beth. Like, who really knows, at this point? The cousins blamed each other. And that was that. Never spoken to each other since. Well, most of them, at any rate.' Katrina pursed her lips.

'My God, that's dreadful! I'm not surprised they haven't got over that. It's hardly the best advert... for either family.'

'Yeah, but you'd think they'd learn, wouldn't you? It didn't help either of them. And then it all kicked off back when we were at school, didn't it?' Katrina turned to Nina, who was chomping through her quinoa with every appearance of delight. She nodded briefly.

'Again? Oh, was that with... Fiona Price?' Beth sat forward. The revelation that the warring families had destroyed one of the biggest landmarks in south-east London was one thing. But that had all been nearly a hundred years ago. The mysterious Fiona Price was part of an altogether more recent scandal. Beth was desperately hoping Katrina might fill in some more pieces of the puzzle.

'Yep, that was all quite weird, wasn't it, Neens? She was a nice girl, in my year, all quite normal – and then the families both kicked off, and the next thing we knew, she'd left the school and that was that.'

'Do you know exactly what that particular fall-out was all about?'

Katrina thought hard. 'Not really,' she said at length. 'I

think it was some boy – when isn't it a boy?' she shrugged. 'You know what, though, babe? Only one way to find out.' She crossed her arms.

'What's that? How would I do it?'

Katrina glanced over at Nina again and this time Beth wasn't imagining the shake of the head Nina gave. Then her friend piped up. 'No, Trina. Don't do that. Don't go getting Beth involved with those chihuahuas.'

Beth and Katrina stared at her for a second. Then Katrina said, '*Piranhas,* Neens. Right. Well, if she wants to know, she'll have to ask them. Wouldn't fancy it myself, though,' she added and shuddered.

'Ask who?' Beth looked from one to the other.

Nina paused, then spoke up reluctantly. 'The Rutlands and the Prices, of course.'

SEVENTEEN

'*Piranhas.*' That word had been echoing around Beth's head all night. Did she really want to get up close with the kind of cutthroats who'd burn down a famous landmark just to get even with each other? It sounded like the kind of encounter she'd usually avoid like the plague. But, if she wanted to get anywhere with the bones, let alone audition some new builders for when she could finally get going again with her shoffice, she really had to take matters into her own hands. Chris Campbell seemed happy to bumble along forever with his little forensic brush, getting nowhere as far as she could see. And Harry was too busy at work to get things sorted. If Beth managed to find out more about Fiona Price, she might be able to cross the shed mystery off her list – and then concentrate on Adua. After all, there was a killer in Dulwich at the moment. It was pretty chilling. And, although she'd seen the police ambling about, there was no more word on this witness that Harry had mentioned. And definitely no whisper yet about the culprit being found.

But it was the weekend, and top of the agenda was not murders old and new, but her boy. After the terrible stuff that had been going on lately, she wanted to spend some proper quality time with him. She had to be sure he was getting over the Gregory King business. And she wanted to check how he was feeling about Adua.

This time, she was the one who insisted they head to the park with Colin for their usual kick-about. She strung it out for so long that both boy and dog were exhausted by the time they made it home, walking the long way round to avoid the site of Adua's death, which now had a few bunches of wilting flowers tied to the railings by the SOCO tents. Beth wasn't going to say anything to Jake, but one of the bouquets was from her.

They sat close together on the sofa both nights, watching comforting old favourite films, with Colin and Magpie refraining from bickering, for once. It felt like the right kind of mourning for Adua, one of the stable pillars of Jake's childhood. And, though Jake remained dry-eyed, while in her presence at least, Beth allowed the tears to slip down her own face as they watched Harry Potter grow into a tortured adolescent with the weight of the world on his shoulders.

Beth sat at the kitchen table on Monday morning, taking stock. Jake had left for school, and she was fully dressed in good time for the advent of Campbell and his crew. She even had a sparse layer of mascara on. It was amazing how organised you could be, if you only got up a good hour earlier than usual. But Beth knew she couldn't sustain this. She already felt tired, and it wasn't even half eight yet. She could have done with Harry's input over the weekend.

On an impulse, she got her phone out and rang his number. She was fully expecting to hear Narinda's silky but curiously unhelpful tones, so almost dropped the phone in shock when she got straight through to Harry himself.

'How's it going, love?' he said. It felt like the first time she'd heard that rough but reassuring voice for ages. She could tell, from his slight abstraction, that there was either someone else in the room, or something he needed to be doing. She had his attention for a very short window and she needed to use it to the full.

'Colin is a bit upset,' she blurted out. Now why on earth had she said that? And in fact Colin was fine. He was currently weighing down her feet beneath the table, with his head pointed hopefully in the direction of the bones and a gentle stream of drool collecting on the floor. Beth was carefully keeping her fluffy socks out of it.

'Yeah? Give him a pat from me,' Harry said briskly. 'Listen, I've got to...'

'It's not Colin, it's me,' she said, shocking herself. It might well have been the most emotional thing she'd ever said to him. Both of them were silenced. She wasn't sure who was the most taken aback.

'Tell me what's wrong,' Harry said, and from the change in acoustics she deduced he'd left the room he'd been in, and was cradling the phone to his ear, having taken her off speaker mode. 'You didn't seem too bad on Friday morning.'

'I know, but that was *days* ago. It's all just getting too much. The bones, Adua... Jake's been so upset all weekend. And you weren't here. And now, on top of all the rest, there's the disco.'

'Disco? What disco?'

Beth realised Harry was completely out of the loop on that. They really needed to catch up. 'Look, there's so much we need to talk about. Do you think you could be home early tonight?'

'Sounds serious,' he said. 'Well, yes. I'll do my best. Don't worry, love. Whatever it is we can sort it out. All right?'

'All right,' said Beth. Immediately, she felt lighter. She smiled, as if for the first time in days. Then there was a ring at the doorbell. 'Damn. That'll be the SOCOs. I'll have to go.'

'OK. See you later, love,' said Harry, and suddenly there was nothing but the buzz of the dial tone in her ear.

Even though she had been about to say goodbye herself, the fact that Harry had vanished so quickly irked her. She swung back the door on the white-suited team with a rather sour look on her face, and caught Campbell looking at her through narrowed ice-chip eyes.

'All right, hen?' he said in his Scottish drawl. Being compared to poultry didn't cheer her up, but Campbell broke into her thoughts. 'Listen, don't worry about the teas today. Looks like you've got a lot on your mind. And we're doing pretty well. We might even be finished soon.'

'Really?' Beth was thrilled. Perhaps too thrilled. Was she imagining it, or did Campbell now look a little crestfallen? But that was ridiculous. She couldn't imagine any householder enjoying having this pack of bloodhounds loose on their premises, given that it almost certainly meant something nasty had happened. And he must have much more pressing bits of mud to dig up.

'You mean you've found everything there is to find? Just those, um, few bones, then?' Beth said, trying to stop herself from grinning from ear to ear. A scattering of bones in your back garden wasn't brilliant, admittedly. But it was a lot better than...

'No, no, hasn't anyone updated you? It's a whole body now. For sure.'

EIGHTEEN

Campbell was standing there, beaming at Beth, as though expecting her to greet the news with a matching delighted smile.

'Christ,' she gasped. 'Are you sure? There's no mistake? A *whole body*, you say?'

'Definitely,' Campbell said, a little less sure of his reception now. 'I mean, you can't possibly have thought it would just be an arm and a few extra bits?'

'I was certainly hoping that,' Beth said weakly. 'Hoping they'd got there... by accident or something.' Even though she'd entertained the possibility the bones might belong to this poor Fiona Price, there was something about having a full body confirmed that felt positively ghastly.

'No, no,' said Campbell, beaming again and looking round at his team as though Beth had told a really hilarious joke. The team, jammed into the kitchen waiting for Beth to unlock the back door, all smiled politely. She elbowed her way through them to let them out, just managing to grab Colin's collar as he attempted to join in as they trooped out into the sea of mud beyond.

'Not so fast, boy,' she said, bending down to him. His big Labrador mouth turned down comically and he looked at her with pleading eyes.

'He wants to become a SOCO when he grows up,' said Campbell, bending to give Colin a quick pat. Colin panted back at him in a most friendly manner, to Beth's surprise. He was a very conservative dog and, after some difficult experiences, he found it hard to trust men. He loved Harry and Jake, it went without saying, but most of their other visitors – even Beth's beloved brother, Josh – were treated with wariness.

'Love dogs,' said Campbell, seeing Beth's raised eyebrows. 'Not really fair for me to have one at home, with the hours I do.'

'Oh, couldn't your family help?' Beth said without thinking. A shadow crossed Campbell's face. 'I'm sorry, I didn't mean...'

'No, that's fine,' said Campbell. 'It's not something that would work at the moment.' He turned away and was out of the door before she could think of anything else to say. She'd clearly stepped on a sensitivity there. But she had more than enough on her plate without worrying about upsetting the SOCOs, for God's sake. An entire body! In her garden! Things were even worse than she'd ever imagined – and she'd spent a lot of sleepless nights recently worrying about the whole bones scenario. Who on earth could it be down there? Who had put them there? And why were they in bits?

She could just see the headlines, 'Death in Dulwich: dismembered skeleton in suburbs' and so on, forever. Her road, her house, her family, even, would always be synonymous with a horrible and grisly mystery.

She slumped at the kitchen table, head in hands for a minute. Then Colin stuck his wet nose onto her leg and she realised that, whatever else was happening, however much she wanted to collapse in a small heap, she still needed to get on with her day.

Beth knew she should make an appearance at the school –

partly to check her son was managing to stay awake in lessons, partly to do the work she was actually paid for. But, as she hurried into her coat and boots and took down Colin's lead, she knew she had absolutely no intention of going near the place today. Instead, after her chat with Katrina and Nina on Friday, she was going to do what she'd been thinking about all weekend: make some enquiries at builders' yards. Campbell might be a whiz at striding around with his small brushes (and her biscuits) but he didn't have a crystal ball. Short of finding a handy identification tag around the other wrist of her body, how could he ever pinpoint who the poor person had once been, or what on earth they were doing in her back garden?

Beth, as usual, was going to have to do it herself.

* * *

Beth parked her Fiat carefully on the little street at the top of the hill in Crystal Palace. There was certainly a wonderful view of the rest of London from here. But the builders' yard itself wasn't much to look at. Even the sign, bearing the one word 'Rutlands', was hanging askew. She cracked open the car door as quietly as she could – and immediately Colin started a mournful barking. Damn. She had rather hoped she might be able to leave him in the car while she did this. He wasn't exactly the ideal Dr Watson to her Sherlock Holmes, as he had a distinct tendency to goose suspects if they were women who took his fancy. Colin had always been a ladies' man, increasingly so now that he was well into his doggy dotage. He'd never met a crotch he didn't like. If he had been a person, Beth sometimes suspected he would have been a bit like Terry-Thomas, all 'Helloooo' and 'Ding dong,' not politically correct at all but with a certain sort of dated charm.

'Oh, all right then, come on,' she conceded, encouraging him to jump out of the car on his rickety back legs. She clipped his lead on before he got any ideas about escaping into Crystal Palace Park, spread out below them. In reality, he wouldn't get ten paces before he had to stop for a sit-down, but she didn't fancy even starting to run down the hill after him.

She pointed him in the much less interesting direction of the two very high gates to their left. For builders who did so much business in high-end Dulwich, Rutlands' premises were distinctly shabby. But perhaps that was par for the course. Builders' supplies were dusty great big bags of things, she supposed – grout and cement and what have you. Plus bits of wood and piles of tiles... probably. Beth had never been to a builders' yard before. She usually just rang up someone who had been recommended by a friend (almost always Katie). And she didn't have much idea what they did, either. Even when her shoffice workers had briefly been in place, what seemed like an age ago now, she hadn't exactly hovered over them. She'd left them to grub up the garden, with the horrific results she was still enduring.

They plodded nearer. The place was big, really big. Colin seemed reluctant, which wasn't like him. Usually, any outing was a good outing. She hoped it was just the notion of the park that was making him pull in the other direction, and nothing more sinister.

Suddenly a series of bangs and crashes came from inside the builders' yard. Then, worse still, there was a deafening volley of bloodcurdling barks. Colin stopped in his tracks as if turned to ice. This was shaping up to be the kind of quest that left Beth doubting her own sanity. She could be in her nice, safe office right now, dealing with nothing more challenging than a festering in-tray. Why was she about to stir up the past in a rough bit of south-east London, with only an ancient Labrador for protection? She might as well turn tail and run now.

But the barking stopped, and Beth forced herself to move forward and peer through the gates. She wondered briefly if she could just pretend to herself there was no one in. But she needed answers to her questions. The key to both her mysteries could be here. She had to press on.

There were evidently people working somewhere. She couldn't see anyone, yet the clangs and bangs only seemed to be getting louder. There was an apron of clear space in front of the gates, but everywhere else was crowded. There were a couple of white trucks bearing the Rutlands' logo (which Beth now realised she'd seen so often in Dulwich streets it was almost as familiar as the red post office vans). There were wooden pallets as tall as her, laden with tiles and wrapped round with ropes. There were two huge versions of the incinerators people used in their back garden. And, against one wall, there were sections from what Beth recognised by now as a shoffice, ready to be installed. Colin whined softly by her side.

She patted his head with a reassurance she wasn't sure she was actually feeling, and pressed the call button on the large intercom by the side of the gates. For long moments, there was no response, though the noises continued. Then there was a blast of static that made both Beth and Colin jump about a foot, and a disembodied voice crackled out.

'Yes?'

'Oh, um, my name is, erm...' Oh God, thought Beth. Am I going to use my own name, or an alias? And why am I only thinking of this now? 'Erm, Beth Haldane, and I, er, well. I wanted to talk to you about a shoffice, erm, one of those home studio things.'

This had the virtue of being the truth, at least. Though if anything went wrong, the Rutlands would now have no trouble in tracking her down. This was one of the many reasons why Harry was always telling her to keep out of things, she realised. And, from Colin's anxious little yelps of protest, he was very much on his master's side.

There was a click, and suddenly the right-hand gate swung

open. Beth edged through, pulling Colin along. He had his tail between his legs now, glancing from side to side as though expecting the worst. Beth hoped he didn't know something she didn't.

They were now standing in the yard, and Beth looked around for somewhere to go where she might reasonably find someone to talk to. At first, nowhere stood out. Then, on her second sweep, she spotted a little shack over in the corner of the yard. There was an old sign above its door saying 'Office', but the writing was so faded that Beth thought she could be excused for not seeing it immediately. She walked forward more confidently. But, just then, there was a sudden rush of air and a black shape shot towards them from one of the stacks of supplies propped against the walls. There was also a deafening series of barks. If Beth wasn't very much mistaken, this was the danger that Colin had been warning her about ever since they'd got here. A very unfriendly guard dog.

The dog was on the loose, and upon them in seconds. Luckily it paused, probably deciding which one of them to eat first, and then began some really top-notch snarling. It had moved so fast initially it had been a blur. But now it was facing them. Beth could see every detail of its very large collection of teeth in excruciating detail, as well as its mean red eyes, enormous snout and powerful, muscular body, ending in legs longer and stronger than hers. It was a Rottweiler. She was electrified by a massive influx of adrenaline. Next to her, she could sense Colin's fear, but the old Labrador stood his ground and started barking back for all he was worth, his hackles rising and his stiff old legs planted as though he was going to protect her to the death. Which would probably be in about twenty seconds' time, at a conservative estimate. But still, it was a kind thought.

Just when it seemed clear that the Rottweiler was tired of snarling and about to move on to the eating part, there was a yell from the little cabin. 'Oi, Cuddles. Enough of that. Get down.'

To Beth's surprise, relief and joy, the dog immediately dropped to the floor, and lay at Beth and Colin's feet, now looking about as threatening as one of Jake's old soft toys. A large woman bustled out of the office.

'Yeah, sorry about him. Hasn't had his walkies this morning. You know what they're like.'

Beth nodded her head fervently, as though Colin also turned into a ravening beast if there was any curtailment of his exercise routine. It would be their little secret that he'd be perfectly happy snuggling up on the forbidden sofa for twenty-five hours a day.

'Um, lovely doggy,' said Beth, stooping for a second as though to pat the dog, and changing her mind rapidly when she met its gaze. However docile it was with its owner, those massive bloodshot eyes still had a murderous glint in them. 'And what a lovely name.'

The woman bent and tickled the Rottweiler on the tummy, and he squirmed around in ecstasy. Colin and Beth exchanged glances briefly. Honestly, some dogs had absolutely no dignity.

Then the woman straightened up. 'So. You ain't here for the good of your health, are you. What can we do you for?'

From the shrewd glance Beth was getting from rather small brown eyes, she knew she had to tread carefully now. She'd basically blurted out the truth just now, and it had seemed like a massive own goal. But maybe sticking as closely as possible to her actual story really was the best way to make the enquiries which, she felt, were the only way she was going to get any closer to solving this mystery.

'I was having a shoffice built, down in my garden in Dulwich,' Beth started, gesturing vaguely down the hill. 'Then, um, well, work had to stop.'

'Unhappy with the firm, were you?' the woman said.

'Oh, er, yes,' said Beth, latching onto this bone-free explanation of why on earth she'd rocked up at Rutlands.

While they'd been talking, the Rottweiler took the opportunity to start squaring up to Colin again, but it only took one whimper from the Labrador for Cuddles' owner to spot his game.

'Bad boy! Inside,' the woman said, pointing to the cabin. The huge black dog slunk off obediently with his head down. 'Don't worry about him. He'll have a little lie-down on his bed, be right as rain in a minute,' she added.

'You've got him so well trained,' Beth couldn't help but marvel. 'I have a friend who could really use some help with her dog,' she added, feeling a bit disloyal to Katie. But if anyone could get the dreadful Teddy under control, maybe it was this lady. Katie taking Teddy to his classes might well have provided the chink that had allowed Jake and Charlie to fall prey to the dreadful Gregory King. It was going to be quite a while before Beth forgave the rascally cockapoo.

'Yeah, just got to be firm with them,' said the woman, but she was clearly distracted by what she'd heard. 'I'm Trixie Rutland, by the way. Whereabouts is this shoffice to be installed? Shall we go inside to discuss it?'

Beth thought fast. Inside, they'd be away from all the chaos of the builders' yard. But they'd be cheek by jowl with the awful Cuddles, and Beth wasn't sure that poor Colin could stand it.

'No! No, it's great to get some fresh air,' she said somewhat unconvincingly, wrapping her arms round herself. The temperature had dropped since they got here, and the colour was beginning to vanish from the sky as time ticked by. 'Let's chat here.'

Trixie's eyebrows shot up. 'Yeah? Whatever,' she shrugged. 'So. Looking to finish your construction, are you?'

'Yes... yes, definitely,' Beth said, managing to sound very unsure. 'I just, erm, wanted to get some background on your company first, um, see how long you've been doing things...'

'Oh, anyone in Dulwich will tell you, Rutlands can get the job done,' Trixie said confidently.

That much Beth was already sure of. Sally Bentinck had sung the praises of the firm long and loudly. But would the job stay done? Or would everything fall down? And anyway, what Beth really wanted to know was whether Rutlands had built her old shed, years ago, or had any doings in Pickwick Road that could have given them the chance to leave a load of bones in her garden. And, of course, whether those bones might belong to Nina and Katrina's erstwhile friend, Fiona Price.

'Yes... Still, it would be really good to know how long you've been doing this type of office for, you know?' Beth tried to make it sound like the sort of question any good householder would ask. 'It would really help me make a decision.'

But it was clear Trixie wasn't really buying it. 'More important to know what we're doing now, isn't it? Rather than what we did back in the day. Though there are plenty of wonderful sheds, excuse me, *shoffices*, we've put up that have been around in Dulwich for years,' she said proudly. 'Not to mention conservatories, home offices, studios, that kind of thing.'

This certainly hadn't been Katrina's point of view. She'd been clear that the long-running feud between Rutlands and the Price family firm had led to a lot of shoddy construction from both companies all round the south-east.

'Would you have records about where you installed sheds in the past, say, about twenty years ago? There was a shed in my garden when we moved in, but it just fell apart,' said Beth, trying to sound casual. If Trixie's response was anything to go by, she failed.

'Can't have been one of ours, then,' said Trixie firmly, giving Beth a sharp glance. 'Now, are you interested in getting this new shoffice of yours finished off, or what?'

'Oh yes, I am. But I really do need to ask a few questions

first. I mean, how would you say you compare on costs with, say, the Prices, for example?' Beth asked.

Instantly the atmosphere froze over. 'The Prices, eh? Been round there already, have you? What they been saying, then?'

Trixie drew herself up to her full height and Beth was suddenly conscious that her big frame, which had seemed quite motherly when she'd been talking to Cuddles, was actually pretty intimidating. Her arms and legs were sturdy and strong, and even her torso was solid. Her bulk was that of a wrestler – all muscle, no flab. And currently she was looking like a wrestler who'd just heard the bell ring for round one.

'Boys!' she yelled.

Immediately, a trio of gigantic men came round the corner towards Beth, Colin and Trixie. Now Trixie seemed as dainty as the sugarplum fairy, dwarfed by the burly figures in paint-splotched overalls.

At least, Beth *hoped* all that red stuff was paint.

* * *

Ten minutes later, Beth was feeling very silly. The Rutland lads had explained they had just finished repainting one of the perimeter fences round the rugby pitches at Wyatt's. She of all people should have known that those fences were painted scarlet. But seeing the three big men covered in what had looked like blood, her heartbeat had gone through the roof and she'd felt increasingly certain that she – and poor innocent Colin – were shortly going to end up under someone's fence themselves.

It turned out, though, that the Rutland boys, and even Trixie, were very similar to Cuddles the dog. Their bark was a lot worse than their bite. By the time Beth had calmed down, and everyone had laughed a lot at her fears and she had tried her best to take it in good part, they had all become fast friends. Beth felt awful that she had no intention of getting the Rutlands to do her shoffice, if Colin Campbell ever left her garden. But sometimes she had to spin these webs in the course of her investigations.

She had got a little further on – after a bit of denial, the Rutlands family had admitted that yes, sometimes they did like to undercut the Prices. But the worst phase of the feud was over, now. It had been a thing, years back, but that was all forgotten, or as near as dammit. They were all just getting on with their lives, these days. There was some scrabbling for business, but that was normal. Although there was a lot of domestic building work going in Dulwich (quite a lot of it generated by the likes of Belinda McKenzie, women who were never satisfied with the palatial homes their stay-at-home personas revolved around) they assured Beth it was totally fine with them if some of it went to the Prices. As long as enough was still carried out by the Rutlands.

Beth wasn't sure if she really believed it. And she got no further with her repeated enquiry about whether her original shed had been built by them. They didn't keep records going that far back, they assured her. But something about the glint in Trixie's dark eyes made her wonder.

Beth was feeling a lot more relaxed with the Rutland family by the time she finally got onto the subject of Fiona Price. But as soon as she mentioned the girl's name, the atmosphere soured as fast as lemon juice stirred into double cream. All four glowered at Beth as though she was something nasty on the sole of their shoe.

'Look-looks like the name rings a bell,' said Beth, as Colin shifted nervously beside her. 'Do you know what happened to her? I'm trying to find out.'

'Why? What are you doing, snooping around in all this? The Prices won't thank you for interfering, any more than we like nosy parkers,' Trixie said, all semblance of friendliness gone.

'But she was one of the Prices? Your cousins? So you all must have known her?' Beth peered around the stony faces of the group, resisting her urge to run screaming out of the place.

'Yeah, so what? Not illegal to know someone, is it?' said one of the lads.

'Not even someone who's disappeared,' another said cockily – and then bit his lip as Trixie lifted her hand and clouted him round the ear. She then turned back to Beth.

'She didn't disappear. She just moved out of London. It has been known. And sometimes, it's good for people's *health*,' she said pointedly. 'Now, if you're not actually buying a shoffice at all, then we have a few things to get on with,' she said. 'The boys will show you out.'

But Beth didn't need an escort, or to be asked twice. She and Colin scampered over to the gate and zipped through it as quickly as they could. As she left, Beth risked a backward glance and saw the three Rutland boys staring after her.

They looked, in fact, like just the kind of people you might mistakenly order a shoffice from – and then end up underneath, spending all eternity regretting your decision.

NINETEEN

Beth's hand was still trembling as she unlocked the door of the car. Then she almost jumped out of her skin as Colin's wet nose snuffled at her fingers. She knew the question he was trying to ask.

'Sorry, boy, no. We can't go straight home and play with those bones. We've got to do a bit more investigation first.'

Colin made a sound halfway between a sigh and a groan but he jumped into the back of the car when she held the door open for him. With a lot of scuffling and scrabbling, he turned round three times as best he could on the back seat before settling himself down for the journey. A while ago, Beth had made the ill-advised purchase of a seat protector, intended to cover the upholstery and keep the worst of Colin's drool off the trousers of anyone unwise enough to accept a lift with her. The purchase had been inspired by Katie, who had said it was a godsend with Teddy. Well, it might work with that little ball of havoc, Beth thought sourly, but not with her Colin. Whether it was the hectic floral print, or the laminated oil-skin-style finish that crackled with his every fidget, Colin loathed it with a passion. But at least it was taking his mind off Cuddles and the difficult encounter they had just had. As Beth crashed the gears in her haste to get away, she heard the soft growling sounds which announced that the old dog was busily trying to eat the thing.

Beth shook her head as they put the Rutlands' yard behind them. She had as little heart for this next stop as Colin, she was wrung out by the encounter with the belligerent Rutland family, but she knew she had to crack on and pay a visit to the Prices too. It was now or never. She really didn't have the nerve to come back and do this again another day. Perhaps they would tell a different story about the long-ago disappearance of Fiona Price. Maybe they would take one look at her, sit her down, and let the entire saga of her garden shed flood out, finishing off by saying, 'And that's when we decided to kill her and stick her in your back garden.'

Even in these delightful imaginings, as she drove down from the heights of Crystal Palace into the suburbs of Anerley, Beth couldn't quite get a handle on why the Price family would have killed one of their own. And there was no proof at all, yet, that the bones in her garden were Fiona's anyway. If they weren't, there was no telling whether it was really anything to do with these builders or not. For the first time, she began to seriously wonder whether Adua had known what went on, so long ago. She'd always been adept at gathering secrets, her big dark eyes winking at all she was hiding. Could she have seen who went under Beth's shed, years before? Is that why she'd been killed?

Beth suddenly realised she could be making herself a target – again – by stirring all this up. What if whoever had bumped off Adua noticed that Beth was now poking about in both the mysteries on her doorstep? Would they turn their attentions to her? This horrible idea was interrupted by an even more horrible chewing noise from the back seat.

'I might be grasping at straws, Colin, but as for you, you're chomping at my nice new seat cover, aren't you?'

In the mirror, she saw him sit up a bit, his tongue lolling out in his trademark grin. She couldn't help giving him a reflex smile in response. She did love the old boy. But then she saw a chunk of something decidedly floral fall from his jaws. Damn it all!

'Col–in! How could you?'

Now it was Beth's turn to huff out a great big sigh. She couldn't help feeling a twinge of annoyance that she'd let Katie persuade her to buy the stupid flowery thing. But Beth didn't have too much time to mull it over. They had arrived.

At first glance, the Prices' premises were much more impressive than their rivals'. The site was at one end of a nice, wide residential road, and perhaps in deference to their neighbours appeared to be very well kept. There was no sign of the chaotic jumble of Rutlands, with its higgledy-piggledy piles of timber and joists. Instead, Price Construction Ltd was tidied away behind large, clean and bright signage, and some good solid wooden gates. Beth found it much less intimidating than the other place. And Colin, by her side as she reached for the intercom, was wagging his tail slightly, which suggested there were no more Rottweilers on the horizon.

It was a disappointment, then, when a very aggressive voice came out of the little speaker.

'Yeah?'

It was amazing how much menace could be stuffed into a single syllable, thought Beth, clutching her coat around her more tightly. She and Colin exchanged a glance and the Labrador's tail stopped wagging.

'Um, I've just come about a, erm, shoffice?' Beth said. It was true, she had. And she did really need to find new builders. So it wasn't that far from the truth... Still, the little duo waited nervously. After what seemed like an age, and with Beth imagining suspicious eyes being cast over them from hidden CCTV cameras, there was a click as the gates opened. Beth walked forward, towing Colin behind her. She was beginning to feel a bit mean for bringing him. But it was an outing of a sort, she supposed, even though it was all pretty terrifying. For her, he was a reassuring presence. And anyone seeing him might well think he would stick up for his owner as, to give him credit, he had done at the Rutlands' place. They wouldn't know most people faced a greater danger of being licked to death by Colin than suffering even the smallest bite.

Before they had ventured very far into the yard, Beth heard the sound of raised voices somewhere within the large and rambling office structure. Where Rutlands had only a tiny shed, the Price operation was run from a conglomeration of Portakabins and outbuildings rammed together. They were painted a fierce sky blue, which was actually rather cheering on this dull day. But the noise emanating from them was anything but uplifting.

'I've told you a thousand flipping times,' a shrill female voice was yelling at an earsplitting volume. 'No, no and no!'

'But listen, Ma,' thundered a man, clearly every bit as incensed as the woman. 'You can't do it that way! You can't cover it all up forever. It doesn't work like that any more, I'm telling you...'

Without even realising she was doing it, Beth started to edge forward to the source of the argument. It wasn't that she couldn't hear the nuances; there were probably people in the far-off centre of Dulwich Village who were receiving all this loud and clear. She just wanted to see who was speaking. The man sounded like the aggressive guy who had buzzed them in. But who was the matriarch? Was she anything like Trixie at Rutlands?

She took another few steps, with Colin doing a sit-down protest. He was wise to the ways of cross humans, these days, and could see no reason for getting closer to the epicentre of the trouble. But, before she could approach one of the small windows and have a proper gawp, the door nearest to her burst open.

In front of her and Colin was a short, wiry man in sky blue overalls, with the Price logo on the breast pocket. It wasn't this that held Beth and Colin's attention, however. His angry piercing blue eyes were compelling, true, and the flush that suffused his thin, slightly haggard face was definitely worrying. But it was the enormous wrench he was holding aloft in his right hand that they were both staring at.

'Yeah?' he said abruptly. Then he seemed to remember the wrench. 'Oh right,' he said, lowering it to his side with a slightly forced grin. 'Um. Not sure now is the best moment.'

At Beth's side, Colin relaxed from action stations mode (teeth bared, head poking forward, all four paws planted) as the man's tone descended from grumpy to merely abrupt. And then the dog sat down with a whump at Beth's feet, and grinned at the big man. So much for his guard dog cover story.

'Um, OK,' said Beth, holding out a palm. 'Right yes, we seem to have stumbled on something...'

'What? Did you hear what we were saying back then?' the man snapped.

'Oh, um, no, no. Absolutely not,' said Beth, shaking her head wildly from side to side. 'Not a word. Really.' She knew she needed to stop, the more she insisted the less convincing she sounded. But somehow she'd got herself stuck. 'Nope. Not at all. Yes, no, no.'

At her side, Colin nudged her gently with his nose and she finally managed to shut up.

'Right...' said the man, looking from her to the dog and back again. Perhaps he was wondering who on earth was in control. And it was justified, thought Beth. *Must pull myself together.*

'Well, I just popped by about my shoffice, like I said. I mean, maybe I should come back tomorrow or something? Make an appointment?'

Beth had been all for getting both builders out of the way today, but she was now feeling that this whole business was too tough on her nerves. Maybe she needed to regroup at home. Or think of another line of enquiry altogether. But the man stayed stock-still, contemplating the strange duo, fixing them with those vivid eyes.

Just when Beth thought she was going to have to turn and flee in earnest, a woman came out of the office. She was in her fifties, with a beehive of candyfloss blonde hair. She was also wearing sky blue, but in the form of a sweatshirt and skirt ensemble, teamed with high heels which seemed, to Beth's mind, massively impractical in a builders' yard. Granted, this place seemed a lot tidier than Rutlands' premises – and Beth instinctively approved of that – but Beth certainly wouldn't have wanted to be capering about the place three inches off the ground. But on this woman, the heels seemed almost a part of her very shapely legs. She strutted over to Beth and looked her quickly up and down. Colin, at her side, seemed to shrink a little.

'What can we do for you, love? Got a lot on today as you can see.'

Beth couldn't see. In fact, the yard seemed curiously still, with none the background activity of Rutlands. Perhaps Prices wasn't doing very well? That could have been what the row had been about.

'Oh, erm. I probably should have rung first. But I thought I'd take a chance. I've got this shoffice I want to build, you see...'

'Why didn't you say, love? Come through, come through,' said the woman, suddenly cordiality itself. She stood aside and ushered Beth towards the outbuildings. 'Honestly, Roger, what are you like? Keeping a customer waiting,' she gave a daggers glance at what was clearly her son, and he hung his head like a child. She gave Beth a little side-eye of solidarity as if to say, 'Men, huh?'

Beth grinned and nodded. She wanted to get into this lady's good books, and fast. It might be the quickest way to find out what the hell was going on in her own back garden.

But at the same time, she was painfully aware that she and Colin were just about to enter the lion's den.

TWENTY

An hour later, Beth was still perusing the biggest catalogue of potential shoffices she had ever seen. There were some here that would even put Belinda McKenzie's mammoth structure to shame. Beth had been slightly elastic with her potential budget. Well, it would be more accurate to say she had told a string of appalling lies, some so enormous that Colin had lifted his head from his cosy mat in front of the three-bar electric fire to give her a sorrowful stare. Colin didn't really hold with whoppers. But what could Beth do? She needed to get Mrs Price talking.

Soon she and Aggie Price were on first-name terms, and she was drinking a nut brown cup of tea that any passing spoon would have had no trouble at all standing up in. Despite her total lack of acting talent, it wasn't a stretch to look as though she was dying to install one of these lovely shoffices. After all, she'd been on the brink of getting one anyway – just nothing as swanky as any of these. The colours alone were very seductive, a range of delicious chalky greens and blues that would go effortlessly with her awful kicked-about garden, would look like a (much) toned-down version of Sally Bentinck's beautiful shoffice next door, and even match the wider verdure of Dulwich Village itself.

As well as all the monster sheds, some with their own attached baby shedlets for storing picturesque piles of firewood, there was even a teeny tiny one in the shape of a shepherd's hut, which for a second seemed really appealing. Then she remembered what she wanted the shed for – to offload Harry's endless blimming whodunits, to regain a bit of space for herself on the odd occasion she felt moved to do some of her extremely neglected freelance work, and possibly a place to store some of Jake's increasingly huge collection of gaming stuff. And *then* she woke herself out of her daydream. She couldn't afford any of these hand-built sheds. The one that was still propped up in her garden in bits was a jerry-built off-the-peg number shorn of all the dovetail joints and fancy finishes she was leafing through here. It was as pared back and simple as a shoffice could be. Because that was what she could actually pay for.

Beth coughed and put down the brochure. 'Of course, you're getting so much demand for these work sheds nowadays, aren't you?'

'Yes, yes,' said Aggie Price absently. 'Look at the trim on this one. Go with your eyes, that would.'

Beth gazed at the page quizzically. The misty dove grey shoffice was gorgeous. But she didn't let herself get sidetracked again.

'Oh, that's so lovely. But I should point out that of course I'll be getting other quotes,' Beth said a little more sharply.

Aggie sat up at this. 'Well, naturally. We wouldn't expect anything else. Any particular firm you've got in mind?'

She said it lightly, but there was suddenly a more watchful quality about the woman. On his mat, Colin flicked his ears back and forth. Beth said as casually as she could, 'Oh, I was thinking of Rutlands. A neighbour recommended them.'

'Rutlands? Are they still going?' Aggie's voice now had a steely undertone.

'I think so... But someone did tell me you'd had a falling-out with them long ago. I don't know if that's true?' Beth's eyes were wide.

Aggie glared at her. Suddenly she slapped the brochure shut. The sound was as sharp as a gunshot in the small, stuffy room. Colin shambled to his feet and panted like an ancient accordion.

'Not going to buy a shoffice at all, are you? What have you really come here for?' the woman asked.

Before Beth could answer, Aggie had clacked to the door, poked her head outside and yelled to her son. 'Roger? Roger! Get in here. Now.'

'Well, it's been lovely looking at your studios, they're really something. I think I'll just go home and think about all the possibilities. That grey one would look perfect...' Beth burbled as she picked up Colin's lead and edged towards the door.

'Not so fast. I think you should tell us what you're up to. I should have known someone like you couldn't afford us,' Aggie Price looked Beth up and down again, and clearly found her wanting.

'Um, well, of course my mother would be helping us out with the money... Sorry if I've stumbled on something sensitive, it's clearly a touchy area, you and the Rutlands, I had no idea you'd be upset,' Beth said in a rush.

Thank goodness, she'd said the right thing at last. Aggie Price subsided a little. 'No, no. I'm sorry. The customer is always right and all that. It's just that, you know, the Rutlands... they're a bad lot, that family.'

Just then, Roger stuck his head round the door. 'Need help, Mum?'

Aggie Price seemed to think for a second, then she waved him away. 'Just get on with your work, lad. I'll talk to you later.'

Roger trailed away. Getting brushed off by his mother seemed to be quite a large part of his working day.

Beth didn't want to lose the moment. 'A bad lot, you were saying?'

Again, Aggie's glance over at Beth was shrewd. Beth tried to look as innocent as possible, as though she'd asked about tomorrow's weather prospects, rather than attempting to delve into a sore point in the Price family history. But perhaps Aggie just needed to vent. Because, before she knew it, Beth was finally getting the full run-down on the Price/Rutland conflict.

Unfortunately, all the ructions Aggie was talking about had occurred, as Katrina had said, roughly a century ago. After fifteen minutes' worth of gripes on who was responsible for which bit of the Crystal Palace conflagration, Colin had put his head down and was unashamedly snoring. Beth, her eyelids growing heavy too, seriously wished she could join in. She knew she should be trying to wrestle the conversation round to the construction of her own original shed, not to mention forcing in a mention of Fiona Price. But the three-bar heater, which had initially seemed so puny, had now contrived to heat the small room to toasty levels, and her attention was definitely wandering...

'So that's it, in a nutshell,' announced Aggie suddenly. Beth, whose head had been dipping lower and lower, sat bolt upright and blinked a few times. 'Now that you know the full family background, perhaps you'd just like to sign here?'

Aggie was now shoving a thick sheaf of papers over the desk towards Beth. On the front page was the ominous word, 'Contract'.

'Oh, um. Well, you know, I, er, always get my other half to look over these things with me,' Beth did her best simper, hoping she was coming across as the type of 'little woman' who knew nothing about business affairs. Colin opened an eye and whined at her. Beth shot him a glance. She'd have to tell him off later. She really didn't need an armchair critic when she was doing her best Meryl Streep impression. Luckily, Aggie knew no better.

'That's fine, of course. Big decision, I know. I always check in with my Chris before signing my life away,' she laughed conspiratorially. Beth got the distinct view that Aggie was lying through her teeth, too.

'Before I go and, er, ask "him indoors",' said Beth, 'I just wanted to check a couple of things. We had a shed before, but it fell apart... would you have built that, by any chance?'

'Well, we've built a lot in your area,' Aggie started promisingly. 'But none of ours would fall apart, love. What was the other thing?'

Beth, put on the spot, felt flustered but knew she had to get it out. 'Fiona Price!' she said, much more loudly than she'd intended. Immediately, Aggie's eyebrows lifted and her mouth turned down.

'What about Fiona?' she said with quiet menace.

'It's just... she went to school with some friends of mine... they're keen to trace her. I just wondered if you had a forwarding address?'

'Did you now?' said Aggie, sharp as a knife. Then she seemed to wrestle with herself. When she spoke again, she was calmer. 'Well. If you give me their names, I'll certainly pass them on. She's not around here now.'

No, thought Beth. Because she might well be in my back garden. But now she was stuck, because she really didn't want to get Nina or Katrina into trouble with the Prices. What could she ask about Fiona that would get her friends off the hook? A family row that had got out of control... maybe she'd set her face against the family business? It was worth a punt. She took a deep breath.

'Um... they heard that she'd decided she didn't want

anything to do with the family firm. I just wondered whether that was true?'

There was no mistaking Aggie's frostiness now. She crossed her arms across her chest and stared hard at Beth. 'And why, exactly, would you be interested in all that?'

Just then, Roger stuck his head round the door again. 'You got the address for the next job, Mum?' he asked, then looked from one woman to the other. 'What's up?'

'This... lady is asking a lot of questions about our Fiona and the row and where she wanted to run off to,' said Aggie, seemingly unaware that she'd accidentally answered Beth's question. Fiona *had* decamped after an argument. It wasn't much, but at last she had something to go on, no matter how small a clue it was.

'Well, I'll just have a think about which shoffice to get, shall I, and give you a ring, erm, at some point...' said Beth, attempting to sidle unobtrusively towards the door.

Roger looked Beth up and down, rather as his mother had earlier, and put his arm right across the doorway to block her exit.

'Not so fast, lady. Where exactly do you think you're going?'

TWENTY-ONE

Beth, for once, found herself blessing Colin's appalling case of halitosis. She'd tried everything to get it under control, buying foods the vet had recommended, swapping him (briefly) to a vegetarian diet and even attempting to brush his teeth at night. But now she resolved to let well alone. Because when Roger Price barred her way, Colin leapt up, and gave the builder a massive blast of his awful, awful bad breath, equivalent to the scent of a thousand decomposing badgers. Roger Price put his hands up instinctively to shelter from the smell, and Beth and Colin were able to nip past him in seconds flat.

Once in the yard, they picked up the pace and sprinted out of the gates. Both were panting by the time they got back into the car. Beth didn't even mind when Colin promptly ripped off another big chunk of his floral cover and got to work on chewing it thoroughly. She reckoned he deserved it.

She was counting herself lucky to have got away from the Prices safely. And she was a lot further on. She now had a reason why Fiona Price had disappeared, and had first-hand knowledge of how unimpressed the Price family was about the whole thing. Fiona had washed her hands of the family and, as far as Beth was aware, she'd never been seen again. So she *could* be the body in her back garden.

Maybe it was time Beth did the sensible thing, and brought in the big guns. Plus, after her tricky time in both builders' yards, she could do with a bit of Harry's reassurance. She'd asked him to be home early this evening – but that seemed like a lifetime away. She wanted to speak to him now. True, he'd be cross with her for visiting the builders in the first place – but she could gloss over that, and just get to the part where she asked for his help in seeing if there was any trace of Fiona Price. She could also find out, hopefully, how he was getting on with Adua's death, too. Maybe it was time for her to suggest to him that the cases could even be linked? It would probably be really useful for him. He could combine both investigations and things would be a lot more streamlined.

She told herself all this as she put in a call to Harry on the car's rudimentary hands-free system while coasting back down the hill to Dulwich. When the answering machine cut in, she wasn't surprised – but found herself becoming infuriated when she heard the message itself. It had been re-recorded, with Narinda Khan's silky voice replacing Harry's usual gruff tones. 'I'm so sorry, DI York isn't able to come to the phone right now,' the woman fluted. Luckily, reception cut out before Beth could say what she thought of that, as the car whizzed into the black spot on Sydenham Hill.

By the time she got back to Pickwick Road and had crammed the Fiat into the last available parking space, she was exhausted. The SOCO guys were long gone, and had posted the key back through her letterbox, as was now the routine. She did her best to ignore the muddy duckboards – and many new smears above the hall skirting board – and made herself a quick tea. Then she shut an exhausted but triumphant Colin in the sitting room with a large chunk of floral fabric to slobber on, and wandered out into the garden. The days were getting shorter

now, and although it wasn't late the trees were already silhou-
etted against a royal blue sky. Just as well, it meant she could see
less of the mounds of mud that currently constituted her plot of
land. She sighed, cupping her mug in both hands for warmth.

'Hi there,' said a voice over the fence.

Beth nearly dropped her tea right down herself. 'God, you
gave me a shock,' she said with a shaky laugh. 'I didn't realise
you were there. But it's nice to see a friendly face.'

'Bad day? Sorry to hear that,' said Sally Bentinck. 'Those
chaps are really making a mess of your garden.'

'Tell me about it,' said Beth sadly.

'On the bright side, you won't have to do any of that digging
to turn the soil they always recommend, come the spring.'

'Well, I suppose that's true,' said Beth, who had never
dreamt of doing that in any case.

'Any news on the find?' Sally asked.

'Oh, well it's finds plural, now. But I suppose you know
that.'

'No! No, I hadn't heard a thing. What else have they got?'

Beth was surprised Sally wasn't in the loop. But then she
realised it must be one of the many consequences of having lost
Adua. She had been the conduit of most of the information
flowing up and down Pickwick Road. They were all at sea
without her, really.

'Well, it's a lot more than just a few bones, now,' she said
with a shrug.

'Is it? Oh God... But it's all ancient, isn't it? From some old
charnel pit or something. Nothing to worry about really,' Sally
shook her head emphatically, making her outsize earrings sway.

'Hmm, maybe,' said Beth carefully. She knew Chris Campbell was working on the assumption that the body had been
buried around twenty years ago. But she was also aware how
tight-lipped Harry always was with his investigations. Campbell was bound to insist on the same level of discretion.

Even if it really had been a charnel pit, that would hardly have been good news. She could just imagine the estate agent's particulars now: *charming semi-detached des res with ensuite burial ground...* 'I'm doing my best to find out where the hell it came from, though. Anyway, how are you? Still loving the shoffice?'

'Yes, it's brilliant,' said Sally. 'I don't know what we'd do without it. You'll love yours when it's finally done.'

'Whenever that will be,' said Beth. 'I'm not holding my breath. Anyway, on a slightly less gloomy topic, I've got to visit my mother tomorrow. She was talking about the carp next door to her... made me wonder about the Sinclairs' fish.'

'Oh, I love them,' said Sally, with all her trademark enthusiasm. 'So beautiful, the way their colours flash. They're amazing creatures, you know. They know to the minute when it's feeding time, they come rushing right up to me every evening now. I think they really look forward to my treats.'

Beth smiled. Fish couldn't possibly tell the time, could they? It was just part of Sally's usual creative licence. 'Well, it's so good of you to look after them. Feels like the Sinclairs have been away for ages.'

'They've certainly taken to cruising,' Sally agreed. 'I got a postcard from them only a couple of days ago. They're in the Caribbean again.'

Beth shivered as a breeze got up and rustled the leaves on the old tree at the end of her garden. 'Well, you can see their point. I wouldn't mind a bit of tropical weather at the moment.'

Sally laughed too and they agreed it was getting a bit too nippy to hang about in the gathering chill. Beth retreated into her kitchen, thinking of the Sinclairs. They were probably leaning over the railings of their cruise ship right now, maybe watching the sun dip below the horizon, waiting for the legendary Caribbean green flash. Even if they were actually stuck on board ship in a force eight gale, it would probably have the edge on grilling unwilling interviewees in not one but two builders' yards in deepest south London.

Beth chucked the dregs of her tea down the sink and went to the fridge to crack open a new bottle of Tesco's Sauvignon Blanc, on special offer this week. Why the hell not? After today's stresses she felt she deserved a treat.

Beth saw Jake eyeing the glass when he wandered down for supper half an hour later. It was unusual for her to be tucking into a drink at this hour and, as the only child of a single parent, Beth knew Jake much preferred a nice, settled routine. She did her best not to show her latest worries and definitely not to cross-question him on whether Gregory King had left the school yet, and they managed to have a jolly meal together.

Being with her boy always cheered Beth. Though Jake was now, in his own mind at least, thoroughly grown-up, he still had his childish ways. Before he even started eating, he doused his plate in tomato ketchup. Beth turned away to hide her smile. Would he be doing that when he was her age, and with a family of his own? She rather hoped so.

They snuggled up on the sofa again that evening to watch a rerun of *Young Dracula*, a series Jake had always loved. Beth was enjoying it so much that she didn't see her phone light up. A text had come in, from an unknown number.

It was just as well the ringer was off. If she'd read it before morning, she wouldn't have got a wink of sleep all night.

TWENTY-TWO

Harry had made a heroic effort and got home before midnight that night – but unfortunately Beth, exhausted by her cross-questioning of the Prices and Rutlands, and knocked out by the quantity of Sauvignon Blanc she had consumed (only three glasses, but that was three more than normal), was deeply asleep by the time he slipped under the duvet and felt for her.

In the morning, she was bleary-eyed, alone, and pretty grumpy about it when she threw off the covers and shambled into the shower. So much for Harry's promise to come home early last night. There was so much she wanted to discuss with him.

And she had another grouse. If it wasn't for the bones, she wouldn't have to get up nearly so early. The prospect of being caught in her ancient pink fleecy number by Chris Campbell for the third time was not appealing. She rushed into the shower, then shrugged on her jumper and jeans and shoved her phone into her bag – she'd check it later.

Then she remembered her first chore of the day. Not, of course, going to work at Wyatt's – though she'd definitely try and fit that in at some point during the week – but popping in on her mother.

Wendy was not free in the afternoons – or at any time that could possibly have suited Beth. As she sometimes reminded her mother, she did have a job. But, as she often had to remind herself of this fact too, she didn't feel she could afford to be too hoity-toity about it. She'd agreed to this quick visit last week, before the whole business had really kicked off in her garden and while Adua was still walking the streets of Dulwich. There was no hope of getting Wendy to reschedule, that always caused seismic ructions and recriminations. So Beth resigned herself to the short drive over to her mother's once she had let in the SOCO troops and set them up with their first dose of tea.

Beth was just about to put her key into the car door (the central locking was a bit iffy these days on her Fiat, along with everything else) when Doug Christie-Smith from down the road, owner of Gold and Silver, the gorgeous Bengal cats, strolled past. He was looking at her with a concerned expression.

'Awful shame about your car, isn't it?'

'What?' Beth did a double-take, then peered at the Fiat more closely. What did he mean? It looked the same as usual. She squinted through the windows. OK, yes, it was pretty messy inside... thanks to Colin having succeeded in his ambition to gnaw the edges off the flowery seat protector. But surely Doug wouldn't be judgy about that, would he?

'The tyres,' Doug said, pointing.

Beth dropped her gaze. Then she saw. 'Christ almighty!'

They hadn't just been slashed. They had been cut to ribbons. If she had ever wondered what was inside tyres, she was now fully informed. The top layer had been more or less sheared away in various places and the innards exposed. Now that she thought about it, the car was even sitting a little lower than usual, since all four tyres were as flat as pancakes.

'You must have made a bit of an enemy, Beth. Cut someone up at a traffic light?' Doug winked at her and started to saunter away. She gazed at him, stunned. Then he turned back. 'Actually, no, it's not funny, is it? Listen, do you need some help? Have you got a breakdown service or anything?'

Beth put her hand to her forehead. Had she even renewed her AA membership? It was the kind of thing that often slipped through the net. Plus the company had the annoying habit of upping its rates all the time, meaning it was much cheaper to leave and rejoin than it was to just let her membership roll over. And sometimes she didn't have the energy to cancel one subscription and take out another.

'I'll have to go and look. God, and ring my mother.'

'Well, let me know if you need any help,' said Doug again. 'Howie and I are just a few doors down if you need anything.'

Beth nodded her thanks numbly. Suddenly all the dark clouds in south-east London seemed to converge on her. Each slow step back towards the house felt like a huge physical effort. She'd been so cocky about getting some extra space with her shoffice, finding a way to make their little blended family work. But someone up there was certainly showing her how foolish she'd been. And, as well as all the problems that had led to, now there was the tyre-slashing on top. To sum up: today sucked.

She was shaking her head as she let herself back into the house. Who could have done this to her little car? Who disliked her enough to commit such an act of petty vandalism? Though it wasn't really petty – four new tyres were going to cost a fortune.

Beth's first call had to be to her mother, cancelling their arrangement. As soon as she fished her phone out of the bottom of her handbag, though, she finally saw the message that had come last night.

Keep your nose out of it, unless you want your throat cut too.

Beth gasped in shock, and sat down quickly as the room swam around her. Who the hell was this from? Was it the tyre-slasher – or did umpteen people hate her now?

Before she could cudgel her brains any further, the phone rang. Beth nearly dropped it. Was it the awful texter? But she could see from the screen that it was Wendy, so she fumbled to accept the call. Beth told her mother about the tyres, but didn't mention the text. The tyres could happen to anyone, it was the sort of senseless crime that happened in cities. The text was personal, though. Typically enough, Wendy was put out rather than sympathetic. Beth had thrown her mother's day off kilter, with her thoughtless positioning of the Fiat directly in the way of a miscreant with a knife. But Wendy supposed it couldn't be helped. She suggested another appointment in three weeks' time.

'Can't you do anything before that?' Beth asked, automati-cally, then kicked herself. She already knew the answer. 'And anyway, don't you want to see Jake?'

'Of course I want to see him,' said Wendy. 'I don't know why you never bring him along any more.'

'Mum! Jake goes to school. If you insist you can only see me on weekdays, in the morning, then he'll always be at Wyatt's and he can't come.' Beth's tone was patient, but, already rattled by the events of the day, she was quickly reaching mother-induced meltdown levels of stress and annoyance.

'Oh, silly me,' Wendy trilled, completely unabashed at her lapse. 'He's still in nappies as far as I'm concerned.'

'Well, don't tell him that when you do finally see him,' Beth said with a tut.

Wendy had one grandchild to keep track of. Beth didn't expect her to keep a tally of the number of days to his next birthday (though that would have been nice) but a vague ball-park sense of his age didn't seem a totally impossible ask. Beth kicked the plastic duckboards as she cut the call short and trudged into the kitchen. But as soon as she was off the phone, she wished she'd been nicer. Her mother might well be getting Alzheimer's. And, even if she wasn't and was just being Wendy, she wouldn't be around forever, and then Beth would be sorry.

Until that day came, Beth had enough on her plate. She hit the phone again and organised the car repair. Chris Campbell poked his head in from the garden. Somehow, the SOCOs all knew what had happened, by that peculiar police sixth sense. And, of course, they'd all trooped past her car on the way in.

'Need any assistance, Beth?' he said kindly, his cheekbones for once looking less than razor sharp. Beth's eyes immediately filled up, to her horror. She was able to soldier along forever on her own, through who-knew-what terrible adversity. But if she ever got a word of sympathy, she tended to crumble like a custard cream dunked too long in tea. She sniffed and, looking around in vain for a tissue, she surreptitiously wiped her nose on a bit of discarded kitchen roll. Campbell averted his eyes and stared out at the wasteland of her garden instead.

'I'm fine,' she said in a high-pitched tone, then crashed around in the sink with a few dirty mugs. 'Want some tea?'

'No rush,' said Campbell gently, giving her a lingering look as he slipped back out of the door. He didn't even take a biscuit from the packet on the table.

By the time Beth had got the car towed to the nearest tyre place, in East Dulwich, she had also cheered up a bit. Blind optimism had helped her through a lot of dark days in the past, and car trouble was fixable, after all. No need to catastrophise. No one had actually died.

Wait a minute, though. It surely couldn't be coincidence that yesterday she'd been asking the rival builder firms about the feud, and only a matter of hours later she'd had a horrible text and her tyres were doing a strong impression of fishnet tights. She'd shaken the hornets' nest that was south London building operations, and this was surely the result. She was rubbing somebody up the wrong way – and as previous investigations had shown her, that usually meant she was on the right track. A quick look at the kitchen clock confirmed her view there was no point, now, in toddling off to work. Normally she would simply have picked up her phone and rung Katie, but she wasn't sure of her reception these days. She made a mental note to sort things out with her friend when she was less harassed. And then she rang Nina instead.

'All right, babes?' Nina answered on the second ring. 'Wossup then?'

'I've just had my tyres slashed. And been threatened,' Beth admitted.

'Nah, mate! Want to talk about it? Coffee?'

'Well, that would be great, if you're sure you have time...' Beth felt a guilty thrill, wanting to chat it all over with Nina but conscious that her friend seemed to spend even less time at work than she did.

'Nearly lunchtime, innit? Working in Norwood today. So see you at the Park Café, opposite Brockwell Park.'

Lunchtime? Beth frowned. Not when she'd last looked. But never mind. She left home for the second time that day with a bit more of a spring in her step. She was lucky with buses, and was soon swooping down Half Moon Lane towards Brockwell Park and nipping off not long after they turned the corner into Norwood Road. The parade of shops lacked the glamour of Dulwich Village but it had the novelty of offering some useful services – there was a little supermarket, a newsagents and post office, and even the wonderful Olley's, Beth's favourite fish and chip place. She headed straight for the Park Café. It was quite basic, compared with the chi-chi Mariella's or, actually, even Aurora.

She pushed open the café door and immediately spotted Nina, who was busily getting on the outside of a massive bacon sandwich. The pink rashers flapping out of the bread reminded

Beth of Colin's tongue. He'd been having a nap in the sitting room while she sorted the tyre situation, and she'd just closed the door on him and left. She hoped he didn't wake up and bark the place down.

'Sit down, hon. Sounds like you've been through the wrangle,' Nina said through a mouthful of sandwich.

It took Beth the usual second or two to decode Nina-ese. 'Yep. I might get one of those,' she said. The sandwich was looking better and better, the hungrier she got. 'Want anything else?'

'I'm all Gucci, hon,' said Nina thickly. Beth took that to mean no, and pottered over to the counter. A few minutes later she was hefting up her own massive sandwich and Nina was the one looking on hungrily.

'Gawd, I should so have said yes to another. I'll just get on with my pud,' she said, unwrapping a family-sized bar of Dairy Milk and chomping down.

'Did you even buy that here? No, don't tell me,' said Beth, laying her sandwich down carefully. 'By the way, have you heard anything about Adua in the playground? I was wondering if maybe she'd had a big row with one of the other cleaners. I know she fell out with Katie's Rosita...'

'My money would have been on Belinda McKenzie's Chloe,' said Nina indistinctly.

'Oh yes, saw her the other day... she had a bit of a look in her eye, for sure.'

'French. Say no more,' said Nina. Beth tried not to look disapproving. 'But she's left, innit?'

'Already? That didn't take long.'

'Belinda caught her smoking in that massive tumbledown shoffice of hers – with her husband Barty. And I'm not sure smoking was all they were doing, if you catch my drizzle. Bags packed same day,' said Nina. 'Turns out Belinda can do manual labour when she wants to. Threw the suitcases onto the street all by herself. Day before Adua copped it, that was.'

'Wow.' Beth digested this news. But although it was as intriguing a nugget as anything in Magpie's bowl, it got her no further with finding Adua's killer. She had to move on. 'With the bones thing, I was wondering... Do you think it was the building firms who shredded my tyres?'

'Well, could be.'

'And of course, I did mention Fiona Price to them. It's about the only lead I've got to go on.'

'So... you mentioned Fiona Price, they didn't like it much, and then this morning you've had your tyres slashed and got a nasty text?' Nina said thoughtfully.

'Yes. I suggested she might have had some kind of big blow-up with the family before she went... I was trying to think why a teenager would run away from home, and that's as good a reason as any.'

Nina shrugged and opened her mouth for another assault on the chocolate bar.

'Do you think you could check with Katrina? Maybe she knows more... she mentioned something about a boy, didn't she?'

'I'll ask,' Nina said indistinctly. 'Don't see why you're so bothered?'

'Well, because of the bones!' Beth hissed. She didn't want the whole café to hear. Nina gnawed away at the shrinking chocolate bar, looking back at her blankly. 'In my back garden,' Beth continued. 'The body. Fiona Price!'

A sudden light dawned in Nina's brown eyes. 'No! NO!'

'Yes!' Beth hunched over the table, trying to keep her voice as low as possible, and astonished it had taken her clever friend this long to get with the programme. 'I know you've always said it couldn't be her because she just "went away" and it was all

OK somehow. But don't you see? It *must* be her. The tyres and the text prove it. It's Fiona Price in my back garden.'

Now it was Nina's turn to stare at her. 'Never fought for a minute it could be her. Wondered why you kept on and on about it. Everyone insisted she was fine and bandy. But I s'pose it really might be her after all.' Nina's eyes were now bigger and rounder than Mariella's finest supersize double chocolate chip cookies. 'Oh my God, poor Fiona.'

TWENTY-THREE

Beth felt she didn't have a moment to lose. She threw down a couple of notes to pay for both their lunches, said a hasty farewell to Nina, and started trotting quickly back up the hill to the bus stop which would take her to the village and home.

In a way it was a relief to feel that, thanks to Nina suddenly agreeing the bones must belong to Fiona Price, she was finally on the right track. She knew who had been in her back garden all this time. But although the mystery was all but solved, she felt terrible for the Price family. OK, so they were very frightening, and they'd done a pretty good number on her car. But no one deserved this. Resolving her own problem would only bring a world of pain to poor Fiona's nearest and dearest. If Fiona Price really was in her back garden, then a young life had been snuffed out in the cruellest way possible, and that should never be cause for celebration.

Beth hovered at the bus stop for a second, before deciding she couldn't wait – she would just run home instead. She was in a hurry to get back and tell Chris Campbell the news that she now knew who the victim was – she didn't have time to play the usual waiting game with London's big red buses. With any luck, once Beth had delivered her bombshell, the SOCOs could be finished, packed up and off her premises by this afternoon. All their painstaking work was aimed at finding an identity for the bones, and if Beth had done that for them, there was absolutely no reason for them to hang around. They could be off, and they could take their filthy duckboards with them. She hoped they'd leave a couple of their boxes of special blue gloves behind, though. They were quite useful for cleaning, and God knew she'd have to do a lot to expunge every trace of their long occupation of her house and garden.

By the time Beth steamed back into Pickwick Road, she was exhausted and dripping with sweat, despite the autumnal chill. She almost skidded on some damp fallen leaves as she zoomed into her tiny front garden and unlocked the front door.

The first sound she heard was the dull chatter of the bunch of SOCOs out back. The second sound was the piteous howling of Colin, a dog who'd been cruelly incarcerated by his evil mistress and who had never deserved such awful treatment. She opened the sitting room door and he bounded out with much more energy than usual, before collapsing at her feet. The fathomless brown eyes looking up at her said two things: *I love and forgive you,* and *don't you ever dare do that to me again.*

'Sorry, boy, but you couldn't have come with me. Doggies aren't allowed in that café, even really good boys. Too much bacon.'

At that magic word, Colin started to bark and Beth cursed herself for a rookie error. She couldn't even let him out into the back garden to let off steam, in case he found himself a tasty bone in her unwanted pick 'n' mix ossuary out there. She clipped on his lead instead and they both trooped out to see Chris Campbell.

Campbell and his team were, as usual, hunched over the now massive hole in Beth's garden. It had started out by the fence, where the first bone was found. But now it covered most of the garden, and was bordered by all sorts of portable benches, forensic briefcases and arc lights, with wires snaking back into the house via Magpie's catflap. It was probably costing Beth a fortune in electricity, she realised as she picked her way as best she could through the maze of obstacles, keeping Colin on a tight lead in case he got distracted by any tempting aromas of decomposition.

When Beth reached the edge of the hole and pushed past two SOCO suits to see what all the fuss was about, she looked down and saw two uncannily green eyes staring back up at her. It was Magpie, an expression of fury on her little black and white face. The cat was no doubt doing her usual trick, and making life as difficult as possible for people in her bad books. The whole crew was probably dying to dig exactly where Magpie was now sitting. Beth felt a fleeting sympathy for Chris Campbell, but when she straightened up and took note of exactly how much of her garden was now hole, and how small the non-hole area really was, she realised she was completely on Magpie's side.

She put a hand on Chris Campbell's arm. He turned towards her, expecting one of his team and with a harsh word or two hanging on his lips. But when he saw Beth, a smile suffused his normally downcast features and the ice in his blue eyes appeared to melt like a glacier in the grip of global warming. Behind him, two of his white-suited underlings nudged each other and, had he not turned a basilisk stare on them, there might well have been an outbreak of schoolyard giggling.

'Just get on with it on your own for a second, you lot. If you can manage that,' he said, dusting off his muddy hands on his overalls. 'What can I do for you, Beth?' he said with one of his funny bows.

Colin looked from Campbell to his mistress and back again, but Beth was oblivious.

'Well, it's some big news,' she announced importantly. 'I think I've found the owner of the bones. So you can all leave.'

Chris Campbell looked at her in such consternation that Beth instantly felt a little less sure of herself. Meanwhile, she could hear the SOCOs' suits rustling as they all straightened up from their tasks and zeroed in on the conversation. 'What on earth do you mean?' Campbell said icily.

'I mean that I've been making some enquiries, and—'

'Just a minute,' said Campbell, holding up one very large blue-gloved hand. 'You've been doing what, now, hen?'

Beth wished he would stop calling her that, her feathers ruffling at the word. 'Well, I've been asking some questions. Finding things out... I've been talking to some local people who know what went on here twenty years ago...'

'Wait a minute,' Campbell interrupted, looking incredulous. 'Do you know how dangerous it is, meddling in a police investigation like that?'

Beth, who could get this sort of thing any night of the week from her own boyfriend (assuming he was home long enough), wasn't interested in taking it from someone else. 'Why don't you stop telling me off and just listen to me?' she said through gritted teeth.

Perhaps it was not the best way to tackle a man who so obviously enjoyed being at the top of his particular tree. Chris Campbell certainly didn't take it well.

'Just hang on there, lass. Who do you think you are, speaking to me like that?'

'Um, the owner of this house, the foundations of which you're probably undermining right now with all this pointless digging. Do you even want to know the identity of the person down there, or not?' Beth gestured angrily to the cavernous hole in her garden.

'For your information, there's nothing down there any more,

except a huge collection of deflated footballs which no one seems to have bothered to clear up,' Campbell snarled back.

'Well, excuse me if I have better things to do.' Beth drew herself up to her full height, partly to reduce the crick in her neck. Not that it made much difference. Campbell was still towering over her, almost quivering with rage. 'So, where are the bones now?'

'In the tent.' Campbell jabbed his finger in its direction. 'Where I was busy making some important deductions. Now, if you've finished interrupting my work, maybe I can get on?'

'You mean you don't even want to know who it is? Really? Isn't that the whole point of you being here right now?'

Campbell opened and shut his mouth and looked down at Beth, exasperation seeming to leach out of every pore. 'Go on then. Amaze me,' he shrugged.

'It's a girl called Fiona Price. She disappeared about twenty years ago, when she was in her late teens.'

'Wrong, wrong and wrong,' Campbell said, turning away.

Beth stuck out an arm. 'Wait. Don't just walk off like that. What do you mean, I'm wrong?'

'One, the bones we've found are almost certainly those of a man. Two, he was put in the ground quite recently. And three, he was definitely not a teenager. Satisfied?'

Beth opened and shut her mouth. Then she ploughed on. 'What? No, I'm not satisfied! When were you going to tell me any of that? How long have you known all this?'

Campbell stared at her through narrowed eyes. 'Oh, come on. We've all known it was a man down there from day one. Surely anyone in their right mind could see that was a male arm bone.'

'No! No, I didn't know. How on earth was I supposed to tell?'

'Um, the size?' Campbell's tone was laden with sarcasm. If

he'd been Jake's age, he'd have added a 'Duh!' to his terse comment.

'Oh. Well, I suppose it was a big bone... But is that enough?'

'There are other tests ongoing,' said Campbell tersely. 'Skull size, dental bone loss, pelvic measurements... but to my mind there's no doubt. And he wasn't a teenager either. Judging by fontanelle fusion alone.'

Beth was silent for a second. Her Fiona Price hypothesis was collapsing about her ears. 'But what about the age? You told me the bones had been down there for twenty years.'

'I thought that initially. But if you'd hung around the other day, I would have shared the results of the Carbon 14 dating with you.'

'Carbon 14? What's...'

'Listen, I don't have time to go into it all right now. Suffice to say it's a radiometric dating method, relying on the half-life of radioactive isotopes. *Not* on gossip from the local coffee shops.'

With that, Campbell swung away from her and stalked angrily off to his tent. Once he was inside, he zipped it shut with an angry flourish, cutting himself off from the outside world. It reminded Beth strongly of the way Magpie was with her catflap when she was in high dudgeon.

'Ridiculous man,' was one of the many things Beth muttered under her breath, picking her way through the obstacles, including various SOCO team members who scattered at her approach. She closed the back door behind her with exaggerated care, though she wanted to slam it off its hinges.

The kitchen was in a terrible state, full of washing-up, and with everything liberally smeared with mud. Beth whisked round with a bleach spray, taking out her anger and frustration on each stain. Then she stood crashing cups in the sink again. If she went on like this, she thought, she'd be lucky to have a single mug left by the time the blinking SOCOs left. But then there'd be less danger of her hurling one at Chris Campbell's head and getting charged with murder herself.

The humiliating exchange in the garden brought waves of painful colour to her cheeks. She scrubbed away at the 'Sexy Mother' mug Katie had once given her as a birthday gift. God knows why that one was out, it was usually stuffed right at the back of the cupboard. The SOCOs had probably all been sniggering over it. They seemed to have a collective mental age of about fourteen. Beth looked up from her labours for a moment and glared out of the window. Out in the garden, various white-suited figures ducked for cover and suddenly looked very busy as they dug stuff up or dusted things on their special folding tables. Campbell himself, Beth noticed, was out of his tent but had his back to the window and was standing ramrod straight. Was it her imagination, or did every vertebra radiate anger and resentment?

So all her efforts yesterday with the Prices and the Rutlands had been completely pointless. And now here she was, with just a selection of scrupulously clean mugs to show for herself. That lot had another thing coming if they imagined she was ever going to make them any more tea.

Campbell had been pretty convincing in his diagnosis. A man, who hadn't been buried long. But it made no sense at all. How could anyone have put those bones in her garden without her knowing? Beth had lived here since before Jake was born, and never once had she seen a stranger with a spade lugging a corpse onto the premises. Maybe Campbell was just plain wrong. He might be used to getting his own way, but could he really tell if a bone was male or female? Tests were sometimes wrong, after all. This Carbon 14 thing probably wasn't totally foolproof. And she was no expert, but there were men with very short limbs, weren't there? And women who were incredibly tall. Belinda McKenzie, for example, would have leg bones that went on for miles.

Fiona Price might have been an anomaly too. She might have had long arms, and something weird going on with her fontanelle, which Beth remembered was the soft bit of skull that babies are born with. It wasn't impossible. Beth got out her phone, to check with Nina. For once, though, her friend wasn't immediately available. Beth left a message, then remembered Nina never listened to her voicemail and texted her instead. *Was Fiona Price tall? If so, how tall?* That should do it.

Then Beth tossed up. Should she go into work today? If she did, not only would she assuage some of her guilt at the miniscule amount she'd been doing recently for her Wyatt's salary – she would also have a chance to keep an eye on Jake. She hadn't heard again from the school so, as far as she knew, things were calming down on the bullying front. But it wouldn't do any harm to keep tabs on him... Just as Beth was getting her things together to head off to the school, her phone pinged.

It was Nina. *Wired question, babe.* Beth smiled. Nina's spelling was as individual as her speech. But her smile faltered at the next sentence. *She was about my height, innit?* Nina's arm bone must look like a chicken wing, thought Beth – conveniently forgetting that her own would be tinier still – so it really couldn't be Fiona Price lying in bits all over her garden. Damn.

Beth texted back her thanks, even though she was actually furious. Not with Nina, of course – she wasn't one to shoot the Messiah, as Nina had put it the other day. But blimming Chris Campbell. He'd been proved right. Damn and blast it all. It still meant, as far as Beth was concerned, that the bones could be those of an unusually tall woman – but they didn't belong to pint-sized Fiona Price, that much was now certain. And there were no rumours of freakishly lanky women missing in the Dulwich area recently, not that Beth had ever heard anyway.

There was no escaping it, she had jumped to conclusions and made a massive fool of herself in front of one of Harry's colleagues, and all his underlings too. This was going to be hard to live down.

The only plus was that she was seeing so little of Harry at the moment. He didn't have time to kiss her goodnight, let alone tell her off for her absurd behaviour. It was scant comfort, she thought, as she stumped upstairs to get a scarf. The weather was decidedly nippy today.

She stood on the landing, gazing out over the gardens of Pickwick Road. *Back at square one.* This investigation was like playing an endless game of Monopoly, and landing time after time on Go to Jail. It was a feeling she remembered well, from Jake's brief obsession with the board game. She'd felt such guilty relief when he'd got into computer games. It was a bit of respite from all the Lego building and hands of Uno that were essential to bring up a boy. But look where her inattention had got her – Jake had nearly ended up as a sex pest, for God's sake. And on top of all that, Adua was still lying dead and unavenged.

Just then, a gleam caught her eye. The waters of the big pond in the Sinclairs' garden were moving. As she watched, one of the koi carp broke the surface, its wide mouth opening and closing like a pensioner struggling with a new set of false teeth. She could see why her mother might feel they were a bit spooky. Beth saw more movement out of the corner of her eye, but it was only Sally's cat, Reggie, sauntering across the Bentincks' lawn. Beth felt a touch naughty, surveying the neighbours' gardens like this – though she supposed they could be doing the exact same thing to her right now. She was sure there must be lots of curiosity about her bones, for instance.

She suddenly remembered Adua saying she liked looking out on the gardens, and Beth could see why. It was a crash course in proving the saying 'No accounting for taste.' Some people went for the rigidly traditional English square of lawn with its pelmet of shrubs, some changed it up with a patio or a decking area. It was just as well no one was particularly into nude sunbathing, because the whole street would know in seconds flat. Only Beth seemed intent on accidentally rewilding her patch.

For Beth's money, the most successful garden by far was Sally's. Her shoffice, standing proud amid lavish foliage, was just gorgeous. Solar lights twined around the extravagant mauve and orange trim. By evening time, they would be twinkling away, making the place look like a fairy wonderland lost in suburbia. Sally had such a gift for design. Not surprising, given her background staging West End shows. Beth only hoped her shoffice would be one-tenth as stylish. That's if it ever got finished. The thought made her redirect her gaze to her own garden, and she immediately wished she hadn't. It looked, more than ever in the September gloom, like a particularly bad day in the trenches, with Chris Campbell as the general barking orders. She dodged out of the way as he looked up at her window. Oh well, she supposed her neighbours were used to her completely ineffectual attempts to tame her back garden over the years. Though things had recently taken a distinct turn for the worse.

Beth's thoughts were tending towards the doom-laden again, and she was glad when her phone buzzed in her pocket. Maybe Katie had decided to contact her at last? Or was it another text from Nina? Perhaps she'd remembered that Fiona Price had had a massively tall sister who hadn't been seen for a while.

She fished her phone out, and immediately went cold all over. The message was about Fiona Price, all right. But it wasn't what Beth had been expecting at all. Again, it was short and to the point. *Stop poking your nose in. Unless you want to be like the Price girl – better off dead.*

TWENTY-FOUR

Beth held the phone away, as though it had just bitten her. What the hell? Who on earth was this person harassing her?

Feeling numb, she fetched her scarf from her bedroom, not even bothering to pick up Harry's dirty clothes and fling them in the washing basket, as she normally would. She was going over in her mind all the possible suspects who could be trying to threaten her. But there were still really only two horses in this race as far as she could see – the Rutlands and the Prices.

It must be one of the two families. And that meant that Beth must be getting somewhere. The intimidating texts were very much in the style of today's tyre-slashing –underhand, nasty acts designed to put the frighteners on her. Well, that had never worked before and it wasn't going to work now, she decided, ignoring the fact that her heart was racing like an express train and her armpits were suddenly damp.

The only thing was that the body wasn't Fiona Price's anyway. There was no point at all in Beth pursuing the idea that it was Fiona under her fence. She realised it was going to look, to this nasty texter, as though Beth had meekly given up the moment she'd been instructed to. This went so much against the grain that for a second or two Beth considered carrying on asking about Fiona, just to annoy whoever had tapped out those horrible sentences. And then, before she'd even thought through what she was doing, she'd pressed the call button, and was ringing the mysterious sender back.

She was shaking slightly as the call tried to connect but, to her immense relief, there was just an insistent buzzing sound. The phone line was dead. It must have been one of those burner phones that were all the rage now amongst criminals. The texter, whoever it was, would have taken out the SIM card, or just destroyed the whole phone, right after sending their message.

Beth wrapped her scarf around her neck a couple of times and trotted down the stairs. It definitely seemed like a good moment to regroup and apply herself diligently to her job. This way, she'd avoid any more contact with Chris Campbell, which would be a boon. She'd found him hard enough to stomach when he'd just been strutting around wrecking her back garden. Now he'd be full of all sorts of self-righteous joy at having got one over on her. At Wyatt's, she'd be away from the noise and chaos of the dig in her garden, and she'd be further from the tyre-slasher and possibly the texter as well. Plus she'd be able to keep an eye on Jake – and she might even be able to get a bit of work done too. You just never knew.

* * *

As Beth walked the familiar route to Wyatt's, passing the pretty Hansel and Gretel brickwork of the Village Primary, the school where Jake had once whooped and played in what now seemed like easier, more carefree times (though back then she'd found them tricky enough), she was mulling over the whole bones saga in her mind. Perhaps she'd had a point earlier. Even if it wasn't actually Fiona Price down there, might it be someone else connected with the Prices and the Rutlands?

She couldn't resist giving Nina a quick ring. 'Listen, do you know anyone else connected with the two building families that's disappeared?'

But Nina was quite huffy, for once. 'I do have a job, you know, Beth,' she said. 'Got to get on, hon. Let's talk later, yeah?'

Well, that was her told, thought Beth. And what did it say for her own work ethic, if notorious slacker Nina was showing her up? Beth quickened her pace, rushing past the village's pocket handkerchief front gardens, all freshly planted for autumn with pretty violas and pansies in shades of rust and purple.

Then her phone rang. For a second she wondered whether it was Nina, having thought better of her sudden attack of diligence. But it was a 'no caller ID' number. A sudden fear gripped her. Was it the evil texter, ramping up the stakes with a nuisance phone call?

She pressed the button to answer and held her breath.

'Hello, hello, Beth, is it?' said a scratchy, slightly familiar voice. 'Found my records in the end, didn't I? Your shed. It was one of ours.'

A minute later, Beth was shaking her head. Nice of Aggie Price to ring her. But even if her shed was built by the Prices, she now knew the body in the garden wasn't Fiona's. She was no further on to discovering the identity of the victim.

By the time she reached the famous wrought-iron gates, she was in quite a stew. It didn't help that one of the first people she saw, after passing the porter's lodge and the Great Hall, was Mrs Montgomery, the Year 8 head. And she seemed to be waving to her. Beth ducked down behind one of the large recycling bins, but it had unfortunate associations, with poor Adua and with her first case at the school, so she scuttled out, keeping her head low, and walked as fast as she could to the side door leading to her office. Phew, that was close.

What she didn't know was that Jake's classroom had a beautiful view onto the recycling area and, as they were having form time at that precise moment, all his fellow students had witnessed his mother's distinctly odd behaviour and spent the rest of the day teasing him about it, with the honourable exception of Charlie. And even he shook his head a little before zipping his lips. Jake was not having a good year so far.

Once Beth had unlocked the archives office and got herself settled at her desk, she realised she'd probably overreacted. Mrs Montgomery probably just wanted to say hi, having recognised her. It couldn't be anything more sinister than that. If it had been, knowing the school, they would have been in touch straight away. They were nothing if not proactive.

Beth shook her head a little to try and clear her teeming mind. The first thing she noticed, once she'd taken a breath, was the woeful state of her office. As well as an inbox that was exploding again, there was actually a mouldering apple core on her desk. This reminded her strongly of the way the archives had been when she'd first been appointed. She remembered how shocked she'd been then at their ramshackle state. She was severely neglecting her duties. As cleaning was her default mode when stressed, and was actually easier than dealing with the backlog, she immediately set to with a packet of tissues from her handbag, hurling the apple core in the bin and dusting everything else down. Ten minutes later things looked a little more respectable. She then got to work on her pile of post and was pleased that it really didn't take long to make serious inroads.

This, of course, was mere displacement activity. Beth knew she should be concentrating on her long-neglected biography of discredited swashbuckler Sir Thomas Wyatt. But no one had ever chastised her on her failure to carry through the project. It was almost as if the school would rather allow its founder's appalling profiteering from slavery to vanish once again into the mists of history.

Normally, this very thought would be enough of a spur to Beth to get her attacking the work with a vengeance. But her mind was still a churning mess.

Looking up for a moment, Beth gazed out of the window. She could just about see a corner of the perfect lawn in front of Dr Grover's office. Despite the autumn winds, there was never a moment when a drifting leaf was permitted to rest on this hallowed turf. Interesting, the way you could see so much sometimes from a window, without even trying... she thought for a second, but whatever memory had been briefly jogged floated out of reach again like a dandelion seed on the breeze. Something to do with a neighbour... but which neighbour?

She sighed and turned back to her work. There was nothing for it but to get on with her research. Now, where had she left Sir Thomas last time? He'd been trying to buy up brothels in Southwark, along a site now known as Paris Gardens, quite close to the Globe Theatre. He'd been pipped at the post by a rival who'd cornered the market in ladies of easy virtue, so he decided to try his hand a bit further afield. Contemporaries were already exploiting the colonies and Sir Thomas, always keen to turn a quick guinea, was intrigued at their tales of the boundless fortunes to be made... Now where had Beth left those documents?

The good thing about an archive that had been used as a dumping ground for centuries was that it contained all the good stuff as well as chaff that really should have been binned on sight. Beth had laid her hands on quite a few telling documents by now. There was one right at the bottom of her in-tray. But the only way to get at it was to move all the stuff on top of it. And the most efficient way to do that was to open every single neglected piece of post and deal with it.

Beth set to. At least she was now doing the work she was legitimately paid for, she thought. There was a satisfaction in that. But, even when her intentions were good, it didn't take much to sidetrack her from the deluge of play programmes, school notices and dry-as-dust correspondence which everyone else in the school insisted on shoving her way.

Amongst the letters from the College School, asking for some pre-Second World War documents to be located and returned – some hope – and enquiries from Wyatt's old boys asking for back copies of the alumnus magazine (Beth hoped her own retirement never got that dull), a few flyers from local businesses plopped out. These were such a waste of trees, thought Beth with a tut, scooping a handful up from the floor. But wait, what was this? In with the mix of pizza leaflets was a larger, shinier offering – a brochure. It had fallen open in the middle, showing a display of gleaming sash windows. They were rather nice – and very Dulwich. Beth's own windows were now either impossible to open or impossible to close. At some point she'd definitely need to get them replaced. When she won the lottery, maybe. Which could be a while as she never got round to entering it. She smoothed the pamphlet closed, then did a double-take. On the front was a gleaming shoffice building, of a size to rival even Belinda McKenzie's mini-Versailles.

For a second or two, Beth allowed herself to dream. How wonderful would it be, to invite Belinda round for coffee, then casually welcome her into a shoffice like this? Belinda would be expecting to sit in Beth's cramped and outdated, albeit surgically clean, kitchen. She would not expect this deluxe creation. The photo showed a glamorous woman inside, tapping away daintily at a laptop while looking terrifically smug. Beth could have a kettle in there, even a freezer like Sally – she could basically move in, and leave Harry and Jake fighting over the remote control and the games consoles.

Then she felt guilty. The whole idea of the shoffice was to

bring them all together, lessening the stress on a tiny house that was crammed to the rafters, given that Jake would insist on growing and Harry was incapable of getting rid of any more books. Colin had done his best to reduce the number of whodunits Harry had brought with him as his dowry, reducing some to papier mâché with his enthusiastic doggy slobbering, but there were still about ten thousand to be found homes for.

There was also the inconvenient fact that a shoffice like this would probably cost more than Beth would get for her entire house. It was not to be. She flipped the brochure shut and was about to sling it in her recycling pile, when something else caught her eye. The name at the top. *Rutlands Construction.*

Having been at Rutlands' rundown Crystal Palace HQ so recently, Beth was astonished their brochure was so ritzy. Their premises had been minimal on the home comforts front. She remembered the terrifying dog, Cuddles, the scruffy crowded yard, the threatening atmosphere – and most tellingly of all, their own office space, which was infinitely inferior to this gorgeous studio they were advertising. Why hadn't they built something like this, to show off to visitors? Perhaps it was the old cliché of the cobbler's children going barefoot, but it gave Beth pause for thought. She looked through the glossy pages much more carefully.

And then, on page three, right at the bottom in a black-bordered box, she spotted it, incongruous amongst the pictures showing types of double glazing and apparently rapturous customers (who looked much too excited about windows to be genuine Dulwich residents, she thought suspiciously). It was a short message, reading, '*In memoriam, Markie Rutland, disappeared 24th March 2001, anyone with information, call 0208 385 0987.*'

TWENTY-FIVE

Half an hour later, Beth was sitting in Mariella's with Nina. To give her friend credit, it hadn't taken Beth long at all to get over Nina's previous scruples about leaving work. Scruples for Nina were definitely, as Shakespeare put it, more honoured in the breach than in the observance, and Beth was very glad about that. Because whatever was going on at Rutlands seemed much more important than either of their jobs right now.

Nina had been to Mariella's with her before, but that was with Katrina. Now that it was just the two of them, and the table they were sitting at was only a handspan away from the tempting counter arrayed with cakes and pastries, Nina wanted to take her time inspecting everything before finally making a selection. Beth waited impatiently. She'd chosen Mariella's as the booths seemed quite private and this was a quiet time in Dulwich anyway, with most of the mummies busy around now selecting their all-important school pick-up outfits or checking their children's extracurricular appointments for the rest of the day, which was almost as crucial. But this sort of hiatus didn't last long – the place would be filling up before they knew it.

Their coffee came, but Nina was still weighing up her cake

choices. Finally Beth lost patience and waved her hand in front of her friend's face. 'Look, do you think Katrina knows anything about this boy?' Beth pushed the brochure over the artfully rustic table, slopping the coffees.

Nina blinked reproachfully. 'Watch it! That cost a fiver.'

'Yes, which I paid,' said Beth drily.

Nina sat back and read the little black-edged notice carefully. Then she sighed. 'I knew Markie, everyone did around the Palace,' she said. 'He was Fiona Price's boyfriend.'

'A boyfriend! Katrina did say something about a boy. So this was him? Where is he now?' Beth held her breath for the answer. If this Markie was still missing, and given that Aggie Price had admitted her family had constructed her shed, then he could be her arm... not to mention all her other bones.

Nina, having eventually plumped for a delicate mauve cupcake topped with Parma violets, took a huge bite as soon as the waitress brought it, seemingly oblivious to the fact that Beth was on the edge of her seat. Beth watched her friend chewing away for what seemed like an age, before she laid the dainty morsel aside carefully and took a healthy swig of her coffee instead.

'I see what you're getting at. But nah, mate,' Nina said, then started looking around again. The place was gradually getting busier as the hands of the large (artfully rattan-trimmed) clock on the wall ticked round to school chucking-out time.

'No? What do you mean? Care to elaborate?' Beth felt frustration welling up inside her. This had been such a perfect solution to her conundrum, she almost couldn't bear it to go south.

'He's in Dagenham, innit babe?'

'Is it? I mean, is he really? How do you know?'

'Katrina. She says he went there to get over his heartbreak.'

Beth thought about that for a second. She wasn't sure if Dagenham would do it for her. But each to their own. And, while she thought about it, wasn't it a little strange that Katrina had kept tabs on the Rutland family's doings, all these years?

Meanwhile, Nina had pushed her plate as far away as it would go. 'No offence, babe, but that cake tastes like my loo freshener smells.'

'None taken, I didn't make it. And you've got a point,' said Beth, thinking of Jane's down the road, where a brownie was still a brownie and violet was only the colour your cheeks went when you got the bill.

It wasn't just the cakes that were making Beth feel wistful as she stood outside Mariella's, once Nina had bounced off to get Wilf. She'd really hoped she'd cracked those blinking bones. But no, here was that blasted, all-too-familiar square one again. Drat and double-drat Dagenham.

It was too late now, really, she reasoned, to go back to Wyatt's. Jake would be leaving any minute and she wanted to be home before him. She'd just nip into the deli, which did service in the rarefied confines of Dulwich as a corner shop, and pick up some of the deliciously melting handmade ravioli she sometimes bought them as a treat.

She was wandering down the chilled aisle, doing her level best not to hurl all the tempting delicacies into her basket, when she bumped into Magenta Bentinck, her neighbour Sally's eldest. Magenta had worked briefly in the art world but had tired of the vicious skulduggery and constant back-biting, and was now much happier in a cut-throat commercial law firm. After the initial 'Fancy-seeing-you-here's, chat inexorably turned to shoffices.

'I'm beginning to wish I'd taken your mum's advice and got Rutlands on the case. Maybe they would have been quicker, and they might not have made the, er, discovery, and we wouldn't have all this palaver,' Beth said wistfully.

'Oh, Mum loves Rutlands but Dad always said they weren't

all that,' said Magenta. 'He thought people only hired them because all the mothers fancied the owners' son.'

'The son? You can't mean... you don't mean Markie, do you?' Beth was agog.

'I dunno, really. Maybe that was his name,' Magenta wrinkled her brow. 'Anyway, Dad wasn't serious. It was just one of his laughs.' She looked downcast, and Beth realised it must be so hard on all the Bentinck children, now their father had moved to the States and more or less abandoned them – for a girlfriend Magenta's age. She was about to say something, falteringly, about how sorry she was, when Magenta changed the subject.

'Isn't it awful about Adua? Do you think the killer's still at large?' she said, lowering her voice and looking around, as though there could be a maniac hiding in the baked goods section. But as usual there were only one or two other shoppers in the deli – Beth liked to think that was because of the stratospheric prices, not because everyone else in Dulwich was more organised than her – when Magenta went on. 'And what about your bones? *Two* bodies, I heard. At least.'

Beth, who'd been wondering how to avoid saying a resounding yes to the question about Adua's murderer, clutched at the yoghurt cabinet for support. She accidentally dislodged an artful pyramid of rhubarb and custard tubs boasting they were made with Devon cream, surely designed to double the cholesterol levels of the daddies of Dulwich.

'What? Two? When did you hear that?'

Magenta put out a hand. 'Sorry, Beth, I thought you of all people would know. Everyone's talking about it.'

Beth went white. She said a hasty farewell to Magenta and, for once, the price of the pasta didn't disturb her one jot as she waved her card at the machine and staggered out of the shop. *More than one body?* She felt sick. And angry, too. Why hadn't that man Campbell told her this latest horror? Granted, she'd been out all day and they hadn't exactly parted on the best terms, but didn't he have a duty to keep her informed?

She was so upset that she rang Harry immediately, forgetting that she was peeved with him over his neglectful attitude of late. Normally this would mean she'd keep a dignified distance, and they would get further and further apart until one of them gave in and made a consolatory gesture (or until Harry noticed there was a problem). But she prodded the number with a trembling finger as she walked back to the house, her mind whirling. It went straight to voicemail yet again, to her fury.

Harry and that dreadful Chris Campbell had led her to believe the bones had only been from one body. But another one? Another person down there? Who the hell could it be? And who on earth had put it there? Either the people who'd lived in the house before her had been monsters, or someone living in Pickwick Road right now was. And, as Beth had found out during her years in Dulwich, you really never could tell.

Why hadn't Harry come out and told her the truth about the bones? And why hadn't Chris Campbell let her know either? He had her number, she'd given it to him when he'd asked. But he wasn't as culpable as Harry. What on earth was the point of having a copper boyfriend if you had to pick up all your news at the chiller cabinet of the local shop?

She bustled into her street, full of righteous indignation, and bumped straight into the Kendalls out for a stroll. They were admiring Sally Bentinck's huge cat Reginald, who was sitting on the wall outside Beth's house and no doubt causing Magpie a lot of territorial anguish. Despite her impatience, Beth did her best to unclench her jaw and grin at the lovely elderly couple. Whatever was going on in her garden certainly wasn't their fault.

'Reggie's such a delight, isn't he?' said Lizzie, rubbing the cat's fat ginger cheeks while he squirmed with joy. Beth was a cat lover but she couldn't help giving Reggie a jaundiced look.

He was a bit of a bully; he and Magpie had had several run-ins over the years and it had taken Magpie a while to get the upper paw. Anyone who even tried to get one over on her moggy was never going to win a place in Beth's heart. She gave him a perfunctory pat then rattled in her handbag for her keys in a businesslike way, trying to convey politely to the Kendalls that now was not the time for a massive neighbourly catch-up. Unfortunately they weren't getting the hint at all.

First the weather had to be considered, and then the latest about the LTN at the end of Court Lane, which had caused such controversy at their dinner party. Beth remained monosyllabic and started to fidget, but the couple had all the time in the world. Then the chat turned back to Reggie.

'We do love him,' said Lizzie. 'And he was poor Adua's favourite, too.'

While inwardly smarting that her own beloved Magpie hadn't, apparently, been Adua's favourite, Beth gave her best sympathetic smile. 'I miss seeing Adua bustling up and down the road. And goodness knows what I'll do when Magpie needs looking after,' she said.

'Yes, Adua knew all there was to know about the pets in the road. And everything else too. She always did say she'd write a book about her experiences when she retired,' Lizzie reminisced.

Beth lowered her voice. She knew Harry hated her doing this sort of thing – but at the moment that was a spur, rather than a disincentive. 'Have you heard anything? About what happened to her?'

'No, dear. We rather thought you might be in a position...' but Lizzie tailed off, seeing Beth's shuttered expression. 'The only thing we did think,' Lizzie said, exchanging a glance with George, 'was that she might have come into money. She got a lovely new handbag just before... it happened, and she had been talking about booking a holiday. So at first, when she didn't come in that Monday, we weren't so surprised. It wouldn't have been typical, but we thought she might have just taken off, gone back to her village for a rest or something. She certainly deserved a break, no one could deny that. The way some of the other families exploited her,' Lizzie shook her head.

Beth mumbled something in apparent agreement, though she knew Lizzie had certainly not hesitated to run Adua ragged, fetching dry cleaning and taking returns to the post office, keeping the house pristine and doing mountains of George's ironing – not to mention serving at all Lizzie's fancy dinners.

'She could be a tad naughty, Adua,' Lizzie continued. 'Sometimes we'd suddenly run out of tea or coffee, when she'd been round. But we didn't begrudge her.' Beside her, George suddenly started coughing. 'We knew things were tough for her back home. And then we got the call,' Lizzie continued, welling up. George patted her shoulder and all three fell silent.

'Buck up, now, Lizzie. Let's get you home. You'll be better after a nice G&T,' said George, winking at Beth. 'We mustn't keep you.'

Beth smiled at them both and Reggie, sensing the more appreciative members of his audience had departed, loped back across the fence to the Bentincks'. But as the couple made their way down the street, Beth looked a bit harder at George Kendall's retreating form. Was she imagining it, or had he been a little less understanding than his wife about Adua's tendency to filch the odd item?

TWENTY-SIX

Beth erupted into her house. She'd wasted so much time with the Kendalls, while she'd been dying to get home and see if that blasted man was still in her back garden. Campbell had so much to answer for, damn and drat him.

As soon as she was in the hall, though, she knew the SOCO team was gone for the day. The line of boxes they usually dumped by the door wasn't there, and there were no spare suits hanging on her coat hooks either. But the filthy duckboards were still very much present, unfortunately. All of a sudden, she heard a whining. Poor old Colin! She quickly liberated him from the sitting room and took him round the block.

Beth's anger was making her jet-propelled, but Colin let her know what he thought of her warp-speed walking. She made herself slow down until she was ambling along, while the dog checked to see that all his favourite smells were still in their rightful places. He was looking very stout; she knew the SOCOs were sneaking him little treats. She'd have to put her foot down about that – as well as the whole street finding out her business before Campbell bothered to inform her.

By the time she returned, in a better mood thanks to Colin's calming influence, Jake was back and already toiling away, apparently, on his homework upstairs. Later they had a pleasant enough evening together, laughing uproariously at the current crop of hopefuls on *The Apprentice*, though, underneath it all, Beth's annoyance at Chris Campbell's high-handed behaviour and his total failure to update her on bodies in her own back garden continued to simmer away like a pot on the back burner.

* * *

It was unfortunate for Harry that he chose this evening to get home before midnight, for the first time in goodness knew how long. He'd hardly got a foot through the door before he'd tripped over Beth's shoulderbag, kicking the contents everywhere. She bustled out into the hall, tutting loudly, and they shovelled everything back in. He wisely said nothing about the rich strata of Haribo wrappers which she carefully replaced. The house was squeaky clean; Beth's handbag contents were another story. He'd got used to her ways over the last couple of years.

'I must get a new bag,' she wailed. Then her face developed a thoughtful look that was all too familiar.

'What?' he said.

'Nothing, nothing,' she said, but she seemed distracted as she shoved the last dried-up old lip balm back in. Then she gave him her opening salvo. 'So. When were you going to tell me about the other body?'

For a second, Harry's mind went completely blank. The awful case he was working on did involve plentiful victims, but he was pretty sure he'd never mentioned that to Beth. Had she found out about it by the peculiar Dulwich osmosis that meant every barrier he put up ended up as full of holes as a Swiss cheese? Or had she found something out about Adua's murder, an investigation that, despite him throwing manpower at it, was getting nowhere fast?

'Body?' was all he said.

'Yes, body,' Beth said, pointing towards the kitchen.

With some relief, he realised she was on about their own back garden. 'You know I can't discuss cases with you...' he started, then held up a palm as a five-minute tirade washed over him. 'Look, I'll make enquiries. How about that?'

Beth stared at him. 'If you're not denying it, it must be true,' she said. 'There's more than one dead person in my garden. I can't believe this! It can't be happening...'

'I'm sure that's not the case... but I'll certainly let you know the moment I hear anything concrete. If I can,' he said, trying as usual to tread the fine line between promising too much and delivering too little. Poor Beth, she had so much on her plate right now. And he hadn't been doing his share in the last few days. Things were just crazy at work. He slightly regretted putting Narinda Khan in charge of scheduling for this case; somehow his hours seemed even madder than usual. She was new to the job, though. Allowances had to be made.

'Can you at least trace a missing person for me, then?'

Again, Harry took a minute before answering. Missing person? He hoped against hope that Beth hadn't ignored all his strictures about conducting her own investigations.

'OK, I know what that raised eyebrow means,' Beth said. 'But seriously, what do you expect me to do? I want all this to be over,' she gestured at the muddy boards, but he knew she meant that to encompass the back garden and its grim secrets. 'Anyway, it's in your own interests. If Chris Campbell can put a name to these bones, then he can pack up and go home. Then you won't have to avoid the place like you've been doing.'

'I haven't been avoiding it, I've just been busy,' Harry said carefully. 'But I don't know why he hasn't just transferred everything to the lab anyway.'

'Oh? Narinda said you thought it was important for him to stay on site.'

'What? No. She must have got the wrong end of the stick somewhere.' Harry ruffled his hair absently, then caught Beth with that faraway look again. 'Listen, all right. I'll check a missing person for you. Just this once. Who is it?'

'Markie Rutland,' said Beth. 'One of the Rutland construction family. And while you're at it, could you also check the whereabouts of a girl called Fiona Price?'

'I said I'd check one person for you, once, and that's two already. Honestly, Beth, is there ever going to be a time when you don't push the boundaries?'

Beth smiled up at him. That little grin was so impish that suddenly he couldn't resist her any more. Then she was in his arms and all was right with the world again. This was where he needed to be, with this funny little woman who meant so much to him. And if his work kept taking him away, then maybe – just maybe – it was time for him to reconsider what he was doing with his life.

* * *

The next day, Beth was rather thrilled to get a call from Harry as she was about to set off for the archives office. She'd been waiting patiently for Chris Campbell and his troops to arrive, so she could double-check the body count in her garden. But naturally on the one day when she was ready, waiting and actively keen to see him, he was ridiculously late.

So she'd decided to revert to old bad habits and leave a key for the SOCO team under the doormat. She'd take Harry at his word and let him talk to Campbell himself. And he did deserve some credit, after putting her worries to bed so very successfully last night... But her purred 'Hello,' into the phone soon turned to disappointment, when she heard what he had to relay.

'Markie Rutland. He's in Dagenham.'

Beth paused on the stairs. 'Oh rats. He's alive.'

'Poor guy. I'll send him your love, shall I?'

Harry's chuckle was warm in her ear. But Beth was already thinking fast. 'Wait a minute... you're certain he's really there? In Dagenham?'

'Yes. Why?'

She could tell Harry's mind had already turned to other things. In the background, a sweet voice piped up asking if he wanted coffee. Beth ground her teeth and said a little more loudly, 'It's just that Fiona Price ran off too...'

'Oh. I see, you had this down as a big romantic elopement that went wrong.' Beth could almost hear Harry tutting, though he was wise enough not to do it into the phone. 'Well, sorry to disappoint you again, but Fiona Price has been seen as well – in Milton Keynes.'

'Milton Keynes? That's really torn it.' Beth was glum. She'd now zipped up her little boots and was looking around for a scarf – it was going to be cold outside again.

'Get real, darling. Things don't just sort themselves out like that in real life,' Harry said dismissively. Before Beth had time to start feeling really cross, though, he carried on. 'Listen. I've been thinking. When this is over, maybe we could go away somewhere? Just the two of us. What do you say?'

For a second, Beth felt her heart lift. Strolling down a boulevard together hand in hand, eating spaghetti by candlelight and kissing – no, that was dogs, wasn't it? But this was just what she had yearned for, over the past couple of weekends. Then, as she closed the front door on Colin's hopeful snout and Magpie's cross glinting eyes, she realised she was being ridiculous. How could she possibly go away and leave those two, let alone Jake? There was no Adua any more to take care of the pets, and as for Katie, who might once have been easy-breezy about taking Jake for a while, Beth was by no means certain that was still going to be the case.

'Can I get back to you on that?' she said. She was sure she wasn't imagining Harry's disgruntlement when he hung up.

The first of the SOCOs was about to trail up the path as she opened her gate. It was Abi, the woman officer Beth had chatted with before. There was no sign yet of Campbell.

'Just to say we'll sort out the shoffice for you before we go, Beth. The boss wanted to keep it as a surprise but I thought you should know.'

Beth thanked her profusely, though she did wonder what exactly that meant. Would they just be tidying up the current horrendous mess? Or would they be putting the whole thing together? Her face lit up with a hopeful smile at that prospect. After that, she didn't have the heart to ask her the questions on the tip of her tongue, 'And exactly how many bodies are down there anyway, and how much longer is this going to go on?' She was pretty sure Abi wouldn't know anyway. Everything seemed to be up to the big man. Beth knew it was irrational, but as far as she was concerned, his name was still mud, even if it did turn out he hadn't actually neglected to tell her about multiple extra corpses in her flowerbeds after all.

Mud. There was just too much of it around at the moment. Her garden was a sea of it, her house was chock-full of it too. As for Jake, his name also seemed to be mud, this time with Katie. It hadn't escaped Beth's notice that Jake and Charlie had not hung out once since Beth had collected him, shortly after the Year 8 disco bombshell from Mrs Montgomery. And then there was the Rosita thing... a question which had caused a rift with her best friend, and had turned out to be unnecessary anyway. And she'd actually been beginning to think she was good at this detective malarkey! What was it they said about getting too big for your boots, she mused, as she kicked at the fallen leaves along Pickwick Road.

'Hey, careful there,' said a voice, reaching out to steady her as she almost slipped and went off the pavement.

'Thanks,' she said, looking up, and up again, to find her saviour was Sally Bentinck's very tall son, Jude, the oldest of the boys. God, the Bentinck kids were a good-looking bunch, she thought. Magenta could have been a model, if she wasn't on her way to being a legal whiz. Jake had been in love with his former babysitter Zoe forever. And Jude, with floppy blond hair and melting brown eyes, was in the same mould. 'How are you, Jude? How's your mum?' Beth asked.

'Oh, thanks Beth. Yes, she's so much better now,' he said earnestly.

'Wait, what? Sally's been ill?' This was news to Beth. Magenta hadn't mentioned a thing yesterday.

'Well, not ill, as such, physically,' Jude said awkwardly. 'But you know how hard it's been for her, since Dad did a runner, in the New Year.' At the thought of his father, Jude's generous mouth compressed into a thin line. 'Anyway, that's why we all moved back in – us boys anyway. Mags isn't far away either, and Zoe's in and out, you know.'

'It's lovely for your mum that you're all so supportive,' Beth said almost wistfully. She hoped Jake would be as caring when she was older. If she didn't handle this awful looming disco with kid gloves, she had a horrible feeling he would leave home at sixteen and never darken her door again.

'Yeah, well. We do what we can,' said Jude modestly. 'Anyway, Mum's pretty busy with all her projects. And she's feeding those fish next door to you again, like she did all last year.' He rolled his eyes. 'But best of all, she's planning one of her surprises. The less said about that the better, though!'

Beth idly wondered what that was about. Sally had always been famous for her amazing parties. When the children had been small, she'd thrown incredible Harry Potter and Alice in Wonderland-themed extravaganzas, which Jake had marvelled at as a tiny boy. She must have another bash up her sleeve now. Beth realised again how annoying it must be for artistic Sally, and the whole Bentick family, living next door to her horrible mess.

'I hope you aren't all too fed up with this SOCO business,' she said. 'I don't think it will be that much longer... They've just said they'll actually sort the shed out when they leave. They're not really supposed to but with Harry, well...' Beth tailed off, realising she was probably not supposed to admit that fellow officers got a much better deal than civilians. She didn't want to get Harry into trouble, so she rushed on. 'After that, it'll just need those little finishing touches.'

Beth knew she was being crazily optimistic here. The SOCOs could be around forever, for all the signs of haste they were showing, and she was worse than useless at design stuff. Her house was cosy, yes, but she had no eye for the clever details that made Sally Bentinck's place unique. It was essential that she put a positive spin on things, though. Even the lovely Bentincks might finally get exasperated. She wouldn't really blame them.

Jude couldn't have been more relaxed, though. 'Oh, don't worry, I'm sure it won't be that much longer,' he said airily. 'I mean, it can't really be, can it? Not if...' His Apple watch beeped and he looked down. 'Oh God, I'm late for a Zoom call, sorry Beth, gotta go. Oh hi, Mum,' he added, as he sprinted up the path to the front door. Beth hadn't seen Sally Bentinck standing there, the hedge had grown so tall. Sally made way for Jude to pass, and then waved her bangles at Beth.

'How's everything?' Beth started to ask, but then her phone rang.

'It's all go this morning,' Sally laughed.

Beth fished her mobile out and saw it was Harry again. 'Sorry, better take this, Sally, see you later,' she said. Not for the first time, she thanked her lucky stars she lived in Pickwick Road. She really had the best neighbours.

'What's up now?' she said to Harry as she started walking up the street.

'And top of the morning to you, too,' said Harry, amusement in his voice. 'All OK?'

Beth considered. 'Since we last spoke ten minutes ago? Not bad,' she said. Things hadn't started brilliantly, and she'd been peeved about his earlier Markie/Fiona news, but it was amazing how friendly faces could perk up your mood.

'Well, I've got some news that ought to really put a spring in your step,' he said. The sound of that familiar tiny lilt in his voice, when he knew something would please her, warmed her heart. Plus she'd seen Harry last night – for some very satisfactory alone time – and this was their second call today. Maybe this was the start of a new dawn, where he'd be a lot more available. She was excited at the idea.

'What's happened?' she asked a little breathlessly.

'It's been confirmed. There's only one set of bones in the garden.'

TWENTY-SEVEN

Beth felt a sudden wash of relief at the news. Just the single set of bones. Then she realised just how odd her life had become. Imagine being thrilled to have a skeleton on your premises! But she was. One corpse now seemed quite tidy and manageable – and an awful lot better than multiple dead bodies.

Immediately she checked herself. When had she become so unfeeling? Obviously she wasn't nearly as bad as whoever had dumped those bones in the first place. But her desire to keep their number to a minimum shouldn't squash her empathy with their owner. Somebody, some poor real person, had ended up in her garden. Fiona Price was out, so was Markie Rutland. But the bones had a name, if only they could speak. And she wondered for a second why Magenta had thought it was two bodies, anyway. But the answer to that was surely the Dulwich rumour mill, grinding out of control as usual. Beth hurried on, to ask Harry what time he'd be back later.

The answer was typically vague, but at least today's excuse was good. Harry's tricky case really was about to come to a head, he said. Beth thought it sounded more and more like a really awful boil. And she hoped the final result would be the same – once the dratted thing had popped, all the poison would gush out and things could get back to normal. Somehow, every time she thought about Harry in his office, she kept seeing a little glint in Narinda Khan's soft dark eyes... hopefully that, too, would be extinguished very soon.

Beth trudged along, careful where she put her feet now, after nearly skidding earlier. Leaves were a trip hazard, true, but it was always a pleasure walking through the village at this time of year, seeing the excited toddlers in their wellies making for the park, where they could stamp and kick to their hearts' content in the waist-high piles of leaves. Jake had loved jumping on the crunchy heaps left by the acer trees in Court Lane, their scarlets and oranges like little flags signalling autumn's descent into winter. It had always taken them ages to accomplish the short walk to Katie's house, even though Jake loved playing with Charlie so much. Beth felt another pang at the situation between her and Katie. She must find a way to get back into her friend's good books.

She dithered. Should she ring her, or maybe text? Or could she just casually drop by, on the way to work? No, no, that might put Katie on the spot a bit too much. Beth compromised and sent a voice memo. She'd only just put her phone away when it pinged. Katie had replied immediately, with a text, making an appointment to meet Beth later that afternoon at Mariella's. Beth studied the wording carefully. Somehow the fact that Katie had answered so quickly didn't seem reassuring. It was more as though her friend had been waiting impatiently for an approach, and had had her reply all mapped out. And was Beth being completely paranoid, or did the proposed meeting seem very... formal? Since when had she and Katie ever needed to make such careful arrangements? It felt very sad and wrong that they had this wedge between them.

Oh well, working on the Wyatt biography would be a useful way of purging her mind of distractions, she decided, trotting past the head's office. Once she'd unlocked the door and settled herself at her desk, she hunkered down and actually managed some good hard research for several hours, even keeping up the pace over a sandwich lunch at her desk. It wasn't until she kicked out a leg while reaching for a file on the shelf beside her, managing to tip over her handbag, that a thought struck her. Harry had knocked her bag flying only last night and it had jogged a memory then, too. Not only that she needed to clean it out urgently. It was something else, something someone had said to her, very recently at that. Something jarring... Now who on earth was it? She racked her brains.

Then, almost automatically, she replaced everything in her bag, gathered up her coat and scarf and found herself waving a quick goodbye to the Wyatt's porter (who was a lot less surprised at Beth's antics these days than he had once been). She was soon running down the familiar Dulwich streets, passing the mummies wending their weary ways to Jane's or Mariella's after an exhausting time at the hairdressers or Lesley Leale-Green's beauty salon.

At last, she was right back where it had all started. In Pickwick Road. She had just reached her gate, and was allowing herself the luxury of bending double and panting for breath while holding onto the post, when Sally Bentinck nearly bumped into her. She was clutching an empty plastic bag.

'Are you OK, Beth?' Sally said, eyes wide and bracelets jangling. 'You look a bit...'

Beth just nodded, she didn't quite have enough puff to give any explanations.

'I've come straight from the Sinclairs', you know,' Sally said, waving the bag. 'Bit earlier than usual today. Just feeding my favourite little fishies.'

'Not so little,' panted Beth, one hand to her chest. If she was going to keep making these mad dashes, she really needed to get a bit fitter.

'Did you get your Fiat fixed? After you had that bit of... car trouble,' Sally asked.

'Yes, yes I did. It was still covered by my AA policy – I remembered to renew it, thank goodness,' Beth said, her breathing returning to normal now.

'Great,' said Sally. 'Well, I'll be going, got some things to do.'

'Oh, hang on a second,' said Beth. 'This sounds odd, but do you know if George Kendall got on with Adua?'

Sally was silent for a second, then gave Beth a piercing glance. 'Funny you should say that. I'm not sure he did.' She smiled and turned. Beth stored the kernel of information away like a squirrel preparing for winter.

'Sorry, one other thing, Sally, do you know when Simon and Trudy will be back?' Cruising seemed like an innocent enough occupation for people of the Sinclairs' age. But were they actually trying to escape something? Like a set of mysterious bones... or a grisly murder. Or, come to think of it, could Simon Sinclair actually be the body? No one had seen either of them for months...

'I heard from them the other day,' Sally said. 'They're on the last leg of the Caribbean cruise. They should be back in the next ten days or so. They've had an amazing time. They'll be brown as berries by the time they get home.'

'It'll be great to see them,' said Beth automatically, with her mind still mostly on that elusive conversation about handbags...

'To be honest, I'll be sad to stop seeing my babies.'

Beth goggled at her for a second. Her children were all in her twenties, and most were still under her roof. But then realisation dawned. 'Oh. The carp,' she said, trying not to sound too taken aback.

'You're not keen on them?' Sally raised an eyebrow.

'Oh, I don't mind them. My mother's not a fan, though. Says there's something creepy about them...'

'Creepy?' Sally broke into one of her trademark peals of

laughter. 'Well, I think they're beautiful. I'll miss seeing them every evening.'

'Don't worry, Simon and Trudy will probably be off again as soon as they get back, seems like they've really got the sailing bug,' Beth said.

But Sally's mood suddenly seemed to have turned wistful, as she retreated down her own garden path. 'Well, goodbye then, Beth,' she said quietly, as she let herself into the house.

Beth took a moment before doing the same. She'd got her breath back, but she wasn't sure she was ready yet to see Campbell and his SOCO squad. As she put the key in the lock, she hoped against hope that things were going to be a bit more under control at home so she could think this whole thing through properly, in the place where it had all happened.

It seemed her wishes were going to be granted. She was expecting to swing the door open on the usual mess of duckboards and the discarded bits and bobs of the SOCO team, coats they'd shrugged off before putting on their white suits, sometimes even bags of shopping they'd picked up in Herne Hill or East Dulwich on the way to the village. But the boards were gone, the coat rack looked almost empty with only her own, Harry and Jake's stuff on it, and the house was quiet and still. Someone even seemed to have tried to vacuum up some of the mud.

Beth, distracted from her sudden inspiration, padded down the hall and into the kitchen. She could scarcely believe her luck. The kettle wasn't boiling away, for once, and there was an untouched packet of biscuits on the work surface. The garden looked even more promising. There was no sign of any SOCO activity at all, the strange little pagoda had been folded away and the plastic duckboards out there had been lifted and removed too. And, most tellingly of all, there was no sign of chiselled Chris Campbell poring sorrowfully over something frightfully important in the corner.

Instead, to her total astonishment, there was Beth's brand new shoffice, plonked proudly by the fence, and looking every bit as beautiful as Belinda McKenzie's. Even if it was a tiny fraction of the size.

There was a string of fairy lights round the entrance, twisted in a beautifully exuberant way, and the woodwork was painted in what Beth could clearly identify as a fresh coat of Farrow & Ball Ammonite, with a Dix Blue trim. It looked better than she had ever dreamt. All right, you wouldn't be able to see it from space, unlike Belinda's. But it would give her little family *actual* space, and that was even better.

Beth was beyond thrilled, and for a second assumed Harry must have somehow made a gargantuan effort to get the thing finished. Then she remembered Abi's promise that the SOCO team would sort things out for her. They must have poured the concrete base the moment she left this morning, and then all helped dragging the bits of the abandoned shoffice into position, knocking it together and even slapping on the paint. How wonderful. So they'd been useful for something after all. Beth couldn't keep the mile-wide grin off her face. She took a step forward.

Suddenly she spotted Magpie surveying her from the tree overhanging the shed. As she watched, as if mesmerised, the cat stretched in a leisurely way, and oh so delicately put out one paw, as if to drop onto the roof of the shoffice.

The tiny doubt Beth had felt, looking at the beautiful shoffice, was now a voice shrieking in her ear. Did any of the SOCOS have a tenth of the flair required to leave the little shed looking this good? There was something wrong. Very badly wrong. Everything stood still for a second, except the cat moving slowly and lazily...

'No!' shouted Beth, in a voice loud enough to wake the dead. Everything in her was screaming that Magpie must not, on any account, touch that roof.

Terrified by Beth's bellow, Magpie jumped straight up in the air and clung with all four paws to the tree trunk, dislodging a twig, which drifted lazily down onto the shed's prettily painted roof. Beth watched it fall, transfixed. The instant it touched the surface, there was a terrible sizzling sound and the twig leapt into the air, smoke wisping from either end. The acrid smell of burning reached Beth where she stood, shaking in the chill.

The entire shoffice had been rigged up as a deadly, Dulwich-style execution machine, like an electric chair – but with much more attention paid to the colour scheme.

TWENTY-EIGHT

On the Sinclairs' side of the fence, a face peeped up for one second, and then was gone. Beth stayed where she was, trembling, exchanging a frantic glance with Magpie. The cat was doing an increasingly desperate imitation of a koala bear. Beth hoped against hope poor Magpie's claws wouldn't slip...

Should she get a ladder? Did she actually have a ladder? Could she borrow one in time? Just as she was racking her brains for a safe method of getting Magpie down – and coming up blanker than Jake's face in a general knowledge quiz – Beth heard several cars screeching to a halt outside in the street. There was also the sound of sirens zeroing in nearby. Usually an annoying backing track to life in south-east London, today the unearthly wails sounded like the sweetest melody.

Beth felt weak with relief. For the Met to have been on the case already, so close at hand, they must have had people in the street itself. And that could mean only one thing. Harry. He must have been having the house discreetly watched. Of course – the tyre-slashing incident. It must have been that which had got him worried. She'd thought he'd suddenly been a lot more

available in the last couple of days. It wasn't just his case coming
to the boil after all.

Bless him. Beth thought he'd been completely zoned out,
these past couple of weeks. But he'd been thinking of her all the
time, and had acted discreetly at precisely the right moment.
For once, she decided it wasn't controlling to keep an eye on
your girlfriend like this. It was just exactly what was needed.

Now she could hear the sound of the front door opening
and heavily shod feet – policemen's feet – pounding through
the hall and kitchen towards her. Suddenly, she didn't care
about the amount of dirt they were tracking into the house. All
she had to do was hope against hope that Magpie could hang on
long enough for them to reach her.

And then, when Harry got here, Beth would finally be able
to tell him exactly who was behind all this.

It was not until she was settled in the kitchen, with Magpie on
her lap, that Beth felt up to answering Harry's barrage of questions. He'd arrived in one of the first squad cars to reach Pickwick Road, and taken charge of operations. First, as Beth stood
white-lipped with anxiety about Magpie, all the electricity to
the street had been turned off. Then a PC with a long ladder
and Beth's oven gloves had taken his life in his hands and prised
the ungrateful moggy off the tree. She'd turned round and
lashed out at him a couple of times, but he'd been very brave
about it, especially when Narinda Khan had taken it upon
herself to swab his wounds with a tube of Beth's crusty old
Germolene.

'Beth, that was too close,' said Harry, when everyone else
had departed and he'd finally let her go. 'Way, way too close.
And I don't understand how you knew not to touch the
shoffice.'

'It was, well, instinct. A hunch... the pieces fell into place,' she said. 'Just in time, too.'

'Well, talk me through it. Please, Beth. Give me a clue about how on earth that mind of yours works.'

Beth smiled at Harry. Usually, he was just angry when she solved a case. But this time he wasn't being defensive. He seemed genuinely interested in her methodology. The trouble was, she wasn't sure it really merited the term. It was a jumble of thoughts, impressions, half-remembered snatches of conversation... which had suddenly added up to a solid and unshakeable conviction.

And they would end in another conviction – that of Sally Bentinck. It turned out Beth's beloved neighbour, the matriarch of the colourful Bentinck clan and theatrical impresario par excellence, had yet another string to her bow. She was a killer.

Beth had watched her being loaded into the police van, her shell-shocked sons looking on. It had been the very definition of an awkward moment between neighbours. But, just before the door was slammed shut on her, Sally had caught sight of Beth, waved a bangled arm, mouthed the word, 'Sorry' – and then blown her an exuberant kiss.

For Beth, that had probably been the most disturbing moment of all. Sally had looked her right in the eye, after plotting to electrocute her. OK, she had apologised, but still... that *really* didn't make it all right.

She shook the memory away and started, falteringly, to work out the answer to Harry's question. 'It was any number of things, really. For instance, Jude, Sally's son, was telling me only this morning how his mum had a surprise up her sleeve... I thought he meant she was having another of her famous parties. But when I saw the shed, I suddenly recognised the way she'd twisted the fairy lights so cleverly round the entrance. Exactly the same as on her own shoffice next door. That meant *Sally* had done all the fancy finishing touches, not the SOCO team. It just rang alarm bells – and I mean, the loudest klaxon you can imagine. Even louder than being in your car with the blues and twos on.'

'Yes, but wouldn't you just think she was doing a nice thing for you? How did you get from the fairy lights to, well, electrocution?'

Beth thought hard. People talked about gut feelings, and she'd called it a hunch herself, but there was logic at work here too. There had been signposts along the way. She hadn't consciously picked up on them, but when the last, deadly trap had been laid, everything had fallen into place.

What had those signs been? She started ticking them off on her fingers. 'It was a whole bunch of things... For instance, carp are carnivorous, did you know that?'

York put his hand on Beth's forehead, but she shook him off. 'I don't have a fever, I'm not delirious. Sally has been feeding those carp every evening at six o'clock for the best part of a year. Why? And what with?'

She stared at Harry, and he goggled back, a dawning horror in his eyes. 'You're not saying...'

'*Carp are carnivorous,*' Beth said again. 'I've seen Sally going up and down the road with a million plastic bags of food for those creatures... the type of bag you'd get from an old-fashioned butcher... and the weight of whatever was inside them, it kind of slapped against her legs... chunks of meat... Do I need to spell it out?' She buried her head in Harry's chest.

'Christ almighty! You mean, she was disposing of a body? All year long? And nobody even noticed.' Harry sounded as stunned as he looked.

'That's the charm of doing things in plain sight. She's got a freezer hidden away in her shoffice. Have a look in it. Rather you than me. Her husband disappeared around the New Year...

I should have guessed, as soon as Chris Campbell realised the body wasn't ancient, or even twenty years old. I got distracted by Fiona Price and Markie Rutland. But there's only really been one person who's disappeared around here in that time. Angus Bentinck.'

Harry slapped his hand to his forehead. 'Jesus, yes!'

'And Sally asked me about my tyres. But how did she know I'd had them slashed? She could have heard from one of the other neighbours, but without Adua passing all the news up and down the street, it just struck me there was another reason why she'd know all about it. Because she'd bloody well cut them herself! Now, when I think about it, I can't believe I didn't twig sooner. I saw her day after day after day, next door with those fish. But I never thought to question what she was feeding them with.

'Then there was the story about Angus, her husband,' Beth continued. 'I swallowed it whole at the time, of course – like the carp. But it was entirely from her side, no corroboration at all. Even the children didn't hear her husband's version of the story. He was just away, in the States, with a younger woman. They were so angry at the way he'd "hurt" their mother that they didn't think to check. She really manipulated them, to the point where they didn't want to speak to him. It's a common enough tale, I suppose – middle-aged man has a crisis of confidence and seeks to bolster his flagging ego with a younger woman.'

'Don't look at me,' said Harry, eyes widening.

'I'm not,' said Beth. 'But because it's so run of the mill, no one thought to question it. All of us, Sally's neighbours, took it at face value. We felt really sorry for her, we rallied round. We took it in turns to check she was OK, we had her over for meals... well, in my case that was probably a penance for her, but I did my best to make sure she wasn't too down, like the rest of the road. And all the time she'd bumped off her husband and was busily cutting him into fish food.'

'Lord. Maybe that explains the latest from Campbell. He was saying the bones had marks on them.'

'I saw that on day one! The arm bone had cuts at the joint. Honestly, I don't know why he took as long as he did to get anywhere on all that.'

'I don't know either,' said Harry. There was something about his tone that made Beth look up, but his blue eyes were giving nothing away. 'Anyway, he got there in the end. That millennium fifty-pence piece. That slowed him down, I suppose. It seemed like it was dating the burial, but that couldn't have been further from the truth.'

'He did get the test results in the end, and they said the bones were much more recent. But that took ages, too. Anyway, the coin was actually another clue! Sally's husband was a collector. He had all sorts of hoards – one of the things that drove Sally mad – and I suppose the coins were part of that. Poor guy. I hate to think of him down there all this time, unmourned. It's just... such an awful fate.' Beth's eyes filled with tears again.

Harry hugged her even tighter. 'Well, we've put a name to him at last, thanks to you. We still don't know exactly how the killing happened – you never know, there may have been extenuating circumstances. Maybe he came at Sally with a knife, or something. Maybe there was more to their relationship than anyone realised.'

It was good that the police were now considering such options, Beth supposed. But she had never seen any evidence of abuse or coercive control, on either side of the Bentincks' relationship. Indeed, right up until Angus's disappearance, she would actually have said they were a very happy couple. It just went to show how little one could ever know about the human heart. Even living next door to Sally, she'd never caught a whisper of anything amiss. And, if there had ever been a heated discussion, she supposed she would have put it down to Sally's exuberant nature, anyway.

'Now we just have to find Adua's killer, and we've cleared it all up,' said Harry.

Beth looked up again in surprise. 'But surely you've realised.'

'God, don't tell me you've got a theory...' said Harry.

'Not a *theory*, no. I know who it was.'

TWENTY-NINE

Harry just sat and stared at her for a beat. Then he shrugged his broad shoulders. Finally, he laughed. 'I don't know why I bother going into work. I should stay in bed and let you sort everything out. Come on then. Amaze me.'

'Well, isn't it obvious?' Beth said, crinkling her nose. 'I mean, when you think about it...'

'OK, OK, don't rub it in, Beth. Just tell me who you think it is.' Harry was starting to look unmistakably stern now.

'Can't you guess? It was Sally, too,' she said simply.

'Oh, great! That'll help my clear-up rates,' said Harry. Beth rolled her eyes and he stopped grinning. 'You're serious? No, come off it.' Beth just looked at him steadily. He rubbed a hand over his face before he spoke. 'OK, say she did. Why would she do that, though?'

'You'll have to ask her, obviously. But I think Adua saw something. I admit, I wondered if Adua had been in some sort of feud with one of the other cleaners round here, but nothing stacked up. Then she could be a bit, well, light-fingered really, and I wondered if that had got her into trouble with an employer... But no one seemed angry, really properly cross about that, not even George Kendall. In the end it was when I went upstairs one day that I started to get an inkling... You can see all the way up and down the gardens from the bedroom windows, just like Adua said at the Kendalls' dinner party – oh, you weren't there. That's probably why you didn't cotton on,' Beth said kindly. Although Harry seemed to be taking all this well, and was really cheering her up in her moment of need, she reckoned it had to be pretty galling that she'd solved everything under his nose again.

'Adua must have spotted Sally in the garden. Maybe she was actually killing her husband. Or just having a terrible argument with him. Perhaps she saw Sally shoving the bones under my fence, when she was having her own shoffice updated. I bet that's when she did it. Or maybe Adua saw Sally in the Sinclairs' garden, feeding the fish with the, um, meat itself.'

Beth swallowed and moved on quickly. 'Or what if Sally only *thought* Adua might have seen something? That would have been just as worrying for her. Adua didn't mention anything straight away, after all. It was ages after Angus disappeared, if you think about it. It could even be one of those cases where she didn't realise what she'd seen at the time, but she gradually started to put two and two together, like I did.'

Harry looked thoughtful. 'What exactly did Adua say that night?'

Beth cast her mind back. 'Well. She was serving us the dinner – you know what the Kendalls are like, they want everything to be super-posh and making Adua serve the food was one of their things. It didn't bother her, she got paid for it. Anyway, we were all just chatting. Adua piped up and said something a bit out of the blue about enjoying seeing everyone's gardens. And even before that, she gave this huge wink. I didn't think much of it at the time but afterwards... I wondered. It was a tiny bit pointed, as though she was trying to get a specific person's attention, though she said it to the whole room. And then there was one of those lulls you sometimes get, but it was... really tense, somehow.

'Then Lizzie Kendall mentioned the other day that Adua had a fancy new handbag. Again, it went right over my head initially. I've been such an idiot about this whole thing, I've been so distracted with Jake and the builders... But it came back to me when you knocked over my bag in the hall, and then I kicked it over again in my office at Wyatt's – I've got to upgrade it soon, seriously.'

Harry was still looking bewildered. Beth tried to make things clearer. 'So, I suddenly wondered where Adua had got the money. If Lizzie Kendall spotted she had a very expensive new handbag, then it must have been something designer label – I don't think Lizzie'd get out of bed for anything less than a genuine Gucci.'

'Honestly,' said Harry. 'Having a new handbag on its own isn't that sinister, is it?'

Beth just gazed at Harry. They'd been together for quite a while now, and yet every now and then he said something that made her wonder whether he ever listened. Or saw. Or learnt.

'These things can cost thousands, Harry. Lizzie Kendall knew Adua was suddenly flush as soon as she saw that bag. She even thought she might have taken off on holiday when she didn't turn up for work, Don't you see? The new handbag is evidence. Someone was giving her cash.'

'Blackmail. Well, you're always suggesting that as a motive, aren't you?' Harry nudged Beth gently with his elbow. 'Looks like you might finally be right.'

'Yes, though I never thought it would be Adua doing something like that. But she must have been getting money out of Sally. And Sally had had enough. So she slit Adua's throat. And that definitely doesn't suggest that killing Angus was purely a matter of survival, does it? Sounds more like she's got into a very bad habit.'

'I think you could be right,' said Harry with his serious policeman face on again. 'Then there were your slashed tyres.'

'Well, if she hadn't done that, you wouldn't have put someone on duty round the corner. And then they wouldn't have been able to get here so quickly... So in a way I've got Sally to thank. And I think she sent me the threatening texts, too. The first was just about getting my throat slit, like Adua,' Beth shut her eyes briefly. 'But the second mentioned Fiona Price specifically. She must have overheard my argument with Chris Campbell that day in the garden. She was trying to warn me off before I found out it was Angus down there. Everyone knows about getting new SIM cards these days, she could have bought one at the Tesco near Herne Hill station.

'And on the doorstep earlier... I'd asked her about George Kendall, whether he and Adua had fallen out. There was just something in her eyes as she answered. A flash of cunning. She deliberately made me think I'd stumbled on a clue to Adua's death. And there could only be one reason why she'd want me to think someone else had a motive.'

Beth paused for thought. 'You know, once Sally saw I hadn't been electrocuted as planned – and I bet she was watching out of one of her back windows – who's to say she wouldn't have come round and just shoved me into the shed herself, to get the job done.'

Harry shut his eyes and then reached for her hand. 'She couldn't have hoped to get away with it, though.'

'I don't know. All she had to do then was throw me over the fence, get me into her shoffice freezer, and start chipping away,' said Beth weakly. 'She's a lot bigger and stronger than me.'

'I'd have looked for you. And Jake would, and Wendy... and Katie, too. She wouldn't have had a hope.'

'That's nice, but by that stage it would have been too late,' Beth said simply. 'I'd have been fish food. Anyway, I don't think Sally cared about the consequences any more at this point. Her son Jude hinted she was really struggling. And now we know just how much.'

They were both silent for a second.

'You know,' she said. 'I really thought the text and the tyres were down to the building firms. But it was only after I mentioned Adua and the fish to Sally that both things happened. She must have thought I was onto her, like Adua.' Beth remembered with a wince.

'She wasn't wrong, thinking you'd got her number, was she?' Harry said. 'But talking about the building firms, the Rutlands and the Prices, it was a waste of time looking into all that old drama with Markie and Fiona for you,' he said. 'You could even call it a red herring, while we're on a fishy theme. Too soon?' he said, as Beth made a moue of distaste. 'Well, it was a waste of Narinda's time, really, not mine. I asked her to take care of it for me.'

Beth stored that up mentally. She hoped Narinda wouldn't resent her for it. Any more than she did already. 'I also thought it might be one of the Sinclairs buried in the garden, at various points. Well, they haven't been seen for so long, one of them could have killed the other and fed them to their own fish,' she said with a shudder.

'I wish you wouldn't treat murder as a bloody jigsaw puzzle. It's going to get you killed, one of those days. Why didn't you tell me, as soon as you started suspecting Sally?' Harry said.

Beth thought about it. 'Things only really fell into place when I saw the shoffice. When I was at Wyatt's, earlier, I realised there was something odd about a conversation I'd had here in Pickwick Road that was crucial – but you'd have laughed at me if I'd said something that vague. Anyway, you've been up to your eyes. Most of the time, I was convinced it was the Prices or the Rutlands... Not to mention the Sinclairs up the road. Or Katie's cleaner. In my wilder moments I even wondered if Nina's cousin had something to do with it, she knew so much about the builders' feuds... I was losing my credibility slightly.'

Harry didn't deny it. 'Even so,' he said. 'You have to start taking this more seriously.'

'More seriously? Does that mean you're not forbidding me from going on detecting, this time?'

'Sorry, what I meant to say is "You're absolutely forbidden from going on,"' he said in his most authoritative voice. Beth tried to laugh, but it was too soon. All traces of a smile were wiped off her face. She was struck by a horrible truth.

It was all very well, talking about cases and detection and all the rest of it... but the culprit this time was her neighbour. Sally Bentinck, whom Beth had been so fond of over the years. Beth had comforted Sally when she said Angus had left – because Sally had been so kind to her when James died. She'd let Beth blub uncontrollably in her kitchen in the early days, she'd invited her and Jake to all those parties... It had all seemed so genuine, so nice. Sally had been the best neighbour Beth could have asked for. It was hard to square that Sally with the person who'd just tried to kill her.

But Sally had been fighting to stay free. She'd already killed twice. The great taboo had been broken. They'd probably never know the circumstances that led to Angus's death. Even if Sally ever revealed what had happened, they would only have her word for it. Maybe Angus really had been planning to leave her. There could have been a younger model in the wings... but as far as Beth knew, no glamorous young thing had ever come forward asking what had happened to her lover. Maybe Sally had simply had enough of Angus, and wasn't willing to split their assets in a civilised divorce. She must have made a fortune in the theatre, whereas he'd been retired for as long as Beth had known them. She might have decided she was going to hang onto everything she had worked so hard for. But whatever her motivation, nothing justified what Sally had done.

Sally was undoubtedly a strong, capable woman. If Angus had picked a fight when she had a knife in her hand, cooking, say... who knew what might have happened. She might well have bitterly regretted her actions. Beth thought back – had Sally seemed haunted? She'd been very sad, yes, in the early days after Angus had 'left' her. But over the last few months she'd been pretty much back to normal, hadn't she?

Adua's death was another thing entirely. That had certainly been premeditated. Flawed though she had undoubtedly been, mischievous Adua had not deserved her fate. Beth shook her head slightly to clear the thought of Adua away. It wasn't that she would ever forget her. It was just that she'd had enough of crying for the moment.

Beth knew that if she were ever up against it, if she felt she was going to be taken out of Jake's life for good, she'd try some desperate measures to keep her liberty, as Sally had. That was not to say she condoned what Sally had done, or even that she herself could ever kill anyone. Katie had once joked she would have trouble stabbing the film on a microwave ready meal, and it was true.

'Do you think you'll get Sally to trial?' she asked Harry. He could only shrug, palms up.

She knew it was by no means a given, even at the end of a case where the evidence seemed to stack up in great bundles all around. Here, you couldn't really say there was a whole lot to go on, if that shoffice freezer came up empty. Adua might have been a witness, but she had been silenced. The fish had probably seen far too much, but had swallowed any qualms they might have had about the new high-protein diet Sally had introduced them to. No wonder they'd grown so huge so quickly. They were witnesses, accessories, accomplices and also the means Sally had used to dispose of the body, but those carp were slippery customers. They'd never stand up in court. It seemed wrong to hope that bits of poor Angus were still on ice next door, but it was probably Harry's best bet for securing a conviction. Otherwise, there was a danger Sally might actually get away with murder.

Beth frowned with concentration. Was there anything else she could dredge up to bolster Harry's case? She was still a little torn. This was Sally, who'd hugged her when she'd thought her world had ended, on James's death. But this was also Sally, who'd planned for her to die horribly in her garden shoffice. And what if Jake had got home early and been tempted to take a look inside? Beth spoke up.

'You should really check Sally's background. I know you'll be doing this anyway...' she said, forestalling any defensiveness. 'But she's so practical, she did theatrical stuff for years, lugging things around, rigging things up, doing the electrics. I bet if you search her computer you'll find an online butchery course or something. She must have googled carp feeding habits. And I know she's got a full set of those Global knives. There was one dropped by the recycling bin, wasn't there, where Adua...' she struggled to finish the sentence, then rallied. 'They can cut through anything. I've seen Sally joint a chicken with one, just like that. Chop, chop, chop.'

Harry, as usual, wasn't committing himself to locking Sally away for a hundred years. But he did say, 'Luckily for us, knives leave quite distinctive marks...'

Beth thought again of that first bone and the damage near the joint. So much of what had gone on recently made her feel sick to her stomach, not least the fact that Sally had always seemed so nice. It made Beth doubt everything. Was she a terrible judge of character? Or was Sally, who'd spent so long around theatrical types, just a really good actor?

'I'm glad it's you, not me, that'll be questioning her. I feel so angry and upset... and stupid. Why didn't I spot there was something wrong with Sally?'

'Why didn't her children, for that matter?' said Harry.

'There are often no clues at all when someone goes to the bad like this. You've heard people saying on the news, "They kept themselves to themselves. We never suspected a thing." That's because, once people step over the line, they do everything in their power to stop anyone else from seeing it.'

'I hope poor Angus didn't suffer too much, anyway.' Her head drooped.

'Listen,' said Harry, putting a large warm hand over her small one. 'As I understand it, all those cuts were made to the bones post-mortem. So it was probably very quick.'

It didn't escape Beth's notice that Harry hadn't specified a cause of death. How on earth could anyone know, now, exactly what happened – unless Sally confessed. So the news about the cuts didn't exactly perk her up – but it was something.

'Perhaps all the stuff that happened to the bones was what made Chris think they were much older than they were.'

'Chris, is it?' said Harry. 'It was "that bloody pathologist guy" a while ago.'

But Beth wasn't really listening. She couldn't help remembering Sally's meaty forearms resting on the fence, when they'd chatted. She'd always envied Sally for being so strong, so capable. Now she wondered what feats those arms had carried out, to convert Angus into a parade of plastic bags of prime fish food.

Thinking about Angus made her sad again – this time that his five children had been deprived of a father. He'd been a good dad, as far as Beth could tell, and the kids were lovely. But they'd had no hesitation in believing Sally's lies about him, which told its own story in a way. Thinking about Jude's hints about his mother's mental state made her wonder how exactly Sally had persuaded the kids not to try and contact their dad. Maybe she'd told them she'd have a breakdown if they did.

'You know, whatever you say, I don't think I'll ever stop kicking myself about this. Here I am, supposed to be a detective, and there was a murderer living right next door and I didn't even notice,' Beth shook her head.

'For starters, you're not a detective. I am. And I didn't see a thing either,' said Harry.

'There's been so much else going on, I just got distracted and didn't stop to question things like I usually would.' Beth took a sip of her cooling tea. 'I expect it was the same for you,' she offered. In truth, she knew Harry had simply not had his eye on the ball. Maybe that would stop, now – along with all the ridiculous overtime he'd been putting in. She nestled her head against his shoulder.

'Is everything sorted, with Katie?' Harry said it casually, but Beth realised he was hanging on her answer. He knew how much Katie meant to her.

'I hope so,' sighed Beth. 'She's been pretty stressed out about Teddy. He's failed the Penge obedience course. And she was furious that I thought her cleaner Rosita might have been involved in Adua's death. But I had to ask the question. And, believe it or not, when you were busy arresting Sally she texted saying she was actually pretty miffed that I stood her up today. I've explained that someone was trying to electrocute me, but she's acting like she's heard it all before. I've already put in some heavy-duty grovelling, but I'll need to do a lot more... I've even offered to let her have Colin to stay again. That did make her laugh at least.'

'Sounds promising,' said Harry, squeezing her hand.

'It was awful that I forgot to tell her Gregory King is almost certainly getting suspended, so we didn't need to get Belinda McKenzie involved. She wasn't happy about being left out of the loop. So now I've had to promise on Magpie's life that I'll turn up and help her "supervise" the boys at the Year 8 disco. I mean, that's going to ruin it for them, but I don't really have a choice.'

'You might enjoy it,' Harry said mildly.

'Lurking around all night spying on my son? I'm not sure about that. But it'll be worth it if Katie and I can be friends again. It's hard, when you fall out.'

'It is,' said Harry. He smiled his beautiful lazy smile, his eyes crinkling up at the corners in that way that still gave her butterflies. 'Don't worry, you'll never fall out with me.'

'But you've scarcely been around, these past couple of weeks. Narinda always says you're busy.' Beth knew she sounded petulant, but she couldn't help it. She *felt* petulant.

'Not too busy to talk to you, Beth,' Harry said quietly.

'Tell her that, then,' Beth insisted. She risked a searching glance at him as she said it, but he didn't seem to register anything particularly pointed in her comment. Good, she thought. 'Oh, another thing – what on earth will you do with the Sinclairs' carp? Is it like a dog when it's attacked someone, and you have to get it put down?'

Harry shrugged. 'You've got me there. I've honestly never had to deal with fish as accessories to murder before. I'm learning a lot, living in Dulwich,' he said, squeezing her hand again. 'And one of the things I've learnt is, you just never give up, do you, Beth?'

She met his eyes. As well as the usual exasperation, Beth was glad to see there was admiration mixed in. She smiled back. 'Never.'

'Just make me this one promise,' Harry said, a satisfyingly long while later.

Beth, a little surprised by his choice of words, took a shaky breath and put her head on one side. He wasn't going to ask *that* question, was he?

'Um. What's that?'

'We're not having fish and chips tonight.'

A LETTER FROM ALICE

Thank you so much for choosing to read my book. I love writing about Beth Haldane and I hope you've enjoyed finding out what she got up to this time. If you'd like to know what happens to Beth next, please sign up at the email link below. Your email address will never be shared and you can unsubscribe at any time.

www.bookouture.com/alice-castle

If you enjoyed the story, I would be very grateful if you could write a review. I'd love to hear what you think. I always read reviews and I take careful account of what people say. My aim is always to make the books a better read! Leaving a review also helps new readers to discover my books for the first time.

I'm also on Twitter, Facebook and Goodreads, often sharing pictures of cats that look like Magpie. Do get in touch if that's your sort of thing. Thanks so much again, and I really hope to see you soon for Beth's next adventure. Happy reading!

Alice Castle

Alicecastleauthor.com

facebook.com/Alicecastleauthor

twitter.com/AliceMCastle

Printed in Great Britain
by Amazon